Timelock

"Oiga," the voice said.

". . . Oiga? . . ."

Fedora's eyes rolled upwards towards the ceiling, searching for a focus. The voice had seemed to come from beyond it; but that, as he now realised, was improbable. It was, after all, a ceiling, and not, as he had at first thought, some weird kind of an off-white fog. It was just that his eyes couldn't seem to find a hold on it. The voice came nearer.

"How are you feeling?"

"Not too bright," Fedora said.

He spoke in Spanish, since the voice did. He spoke it well, but at the same time he knew that it wasn't his native language. His lips seemed to move too sluggishly to form the words; it was as though they were the first he'd spoken for a very long time. How long? . . . But what was this, anyway? It had to be an illusion, like the other. The voice was near at hand and always had been. He turned his head on the pillow, and now his eyes came into focus with no trouble at all. He blinked. He hadn't expected it to be that near.

Other titles in the Walker British Mystery Series

Peter Alding • MURDER IS SUSPECTED
Peter Alding • RANSOM TOWN
Jeffrey Ashford • SLOW DOWN THE WORLD
Jeffrey Ashford • THREE LAYERS OF GUILT
Pierre Audemars • NOW DEAD IS ANY MAN
Marion Babson • DANGEROUS TO KNOW
Marion Babson • THE LORD MAYOR OF DEATH
Brian Ball • MONTENEGRIN GOLD
Josephine Bell • A QUESTION OF INHERITANCE
Josephine Bell • TREACHERY IN TYPE
Josephine Bell • VICTIM
W. J. Burley • DEATH IN WILLOW PATTERN
W. J. Burley • TO KILL A CAT
Desmond Cory • THE NIGHT HAWK
Desmond Cory • UNDERTOW
John Creasey • THE BARON AND THE UNFINISHED PORTRAIT
John Creasey • HELP FROM THE BARON
John Creasey • THE TOFF AND THE FALLEN ANGELS
John Creasey • TRAP THE BARON
June Drummond • FUNERAL URN
June Drummond • SLOWLY THE POISON
William Haggard • THE NOTCH ON THE KNIFE
William Haggard • THE POISON PEOPLE
William Haggard • TOO MANY ENEMIES
William Haggard • VISA TO LIMBO
William Haggard • YESTERDAY'S ENEMY
Simon Harvester • MOSCOW ROAD
Simon Harvester • ZION ROAD
J. G. Jeffreys • SUICIDE MOST FOUL
J. G. Jeffreys • A WICKED WAY TO DIE
J. G. Jeffreys • THE WILFUL LADY
Elizabeth Lemarchand • CHANGE FOR THE WORSE
Elizabeth Lemarchand • STEP IN THE DARK
Elizabeth Lemarchand • SUDDENLY WHILE GARDENING
Elizabeth Lemarchand • UNHAPPY RETURNS
Laurie Mantell • A MURDER OR THREE
John Sladek • BLACK AURA
John Sladek • INVISIBLE GREEN

DESMOND CORY
Timelock

WALKER AND COMPANY · NEW YORK

First published in the United States of America
in 1967 by the Walker Publishing Company, Inc.

This paperback edition first published in 1984.

ISBN: 0-8027-3052-3

Library of Congress Catalog Card Number: 67-23099

Printed in the United States of America

10 9 8 7 6 5 4 3 2 1

Acuña, too, was driving to Barcelona. And he, too, was unconscious; or more precisely, asleep. His chauffeur had taken the no. 2 highway from Madrid and was, at the time of Fedora's sad collapse, nearing Zaragoza; he had just negotiated the rather awkward stretch that leads into La Almunia and was now, once more on the open plains, making up for lost time. From here on, he hoped to average a steady sixty kilometres or so an hour; he knew, in any case, that he'd *better*. Acuña was comfortably asleep in the back of the car, but at 5 a.m. on the dot he'd be waking up, and when he did he'd find himsef in Barcelona. Or else. . . .

Acuña was a very important man. He was, among other things, chief security advisor to Muñoz Grandes, who was Deputy Head of State to General Franco. That was his official post. He had a number of less official posts that the chauffeur knew about, posts guaranteeing him a yearly income of some five hundred thousand pesetas, but these posts somehow didn't get talked about much—certainly not by the chauffeur, who knew the value of discretion. As for his private life, that didn't get talked about at all. It centred mostly on a flat off Recoletos where not one but *two* young ladies were together enabled to lead (as the chauffeur was convinced) the life of Riley, this in return for their doubtless highly skilled services from two to five p.m. daily. *Daily.* Acuña was short and very, very fat and hideously ugly; he had to be, moreover, pushing sixty. Hence the chauffeur's discretion, it may be said, was tinged with a certain admiration. And when all was said and done, it gave him something to think about on these long and boring night journeys. Food, so to speak, for the imagination. Acuña usually slept. No wonder.

... But always woke at five. On the dot. The chauffeur glanced briefly at the clock on the dashboard and compressed his lips; the road, as they travelled eastwards, was getting greasier. But so far, they were making good time.

By 4.45, they were through San Feliu and the lights of Barcelona were a hazy glow in the sky to the north-east. Twelve minutes later Acuña, on the back seat, stirred and then opened his eyes; he was awake. No yawning. No stretching. Hardly a movement. He was awake; that was all. The black car fled down the wide streets, the pavements to either side brushed orange by the overhead lights, shining wetly in the reflected beam of the headlamps. The air was damp. It made quite a change from Madrid.

"Where are we?" Acuña asked.

He didn't mean, *Barcelona*. He knew that already. He wanted to know exactly. "Going down Regencia, sir, towards the port. We'll be at the Torre in about four minutes."

Acuña grunted. After a while, he raised a hand to massage his unshaven chin. The tyres hissed on the road; the tall buildings drifted by. They passed a bicyclist, then two more; then a solitary taxi, going the other way. The car turned sharp left, ignoring the red admonition of a traffic light; Acuña took out and lit a short thin cigar. In the Plaza de la Torre, the car came to a halt.

The chauffeur opened the door. Acuña got out.

"I'll phone you if I need you again today."

"Yessir."

No case, no coat, no hat. Acuña waddled towards the front door of the house that stood at the corner, not acknowledging the chauffeur's farewell salute. The door opened while he was still some ten paces distant from the front steps; a dark-suited figure showed briefly inside, silhouetted against the light that burned in the narrow hallway. Acuña didn't nod to *him*, either. He walked unhesitantly in, and the door closed behind him. The chauffeur spat on to the pavement, clambered back into the Dodge and let in the clutch; the garage attendants at the Avenida would be on duty and waiting for him and so, with any luck, would be a cup of hot coffee. It hadn't been too bad a trip. Routine.

"Anything from Recoletos?" Acuña asked.

"No, sir." The man in the dark suit was trotting along at his heels like a well-trained gun dog. "Nothing."

"Put me through."

"*En seguida, señor.*"

Acuña went through into the Divisional Coordinator's office. A desk piled high with papers; a telephone. He sat down. The man in the dark suit picked up the telephone and commenced to dial. At Recoletos, they'd be waiting, too.

The flat in Recoletos wasn't exactly what the chauffeur thought it was. It was the communications centre of the Spanish Secret Police; a very efficient organisation, in many ways. Acuña thought so, anyway, and he was in a good enough position to judge. He was the head of it.

"Where's the Coordinator?"

"On operations, sir. He expects to be back before ten o'clock. You'll find his memoranda, sir, on the desk."

"Ugh," Acuña said.

There was no shortage of papers on the desk. There was a whole mountain of them. Acuña started to go through them. The Madrid call came through almost at once, and he gave brief instructions without lifting his eyes from the folder open on the desk in front of him. When he had finished reading the folder, he laid it to one side and took another. Time went by. At irregular intervals, the man in the dark suit came in from the next-door office, carrying new folders, messages, telegram slips and one one occasion an Interpol Blue. Acuña took no notice. At ten o'clock, he was still sitting there; the pile of papers had shrunk to perhaps a quarter of its former bulk. He went on reading, reading, reading. Nothing disturbed his concentration. This, after all, was his job; he was used to it. Papers, papers, papers.

Routine.

... Only this time it wasn't, quite.

Acuña was the head of the Secret Police, and had been for years. He was an expert at counter-espionage; he had to be. The Russians had a very high opinion of him; or very low, according to how you looked at it. They didn't like him at all. Nor did Franco. But his record was impressive. In his own mind, though, he was really little more than a jigsaw man. Jumbled pieces came to him; he tried to fit them together. Sometimes he could and more often he couldn't. In the former case, action would be taken; sometimes in accordance with his recommendations and sometimes not. In the latter case, nothing happened at all. He just went on trying. Acuña hardly ever made a move until he was sure. Completely sure. They said he was cunning, but really he was only cautious.

He liked, when he could, to work with younger men. Less experienced, more impulsive. They provided the thrust, packed the cylinder with petrol vapour. Acuña was the brake. He braked at the right moments and he did the steering. What matters in the long run is to get there. The way you brake, the way you steer, you maybe use up a lot of petrol. That didn't matter. There would always be young men with brains and courage and energy, and Acuña knew how to find them. That was the least of his problems.

At one minute past ten, the latest discovery came in. The Coordinator of the Catalonia Division: Paco Rivas. Thirty-three years old; tall for a *sevillano*, six foot one, and with plenty of bulk to set off the height. Bulk, not fat. Just over fourteen stone, with a deflated chest measurement of thirty-eight inches. Dark wavy hair and a creased, sun-tanned, intelligent, extremely active face. Far too active to be ever called studious, though he'd studied at Madrid and at the Sorbonne and had a Ph.D. Vienna in clinical psychiatry. The face guaranteed the energy and the body the stamina; Rivas, Acuña hoped, would last a good deal longer than some of the others. Three or four years, with any luck. Though it depended a good deal, of course, on who Rivas had to tangle with; you could have called him unlucky, in that respect. That was why the present jigsaw wasn't a routine problem. Not exactly.

Acuña blinked at him with his flat and red-rimmed eyes. "Well, now," he said.

"It's not too good, *jefe*. Not too good."

"Let's have the picture. As you see it."

"It's still not perfectly clear." Rivas hadn't been told he could sit down, so he remained standing. "Things have been going on at Villafranca. We don't know what. There's been a fire there, and at least two bodies have been recovered. We don't know whose. Ortiz is almost certainly dead. He was in that aeroplane accident and we're waiting the assessor's report. Since it crashed in the sea, it may be a long time in coming. We're assuming sabotage. Ortiz's wife is now in France. We missed her at the frontier, probably by about twenty minutes. The Englishman has to be still in this country; at any rate, we've no report as to his having left. We're hoping to regain touch with him this morning. And there's one thing at least we're quite sure of. It's Fedora."

"Yes," Acuña said. "It's Fedora." A faint shadow of expression crossed his face, but not of any recognisable emotion. It was just a brief departure from total impassivity; that was all. ". . . Sit down," Acuña said.

Rivas did so, promptly, crossing his knees with a movement so abrupt as to be almost a jerk. "And that has to mean Feramontov. At the other end."

"Ortiz, dead. Madame Ortiz, in France. Fedora, out of contact. And Feramontov never in it. Yes. Go on."

"It's not good. I know it's not good."

"Go on," Acuña said.

"We've reason to supppose that Feramontov was picked up by Ortiz's yacht. Well, the yacht got to Alicante last night. I've sent an agent there to question the skipper and to pick up any other loose threads. There's not much—"

"Who did you send? Alonso?"

"No. My brother."

"Maybe," Acuña said, "you should have gone yourself."

"There seemed to be so much to be cleared up right here."

He didn't say it as though he felt uncertain, but his eyes turned away from Acuña and towards the window. The square outside was still deserted; it wasn't raining, but there was rain in the offing. Not a bright morning, by any means.

". . . To sum the whole thing up," Rivas said, "I thought there was a chance—no more than that—that Feramontov might try to contact Ortiz. So I put someone in at Villa-franca, just to keep tabs. At the worst you could say that I should have put in someone more experienced . . . but it was an off-chance, anyway, and Alonso fitted pretty well into that set-up. As it turned out, there wasn't much wrong with the reports that came in. I hadn't allowed for Fedora showing up, of course. Just possibly a more experienced operative would have got on to him sooner, but I can't really blame Alonso for that—the fault was mine, if anyone's. I saw Ortiz as the objective, really, with Feramontov as a barely possible ultimate target. What happened was that the people in Madrid didn't take the reports very seriously, because they didn't see how Feramontov could be anywhere near Barcelona. But it *was* Feramontov. So they were wrong."

"I wouldn't say wrong," Acuña said. And Rivas' eyes came back to him. ". . . Who else could it have been?"

"Oh, it was Feramontov all right. In and out again—the typical technique. All I meant was that the Madrid boys had their reasons. They thought we had him holed up down in the south, they thought he couldn't make a break without being nabbed. Our cordons don't slip—*you* know that. They weren't wrong in making that assumption."

"But then how did he do it?"

Acuña said nothing, and so Rivas confronted the problem. You could see him doing it. It took him just eight seconds. Then, unexpectedly, he made a circle of left thumb and fore-finger, thrust his right forefinger through it. ". . . You don't mean a leakage?"

"Of course."

"But that's not possible."

"There's no other explanation. And *if* there is, it goes to confirm what I've been suspecting these past six months. One moment he's bottled up, the next he isn't. So there's a leak. There *has* to be."

He had been sitting on a hard chair for just over five hours. Now he shifted position a little, easing gently forwards his huge posteriors; the first indication he'd yet given of any kind of physical discomfort. "That's bad," Rivas said. "That's really bad."

By way of reply, Acuña snorted.

"High level, I suppose?"

"I'd say the highest. Ministerial, maybe. I don't know yet. But," Acuña said, "I will."

Rivas pushed out his lower lip, pondering deeply. *Leak,* he thought; a four-letter word. In the Secret Police and in similar organisations, the only one that really matters, Top Priority Taboo. You're supposed to grow pale at the sound of it; he wasn't sure he hadn't. Because the Secret Police had enemies, hundreds of enemies, and dangerous ones, and in that one word *Secret* lay their sole protection. To set the one word against the other is like setting a ferret on to a rabbit. It was bad, *really* bad.

"I don't see how we'll ever catch Feramontov," he said, "if he knows just what we're planning to do as soon as we know it ourselves."

"I don't say *as soon as,*" Acuña said comfortably. "No, I imagine that there's some delay. As much as twelve hours, perhaps. It can't be *that* easy."

"But even so."

"Quite," Acuña said. "Even so. Of course, there's another way of looking at it." He took out another of his cigars, bit the end off it, spat inelegantly into the wastepaper basket. "We find the leak, we find Feramontov. We leak the wrong information through to him, and he's in the bag. Had you thought of that?"

"I can't say I had," Rivas said. "Leaks. I *hate* leaks."

"We've had them before. No doubt we'll have them again. And they can be useful. It's a matter of thinking of the best way of . . ." The match sputtered in Acuña's fingers; he blew out a symbolical wreath of smoke. As he did so, the telephone rang.

Rivas reached for it, listened in silence for a moment. "Yes," he said. "Put the call through." And looked up. "Here's Alonso on the line. Now we may learn a little more about something or other."

The hotel was not expensive though it overlooked the beach, the sloping beach of Alicante with its fringe of palm trees. The name of the hotel was the Albuferete. That morning, as in Barcelona, the rain had held off; but the *levante* was blowing, bringing with it grains of dust and of fine, stinging sand, so that most of the hotel windows over-looking the beach were closed and shuttered. Not all of them, however. There was an open window on the first floor; and through this a cool draught entered, lifting now and again the calico curtains, raising a tuft of hair from the forehead of the man who lay on the floor beneath them, leaving on his upturned face the filmiest imaginable deposit of white dust.

The other man in the room stood a little to the left and clear of the open window, staring down at the corpse. A tall, well-built young man who looked very much like Rivas and was, in fact, Rivas' younger brother; there were five brothers altogether, but only two of them were policemen. This young man looked like Rivas, yes; but principally he looked unhappy. He was worried, not so much about the corpse as at what the corpse implied. It implied that there might quite soon be four Rivas brothers, and only one of them a policeman. Which didn't make for a cheerful frame of mind.

He had already searched the room, and what there was to find he had found. On the whole, though, he would rather have not. There had to be a reason for the corpse on the floor, and the chances seemed high that the reason was now in his coat pocket. He took the reason out and looked at it; then went over to the writing-desk in the corner of the room and, taking one of the hotel envelopes, slipped the reason inside. On the envelope he wrote the name and address of a dentist who worked in Barcelona, then stuck on it a sixty-centimo stamp. Then he licked the flap and sealed it. He sat at the desk, thinking, a little while longer. Then he got up, sliding the envelope into his pocket, and left the room, taking care not to pass in front of the window (his guess was that the bullet had come that way, conceivably when the dead man—then alive—had gone across to close it) and taking care to lock the door after him. He walked downstairs. There was a postbox by the receptionist's desk, as he had already noticed, and as he went past he pushed the envelope through the slot.

He had telephone tokens in his pocket and the kiosk was the far side of the hall. The number answered at once.

"... He said someone had been to see him," he said without preamble. "Well, someone's called again."

"He's dead?"

"Shot through the head. I'd say with a rifle."

The window to his right gave not on to the beach but on to the side street, just south of the main hotel entrance. He surveyed the street while he talked. There was a little green Renault, empty, parked outside the hotel, and an army jeep with a uniformed driver. The driver was sitting at the wheel and reading a paper. Twenty yards farther up the road, someone else was reading a paper; leaning against the wall, legs casually crossed. A man in a grey cotton jacket. He could have been alone, but almost certainly wasn't.

"You'd better watch it," the telephone advised him.

"I'm watching it."

"Did you find anything?"

"Something, yes. I don't know how useful. I've posted it to Centre."

"That was wise."

The telephone clicked in his hand. Not very helpful. But then, he hadn't expected it to be. He was on his own now, even if the fellow with the newspaper wasn't. On his own, among a hundred enemies. He fumbled for a cigarette and lit it.

They wouldn't come in for him. Or he didn't think so. They'd wait outside. His hands, he found, were sweating more than he'd realised; enough to stain the cigarette paper. He heard a sound beside him, looked round.

An Army officer was coming down the stairs, carrying the inevitable leather briefcase. A lieutenant-colonel. Eyeing him with the usual disinterested military glare. Rivas stubbed out his cigarette quickly; some people were fussy. He said,

"Excuse me, colonel . . ."

"Yes? What is it?"

The fussy kind, all right.

"Would you be so good as to examine this?"

He held out his Special Service pass. *All government officials and State empoyees are hereby requested to recognise and render all possible assistance, etc., etc. Signed, squiggle, squiggle. Jefatura de Policia.* The colonel withered it with one pale blue glance; he'd seen police passes before. "Well, what can I do for you?"

"Is that your jeep outside, colonel?"

"It is."

"In that case, perhaps you'd be kind enough to give me a lift."

"A lift to where?"

"To the Comisaria."

The colonel was already moving on. "All right. Very well. I suppose so."

"I appreciate the favour." Rivas fell discreetly into step beside him; left, right, left right; full regulation pace of one metre exactly. "It's only fair to warn you, sir, that I may be, er . . . shot at. On the way."

"*Shot* at? Don't be a damned fool. This is Alicante."

"Possibly as we leave this building."

"Shot at, hey?" the colonel said. Left, right, left, right. His pace not altering by so much as a millimetre. "By God. I'd like to see 'em try."

Rivas, who wouldn't, thought it best to say nothing. He marched with the colonel down the steps and across the half-mile or so of open pavement that separated them from the jeep. His stomach muscles were clenched so hard as to be painful. "In you hop," the colonel said. "Lie on the floor, if you want."

"I can't do that, sir." The question of personal prestige apart, there wasn't enough room.

"I suppose not," the colonel said. He sat down beside Rivas and drew from its holster a Luger pistol. "*A la Comisaria, Gomez.*" He flashed his eyes belligerently up and down the street. The driver switched on the ignition. The man with the newspaper had gone away.

"Drive on," the colonel said, satisfied.

Off they went. Sharp right at the corner, sharp right again. Rivas, staring straight in front of him. It began to look as though it was all right. It would have happened by now, if at all. So he'd been lucky.

"Well?" the colonel said. "Nobody did any shooting that *I* could notice."

"No, sir. I'm extremely grateful."

"Lot of damned nonsense." He seemed disappointed.

Left, and on to the main road. Rivas began to relax. It was all right to be lucky sometimes; that was allowed. But it didn't do to make a habit of it. He began to think about the dead man, about the phrasing of his initial report. He found this rather difficult, however; something was still disturbing him. It took him some little time to realise what it was.

"If I may say so, sir, with due respect . . . you're pointing that thing at *me*."

"I know," the colonel said.

The jeep turned off the main road again.

"Look at it from another point of view."

"Yes?" Acuña said, looking at his wrist-watch. Half past

two. Getting on for lunch time. "Which?"

"If Feramontov isn't on his own, well, then he's working *for* somebody. Nobody's going to help him, I mean, out of pure kindness of heart. He's worked for a lot of different people in the past. . . . The question is, who is it *now*?"

"Not the Russians," Acuña said. "Which is nice to know."

"Exactly. He's on their black list. And that being the case, who'd want to touch him? There can't be many people who're *that* un-fussy."

"So who would you suggest?"

"Well, there's Egypt." Creases across the elder Rivas' forehead, signalling perplexity, subtlety, the hideous tortuousness of thought. "But I can't see them buying from the Moscow black list; they usually play it much cooler than that. The Moroccans. . . . Well, yes, maybe, but I don't know what they'd want to use him *for*. And then there's Argentina. Peron's crowd. But that's preposterous. Wildly unlikely. So there may be something in it."

"And France?"

"*France?*"

"France."

"Oh. You mean the bad boys."

"They're very bad boys indeed," Acuña said. "Half of them are right here in Spain and the other half are sitting on our bloody doorstep. And Madrid, of course, stiff with *simpatizantes*. That's what makes a leak that much more likely."

"Ortiz. And his wife was French. I'll admit there's a link-up."

Acuña leaned back, closed his eyes. Yes, he thought. There *was* a link-up. There was a piece, in other words, that looked as though it might fit. But that didn't have to mean a thing. When you have a space, a vacant space, there are *always* pieces that look as though they may fit. And if there aren't any, then the mind creates them. That's why you have to be careful. Cautious. You have to be sure.

"I have a feeling," he said, "that we're going to have to

throw all the old pieces away. Egypt. Morocco. France. They belong to another game. And Feramontov's stopped playing it. I've got a feeling we're up against something new. Completely new. That's what I think."

You have to be certain. Yes. But certainty isn't a matter of reasons, of logical analysis. It's a matter of intuition. You know or you don't know. It's as simple as that.

"Nothing's ever new," Rivas said. "Or so you used to tell us."

"*Plus c'est la même chose*, perhaps. That doesn't make change any less of a reality. It happens. And when it happens, you'd better move with it. Or you'll go," Acuña said, "where the dinosaurs went."

Change. Evolution. But minds evolve, as well as bodies. People learn. They learn from each other. In France, *les mauvais garçons* had learnt from Hitler; they'd tried to overthrow the ageing, adulated general who had constituted, at the time, their country's legally appointed government, and they had failed; but it had been a much nearer thing than many people supposed. Evolution takes no note of failure. It establishes a new combination, a fresh alliance, and it tries again. France didn't have a monopoly of ageing and adulated generals as Heads of State. Spain had a splendid specimen, had had one for twenty-five years. It was obvious as only hunches can be. They ought, Acuña thought humourlessly, to have special stickers on their windscreens, saying DINOSAURS MUST GO : but no, they couldn't be as obvious as *that*. They worked in secret, deep underground, but they were bad boys for all that. Very bad boys indeed.

On the desk, the telephone rang. The telephone was always ringing.

The call was long-distance from Madrid. The voice at the other end of the line was soft and furry, a voice that massaged, with nothing in its level intonations to suggest that it might also squeeze, might tighten to a stranglehold. Feramontov listened, as was his custom, and said little. He had never met the owner of the soft and furry voice, but he had heard it on occasion say certain things; things that might have inspired in him a certain respect, had he been familiar with that concept. He held the telephone loosely in his hand; a long, brown, bony hand; narrow-knuckled; the nails neatly trimmed and slightly pinker in pigmentation than those of the average European. It could have been the hand of an Arab, but it wasn't. It was Feramontov's. He held the telephone loosely, and he listened.

"You feel you can arrange reception of the goods, then," the voice was saying, "in about three weeks' time? We can't conclude the transaction very much later, for reasons you're familiar with."

"That'll be all right," Feramontov said.

"Good. It doesn't seem likely that I'll be contacting you again before the 28th, unless of course there are new moves from our competitors. I hear they got left well behind on our last operation, but I'd like your assurance to that effect."

"They showed signs of catching us up in Alicante," Feramontov said. "We took the matter in hand. I have one of their representatives with me now. Things can safely be left to me."

"*Whose* representatives? I believe there's a British firm showing some interest."

"No," Feramontov said. "Not *him*." His grip on the receiver had tightened momentarily; he relaxed it with a conscious effort. "One of our home competitors. The other I take to have been an ... intervention, merely."

"Interesting, though," the voice said. "And possibly useful. I imagine our Spanish friends won't have liked it very much. It may even distract their attention for a while, and that of course may suit our book very nicely."

Feramontov's lips were still drawn back a little from his teeth. He was beginning to have a *thing* about the British firm; he knew it, and didn't much care. "They've been left nothing else to work on," he said. Then—since the conversation was, in his view, concluded—"I'll hear from you by the

28th. If not before." And placed the receiver carefully on its hook.

He stood motionless for a moment, deep in thought; then placed, no less carefully, his khaki officer's cap centrally on his head; flicked at the brim; and walked out of the Telegrafos building and into the street. His driver, standing by the jeep, came to attention and saluted. Feramontov clambered in. The motor coughed, spluttered, then finally turned over. The jeep moved away down the lamplit street.

Secret Police agents, on operations, report in on a six-hour time-check. Failure to report is tabulated at Central, and after three successive failures the agent is reported missing. The younger Rivas, therefore, went missing at 12 midnight precisely. The letter that he had posted wasn't delivered at Central until eight hours later, but when it did a Special Messenger took it straight to Acuña. Where was Acuña?... A silly question. He was sitting on a chair, at his desk.

Alone, as it happened. The elder Rivas was on operations again. He hadn't been told about his brother yet, and when he was it would be in the usual way. Through a two-X bulletin. That would be the way he'd expect.

Acuña opened the envelope and looked at its contents. It hadn't meant a thing to young Rivas and it didn't mean a thing to Acuña, either. But a man had died because of it, one man and maybe two, and it was all he had. It didn't mean anything, but it was a good deal more than nothing. It was what he had to work on.

He thought he knew how.

He rang the bell and the man in the dark suit came in. "I want," Acuña said, "that last report from Alonso. And I'll see the Coordinator... when he comes in."

2

"*Oiga*," the voice said.
"...*Oiga?*..."

Fedora's eyes rolled upwards towards the ceiling, searching for a focus. The voice had seemed to come from beyond it; but that, as he now realised, was improbable. It *was*, after all, a ceiling, and not, as he had at first thought, some weird kind of an off-white fog. It was just that his eyes couldn't seem to find a hold on it. The voice came nearer.

"How are you feeling?"

"Not too bright," Fedora said.

He spoke in Spanish, since the voice did. He spoke it well, but at the same time he knew that it wasn't his native language. His lips seemed to move too sluggishly to form the words; it was as though they were the first he'd spoken for a very long time. How long?... But what *was* this, anyway? It had to be an illusion, like the other. The voice was near at hand and always had been. He turned his head on the pillow, and now his eyes came into focus with no trouble at all. He blinked. He hadn't expected it to be *that* near.

"Now there's nothing to worry about," the girl said. Her tone was resolutely cheerful, like a chaffinch's. "We gave you a little injection, just to bring you round. The effects'll all pass off in five minutes or so. Just lie still and take it easy."

She spoke from a range of about six inches but she was not, Fedora now realised, actually in bed with him. Which was just as well, since she appeared to be some kind of a nun. It would be a nursing order, no doubt. Our Lady of Balenciaga. Or something. Fedora didn't feel in the market for resolute cheerfulness, though. Silence and sympathy were what he wanted. His arm was hurting. So was his head, but not too badly. It had been worse before. When?... Oh yes. He had it now. A fleeting vision of the car bumper swerving up towards him, of his right wrist jarring on the road ... mud and grit. ...

He opened his eyes again, trying to adjust them to the new realities of colour and movement. The nurse was reaching for the tray that stood on the bedside table; glass, hypodermic syringe, used ampoule, cotton wool. "How long have I been here?" Fedora asked suddenly.

"You were brought in very late last night. It's now just after three in the afternoon." Stiff linen rustled as she moved away. "The doctor will come and talk to you in five minutes' time. *Mientras tanto. . . .*" He didn't see her smile because he was looking down at his arm, at the bandages that encased it; but he sensed it somehow. It didn't mean anything, of course. It was the usual professional smile, resolutely cheerful and a shade overworked. ". . . Be a good boy. Everything's all right."

It wasn't, though, Fedora thought. At first there had been only a sense of unease, of inexplicable urgency, of something needing to be done; then, though at no definable moment, an awareness of exactly what that something was. He had to be in Alicante; he should have been there that morning; this was the worst of possible times to go *hors de combat*. Even so, it mightn't be too late. Provided he got moving right away, there might still be time. He lifted his arm some three inches from the mattress, flexed it a little at the elbow; everything moved all right. It could have been worse.

His eyes were beginning to hurt him, though. The blinds had been drawn across the window to his left, but the sunlight that squeezed in through the narrow apertures seemed to be exceptionally bright. An effect of the drug, probably; perceptions heightened but incorrectly synchronised. To bring him *round?* . . . That was unusual, surely. An amphetamine, maybe. Pulse rate? . . . He couldn't check. The bandage covered the whole of his right hand and wrist and most of the forearm. He breathed slowly and deeply. His reactions seemed normal enough. His head was clearing very fast.

... But all the same, something odd. He didn't know what.

He lay still, as the nurse had instructed, moving only his eyes, taking slow stock of his immediate surroundings. A small, bare room with whitewashed walls; a private ward, obviously, in some small hospital or Red Cross centre. A small cupboard in the corner by the window, a key projecting from the keyhole; his clothes would probably be inside. He followed for a moment the train of thought that this suggested, but abandoned it almost at once. It would be ill-advised. He might run into something he couldn't handle, like maybe a one-legged midget. He continued his cautious reconnaissance.

Over the bed, a wooden crucifix. Nothing else on the walls. The cords of the window-blind were badly worn and the sill was of brick-red tiles. Everything was very clean, but the usual hospital smell seemed to be lacking. But then this wasn't one of the big Barcelona hospitals, he'd already guessed that. Probably the *casa de socorro* in one of the outlying villages. Laura had had *that* much sense, anyway. Though the formalities might well be troublesome, wherever she'd taken him. Forms to fill in, papers to sign, bills to pay. Fedora inhaled more deeply than before and sighed windily.

The door handle clicked noisily and a man came in. Tall and thin, with a knee-length white jacket and wire-framed spectacles. He had that intangible doctor's air of needing to be somewhere else rather quickly. "Mr. Fox, isn't it?"

"That's right."

"You speak Spanish?"

"Yes."

"Ah. Good." The doctor approached the bed with gangling, wading strides like a stalking heron; touched, in rapid succession, Johnny's neck, left temple and left wrist. The latter he retained for several seconds. "I am Dr. Baez. Are you in any pain?"

"No," Johnny said. "Not really."

"Good," the doctor said again. He relinquished Fedora's wrist, sat down on the edge of the bed. "It would be better if you didn't talk too much. So let me try and anticipate your questions. You've had a very nasty knock on the back of the head and you've been suffering from concussion. You'll feel the effects of it for a few days yet, but it's nothing serious. There's just one question that I must put to you."

"Yes?" Fedora said. *Nothing serious.* That was nice to know.

"You have what appears to be a double abrasion. Our impression is that you received a heavy blow some time before your accident last night. Is that the case?"

"Yes," Fedora said. "That's the case."

Baez folded his hands on his lap, as though restraining a gesture of impatience. "You didn't notice anything wrong prior to the accident? Eye strain? Fogged vision? Headaches?"

"I had a very bad headache. Yes."

"Then why the hell," Baez said, "didn't you go and see a doctor at once? . . . All right. No need to answer that. But in my opinion—and it's best to be frank—you should never have been driving that car at all. Criminal negligence, I'd call it. And if the police decide to charge you, I'll have no option but to say so. You realise that?"

This had to be the new psychology, Fedora decided. Give the patients something new to worry about, take their minds off their injuries. "Surely," he said, "there can't be any question of that."

The doctor shook his head. "I don't know so much. Of course, you're a foreigner. They stretch points for foreigners. And again, you may have learnt your lesson already. I certainly hope so."

No. No, it wasn't the new psychology. Baez was cross, that was all. Baez was a cross Spaniard. Fedora usually rather liked cross Spaniards; he could so easily see what they had to be cross about. "I'm sorry," he said. "It was just that I had . . . Well, I still have . . . very urgent business. . . ."

"Always the same old story. Business, business. I notice you still haven't asked after your passenger, though. You young people don't seem to have any sense of responsibility at all. Once you're at the wheel of a motor-car—"

"*What* passenger?"

Baez stared at him. "I understand the name is—"

"Laura? I thought," Fedora said, "she'd brought me in."

"Good God, no. Oh, no real damage. Cuts and bruises, mostly superficial. She was lucky, though. You *both* were. The car's a complete write-off. Not that that'll worry you much; I've no doubt you're properly insured."

"I stopped the car," Johnny said slowly.

"What do you mean, stopped?"

"I remember it perfectly. I stopped the car. I got out. Then I fainted, or something. How could Laura...?"

"Where?"

"What?"

"*Where* did this happen?"

Baez was watching him now very much more closely. A heron, poised to stab. Fedora, aware of this new intenseness, felt a muscle twitch high up in his cheek.

"On the Villafranca road. I don't know *exactly* where. Before you reach the main road and turn off for Barcelona. ... We were heading for the station. Does it ... matter?"

"Barcelona," Baez said. "I see."

There was something odd, of course. There always had been. "Where *am* I now?" Fedora asked. "Something's wrong. Isn't there?"

"No, no. Not *wrong*, no." The doctor's manner had changed insensibly; he was no longer ready to pounce. His tone, indeed, was almost one of reassurance. "Nothing, that's to say, out of the ordinary. You ask me where you are. Well, you're in Cordoba."

"But I *know* Cordoba," Fedora said. Even to him, it seemed an inapposite remark.

"This is the Red Cross hospital in Cordoba. Last night you smashed your car up about three miles out of town, coming in on the Sevilla road. You had a passenger and you seem to remember the passenger. Do you remember anything else?"

"That was Barcelona," Fedora said.

"You lost consciousness in Barcelona?"

"Yes."

"What day was that?"

Fedora knew that he wasn't showing up to great advantage. "Let's put that another way," he said, lunging bravely in the direction of rationality. "When's today?"

"Today is Tuesday," Baez said. "May the twenty-fifth."

"May the twenty-fifth. I see."

"And . . . you were going to Barcelona?"

"On May the fourth, I think. Yes. May the fourth."

"We seem to have lost three weeks," Baez said. "Almost exactly."

"But that's not possible."

"You've heard about amnesia?"

"Everyone has."

"Yes. But I know what you're thinking. That happens to other people, not to *me*. That's what *everyone* thinks. But it's not all that unusual, you know, especially after blows of the kind that you've sustained. There's nothing to worry about, nothing at all."

It sounded as though it had to be true, but Fedora didn't yet believe it.

"It's a purely temporary condition. As the effects of the concussion wear off, you'll find things start coming back to you. Total amnesia is another matter, but it seems quite obvious you . . . What's your name?"

"Fox," Fedora said. "John Fox."

"How old are you?"

"Thirty-seven."

"Married?"

"No."

"And what exactly are you doing in Spain?"

"At the moment I'm on holiday. That's to say, I was on holiday at Villafranca. What I'm doing down here I don't know. Normally I work for a British firm in Madrid. Technical publications. I was supposed to be—"

"All right," Baez said. "That's quite all right. And the girl in the car?"

"We met at Villafranca. Her name's Laura."

"Laura what?"

"I don't know."

"Don't know?" Baez looked up. "Or don't remember?"

"I never asked," Fedora said. "It didn't seem important at the time."

"I see." For the first time, a faintly human expression appeared on Baez's face; it was even possible that the thought of smiling had occurred to him. If so, he repressed it. "Since I treated the young lady in question, I think I know what you mean. Generally, then, you remember who you are and everything about yourself. It's just that you reach this point when, as you say, you fainted on the way to Barcelona . . . and after that, nothing. Right? . . . You're sure?"

"That's it."

"Try again."

Fedora tried for a few moments. ". . . No. No good."

"The lady tells me you were driving here from Sevilla. Does that suggest anything to you? . . . Sevilla?"

Sevilla. Sevilla.

"No."

"What were you doing in Sevilla?"

"It's no good." Fedora's fingers plucked in irritation at the blue coverlet. "All I feel is a vague sense of time having passed. You know what I mean? . . . The way I remember it, last night I was driving into Barcelona. And yet I sort of feel that it was much longer ago than that. That's all."

"It *was* much longer ago," the doctor agreed. "Three weeks ago, to be almost exact."

Fedora said nothing. There was nothing to be said.

"On the face of it, it seems possible that you've been wandering round all that time with severe concussion—though you probably didn't know it. I can't believe you consulted a doctor at any time. He'd have had you right where you are now, tucked up in bed. And in a flash. So you've probably only got yourself to blame." Baez was evidently returning to his old form. "The best thing you can do now is get some sleep, and if you're still feeling this way tomorrow morning I'll bring in one of the local specialists. He'll cost you a packet and it'll serve you right." Baez stood up, made his angular way towards the door. "I'll see you again when I make my evening rounds. If there's anything you want in the meantime, ring for the nurse."

"Thank you very much," Fedora said.

Baez went out and the door closed behind him.

Sevilla. Sevilla.

No.

Alicante, yes. I was going to Alicante when it happened.

That was the only good thing about the present set-up. A missing day is one thing, three missing weeks quite another. The urgency's gone. I needn't worry about getting to Alicante any more. It's far too late.

But for all I know I've *been* to Alicante. Oh, this is absurd. This is just ridiculous. And also, dangerous. That's the trouble. I'm in a hole and I have to climb out of it. Somehow.

Why was I going to Alicante?

Yes. Let's get things in order.

What's your name?

It isn't John Fox. I'm Johnny Fedora. I work in Madrid all right, but not as a technical translator. Or not entirely. I work for a firm called Eminex and I'm on loan to British Intelligence. Securace. Cartwright's outfit. And I've come to Spain to kill a man called Feramontov.

There was a trap. At Villafranca. We laid a trap, me and ... *God.* What was his name?... Yes. Boyd. With a man called Ortiz as the bait, as the goat to call Feramontov's tiger. It didn't work. It was a *fracaso.* Boyd and Ortiz got dead both, and a lot of other people too. Feramontov took the bait and got away in Ortiz's yacht.

The yacht went downcoast to Alicante. I made a lot of phone calls and I found that out. So I started off for Alicante to talk to the captain of the yacht, a man called Durand. That was when it happened.

A man called this. A man called that. It doesn't seem to have any reality, damn it. But it happened, it all happened. It happened to *me*.

And now *this* has happened. I've lost my memory. I'm in a hole and I have to climb out of it. Yes, but how?

... Let the free length of the cantilever be l. Depression of any point on its axis at a distance x from fixed end be y, when load W is applied at free end. Then we write

$$y = \beta\frac{w}{y}\, l^8\, \mathrm{f}\left(\frac{x}{l}\right)$$

—Y representing Young's modulus and the quantity β depending on the transverse dimensions of the cantilever. Yep. Now we apply Rayleigh's reciprocal. That gives us the degree of depression of the free end when load W is applied at point x. But say we derive an alternative expression. Say that $OP = x$ and load W is applied at P_1, then the form of the cantilever, at distances (ξ) from O less than x, can be given as

$$y = \beta\frac{w}{y}\, x^8\, \mathrm{f}\left(\frac{\xi}{x}\right)$$

No. That's not right.
Yes, it is.
Okay.
Now we give the inclination of the axis to the cantilever over the length OP. How? ... Yes. $\dfrac{dy}{d\xi}$ So then the inclination at P is given by ...?

The hell with it, Fedora thought. It has to be years since I blew up a bridge. *This* isn't the way. Try something else.

The brain is something like a telephone exchange. When the wires go down, you test and keep on testing. That's what the lecturer said. It sounded easy, then. Everything's easy, in those quiet back rooms off Whitehall. Check the wires. Keep on testing. Think of things. Describe them. Easy.

Here's a *very* pretty little thing. It's called a quartz crystal resonator. Now I'll tell you what it's for. It's a device that gives an accurate frequency impulse in all kinds of electronic systems. It all has to do with the piezoelectronic effect, which arises when a crystal is mechanically deformed and produces a voltage. Quartz has a very elastic crystal structure, so it vibrates in selective modes with a very low internal friction. You can't say that one part of it is a capacitator and another a resistor and so on, it works as a whole and that's the beauty of it. Sometimes you can stop it functioning and can then say you've done a good day's work; for example, at the central computer in the *K-polizei* HQ in East Berlin. I may have done a good day's work quite recently, for all I know. I've had twenty-one chances to do so, or so it appears. *Twenty-one days,* for God's sake.

Something like that has happened to me. Inside my head. The crystal structure isn't vibrating properly. Oh, I know all the answers, or most of them anyway. I could go to London right now and take one of my routine six-hour grillings, bright lights and all, and not one of the Colonel's boys would be able to catch me out in anything that mattered. Unless, that is, they thought of asking me something really difficult. Such as, *What were you doing yesterday?* . . . Something like that. Then they'd have me stumped all right, all right.

Stop.

Check the wires. Keep on testing.

"He's all right, then?"

"He's fine," Baez said. "Yes. Fine."

"And . . . can I see him?"

"I don't see why not."

She stood up.

". . . There's just one thing," Baez said, "perhaps I ought to mention . . ."

Now, now, Fedora. No panicking. You're rushing things, that's the trouble. Got to check at the fences. *Anda con calma.* Suppose you lie straight and stop sweating. And go back to where we started from.

Nothing personal. That's the main thing. Try to remember things, yes, but nothing personal. Theorems, all that jazz. Theorems are excellent. Then let yourself in on the deal, little by little. Standard recovery technique from drug treatment, as outlined by a plump little man in Whitehall. It might work for this loss of memory kick, as well. In fact, it *will* work. Convince yourself of that. It's important. This is the way to do it, tried and trusted method, wise mothers buy it for their babies. Never fails. Just stop sweating, that's all.

Now, then.

What was the Red Chapel?

Yes, that's going back a bit. Before my time, really. It was a German underground resistance movement, KPD based. Some contacts with the West as well, and with Switzerland through Hausmann and Rössler. Not very effectual, except in the Intelligence field. Got largely wiped up, winter of 42-43, by the Gestapo, who gave it that damned silly name. Schulze-Boysen, tortured to death; Arvid von Harnack was executed and read Plato in the death-cell. His wife was American. She was killed, too.

Next question?

What was the Jojo job?

I'm glad you asked me that. It was an abortive attempt to assassinate General de Gaulle in September 1963. It would have been a quasi-military operation, with the killers moving up from Spain in an armour-plated Citroen, but it fell through because someone talked. Jojo was the code name for Jeanne Morin, who mistress-minded the whole thing and made a right mess of it, though she did get away in time herself. Nothing got into any of the papers; but somehow after the Jojo job everyone seemed to know what a *barbousse* was, and they hadn't known before.

So good luck to *her*.

What is article 301 of the Swiss Criminal Code?

I know that one, too. Oh, I'm quite a little mine of useless bloody information. Useless, that is, while I'm lying here flat on my back. Still and all, it's amazing, the amount of miscellaneous lumber I'm carrying around with me all the time. Suppose I'd had a proper education, had been to a public school and all that. Eton, even. Why, there'd have been no stopping me. I'd be someone really important and could maybe work it all out with a half-dozen matchsticks. Instead of which, here I am, lying on my back. . . .

You said that before.

Back to your homework.

Deep breaths. One. Two. Three.

Start again.

Who was Otto Hartmann?

That's an easy one. Colonel of the SS, member of the Kreisau Circle, believed to have handed on information to the High Command of the Wehrmacht and hence to have been responsible for the death of Helmuth Count von Moltke. He was executed in the South of France, July 1944. *Who killed him?*

Me.

He was the first man I ever killed.

One. Two. Three.

Who was Feramontov?

Oh, an interesting type. A many-sided character. We know all about Feramontov.

Except where he is now.

That's what we'd all like to know.

Where is he now?

All right. Don't push it too far. Leave it at that.

Come on, come on—where is he now?

Moscow. London. No. Somewhere in Spain. Alicante? Sevilla? How would *I* know where he is now?

You *do* know. You know you know. So come on. Where's he hiding? You've been after him for days. Weeks. Months. He's yours. So come on. *Where is he?*

I don't know. I can't. I can't remember. It'll come back all right if you don't push me. Just leave it at that.

There isn't time, Fedora. It's there, you know it's there. You've got to find it. All you have to do is try—really try. Now. Concentrate. Where? . . . Where? . . .

Barcelona. Brindisi. Beginning with a B?

Maybe something to do with a colour?

Or was that the Red Chapel?

Kapelle Rote, a German underground resistance group. There was von Harnack. Schulze-Boysen. And Rittmeister. He was a psychiatrist. My God, that fellow just now. What was *his* name?

Baez. That was it. Baez.

Hold on to it now. Hold on to yourself. Just hold *on* a while, that's all. Take it easy.

B in it somewhere. Ljubljana? Rabat? No, Spain. Spain. There's a B in Cordoba, but it's not that. Can't think of *any.* Not a common letter, in Spanish place-names. No bells ringing. B as in bells. Belalcazar? Belmont? Marbella?

Bel? Bel?

Or Boyd. Arnie Boyd. They sent him out to work with me here. Now he's dead. And I might as well be, for all the . . .

Bel. Bel. Belshazzar? . . . Bel? . . . Bel? . . .

Johnny's eyes were closed now; his lips moved, phrasing the same soundless syllable over and over again. Sweat formed a thin film on his forehead beneath the bandage, on his cheeks, at the base of his neck. The patient wasn't taking it all that well; Baez, had he seen Fedora now, would not have been pleased. Not pleased at all.

"Hullo," Laura said. "How are you feeling?"

"Well, something rather awful has happened."

"I know. The doctor told me."

There followed rather a lengthy pause, Laura's kisses tending to be rather protracted, not to say smoochy, affairs. Few people, however, complained on this account; and Fedora, never. "Well, now," Laura said, sitting, as had Baez, on the side of the bed. "You seem to be in *fairly* good shape."

"How about you? The doctor said . . ."

"I'm all right. Except . . . You hadn't noticed?"

"What?"

"For heaven's sake. Johnny. You *must* be hazy."

"I don't see . . . Oh Lord, yes. My word, that's quite a shiner. My attention was elsewhere, so to speak."

"A beauty, isn't it?" Laura said complacently. "And you should see my ribs. A *mass* of bruises."

"How soon can that be arranged?"

"What? . . . Oh, *that*. I don't think I ever met a man with so one-track a mind."

Her tone remained complacent as before; Johnny gathered that this wasn't a complaint, either. She stared at him with large, serious eyes (one of them considerably less large than usual. As black eyes went, it was indeed something special), and Johnny stared right back at her. He hadn't, of course, forgotten her face, but in his perturbation he had forgotten that he liked it so much. The jaw-line maybe a little too broad, the mouth maybe a little too wide, but that was the way it had been and the way it always *should* be. Funny face. You derived quiet pleasure just from looking at it. And kissing it, of course, better yet.

"I may have a one-track mind," Fedora said. "If so, it seems to have got sort of derailed."

"Just as well they told me. I'd never have guessed."

"Well, but look. Exactly what's been happening? Have you been *around* all the time these last three weeks? I'll bet," Fedora said, struck by a thought, "there's been some things going on that'd be fun to remember."

"Mmmmm. Recapitulate, even better. You really don't remember a thing?"

"Not a thing. We were on our way to Alicante, and I blacked out on the way."

"That's right. You were out for all of ten minutes. I wanted you to see a doctor, but you insisted we go on."

"So we went to Alicante?"

"Oh yes."

"And?"

She picked up his good hand, squeezed it. "The doctor said you shouldn't talk too much. Don't you think maybe later on . . .?"

"I'm not talking. *You* are. And it's important."

"Yes, I gathered it was. All I can tell you is that you went to see a man in a hotel. Called the Albuferete. The man's name was—"

"Durand."

"*Yes.* Oh. You remember that from before."

"I *did* see him? You're certain?"

"Well, you told me you had. I didn't go myself. You wouldn't let me."

"I didn't tell you what we'd talked about?" No, Johnny thought. I wouldn't have. Damn it.

"No. But we left in a hurry. That same afternoon. For Sevilla."

"And in Sevilla?"

"Well, you had business to attend to and I did some shopping. I went through Sierpes like a whirlwind. And we went to a bullfight . . . We spent a lot of money, I'm afraid."

"I'm sure," Johnny said, "it was worth it."

Business, he thought. *What* business?

"The man you talked to . . . Durand . . ."

"What about him?"

"He was shot about an hour later."

That sort of business. A few seconds' silence, while Fedora pursued such implications as he could perceive; this, without liking them particularly. "It was in the paper," Laura said. "I think you still have the cutting somewhere. He was killed in his room in the hotel."

"Why did we go to Sevilla?"

"You said you were losing your sun-tan."

"No. Really?"

". . . You didn't say. I assumed it was because of what Durand had told you."

"Yes," Johnny said sadly. "That's what I was thinking."

The sunrays entering through the cracks in the blind were now touching the coverlet. Laura got up and moved over to the window, pulled the shutter up on its roll of cord. The white wall opposite turned gold and cream in the evening sunlight, and Fedora could see there the shadows of the motionless fronds of a palm tree. It was nothing like as hot as it had been.

"I hope I apologised," he said.

"What for?"

"Things just seem to happen that way. I know it's unpleasant."

"People getting dead, you mean?"

"Yes."

"Of course," Laura said, sitting down beside him again, "I can't help putting two and two together. You haven't told me much. But if it's useful . . ."

"I wish now I had. But it's difficult."

"I know. You're some kind of British government agent, Intelligence or something. The only time we ever talked about it, I asked if what you were doing was in any way against Spain. . . . Well, I *had* to ask that . . . . And you said it wasn't. And that was all I really wanted to know. I'm afraid it doesn't help much, though."

"I wouldn't have lied about it," Johnny said.

"No. You don't tell many lies, as a general rule. I've noticed that."

"That was in Alicante?"

"No. In Sevilla. Just before . . ." A hesitation, rather than a pause, lasting barely a second. "Before we left for Cordoba. Before we came *here*."

"Where are you staying? A hotel, or something?"

"Yes. We had a reservation."

"A double room?"

"Of course."

"You've got," Fedora said, "to get me *out* of here."

"Tomorrow."

"Is that what the doctor said?"

"Yes. And besides, it's what *I* say."

"Good," Fedora said. "That's good."

"The doctor also said you weren't to worry. It may not all come back at once. But it'll come back all right." Her fingers touched his wrist again, briefly. "So far as I'm concerned, it'll *always* be there. Always."

Well, well, Fedora thought. So progress has been made. Of course, if they'd been *that* good, it made the whole thing that one damned intolerable degree more frustrating. He groaned audibly.

". . . And if it's the job that's worrying you—whatever the job was . . ."

"Yes?"

"I'm almost sure you don't *have* to worry. Whatever it was, you finished it."

Johnny stared at her. That surely wasn't possible. Finished it? . . . *Finished* it? . . ."

"Yes," Laura said. "I've got reason to think so."

No. It wasn't possible. The job would finish when Feramontov was dead, and not before.

But then, how do I know he *isn't* dead?

I couldn't have *killed* someone and not remember it. Least of all Feramontov. Or could I have?

Barcelona, Alicante, Sevilla. I've been following a scent all right. Maybe not even a scent; just an intuition. That's the way I very often work. A *feeling*. I know that feeling. And I've got it even now, that's the trouble. It's there somewhere down in the depths, beneath the rational mind; too deep down maybe to be affected by . . . what's happened. It's still there, I'm sure of it. The job isn't finished.

Beneath the rational mind, perhaps. But it has a rational base. Intuitions always have. I *know* something, I'm sure I do. There's something that I know.

But I've forgotten what.

3

Fedora slept better than he had expected to, and woke to find the morning well under way. His window, of course, was now shaded and the room was pleasantly cool; propped up on a pile of pillows, drinking white coffee and chewing a meditative *tostada,* he could turn his head to see the dusty green fronds of the palm tree, the crumbling sunbaked stone of the wall beyond and, in the far distance, a skyline of gently rolling hills. Cordoba; a nice town in the spring, and at most other times, for that matter. He wondered what the hell he was doing there. He had forgotten to ask.

Anyway, what was the use? He'd come to build up his sun-tan. Or his sex-appeal. Or whatever. He'd never have told Laura the *real* reason why. The thing to do (as he realised this morning) was to get back in circulation. He felt pretty good today. No headache, no pain in the arm, no nothing. They'd begun the morning without waiting for him; that was the way the world was organised. He had to get back in it, and pretty quickly.

"I know a man," Laura said, "who knows a man."

"With the power of hoodoo."

"No. Not exactly."

"You're supposed to say 'Who do?' and I say 'You do,' and you say . . . Never mind." Fedora gave it up. "Scrub round it."

"Yes, I think I will. The thing is I rang him up last night."

"Rang who? . . . There I go again."

"The man," Laura said, "with the power."

"What power?"

"He shrinks heads."

"He shrinks heads. That," Fedora said, "is hoodoo."

"You do."

"No, *I* say *you* do. *You* say *who* do. Let's start again."

"To hell with it," Laura said. "He's coming all the way from Madrid specially to see you. This *very* afternoon."

Fedora gaped at her, his mouth full of the final remnants of the toast. "You're serious?"

"Of course I'm serious. He's a psychiatrist. One of the best. I mean, why not? You can afford it."

"Well, that's nice to know. You think he can help?"

"Dr. Baez thinks so. Which is more to the point."

". . . But a *psychiatrist?* What can I talk to him about?"

"You can tell him about the man."

"What man?"

"The man with—"

"All right. *I* know. I thought you said you were serious, is all."

"I cheated."

"Yes. You did."

"It's worth trying, though, isn't it? You need some kind of a specialist. That's obvious."

"What I need," Fedora said, "is my clothes."

"I brought some for you."

The hotel was only a couple of hundred yards from the hospital; Fedora, who still felt reasonably chirpy, decided not to bother with a taxi. So they walked together down the Avenida, their footsteps kicking up little puffs of dust that faded to nothing in the morning sunlight. Laura wore brown low-heeled shoes and beige-coloured terylene separates that seemed almost to merge into the colour of her skin, to create a rather strange kind of anonymity. Though perhaps that existed mostly in Johnny's own mind; there was still a faint atmosphere of unreality to his surroundings, even to Laura herself, a strange half-remembered-dream quality. He hoped, however, it would soon wear off, now that he was back in action. Well. Back, anyway. Moving around. ". . . I'm awfully stiff."

"I expect you are. It was quite a nasty smash-up."

"What happened, exactly? Was it like that time in Barcelona?"

"No, not really. We just went off the road, that's all. You missed the turning. The car people were very nice about it, luckily."

"We hired the car?"

"Oh yes. Almost first thing. when we got to Sevilla."

They walked up the hotel steps. Big green awning, green-shaded entrance hall; a grey-uniformed pageboy with a pill-box hat. The reception desk with a stuffed bull's head on top of it. "I'm afraid I'm going to be asking a lot of questions," Johnny said.

"Not if the head-shrinker does his stuff."

"I'm not optimistic."

The receptionist. Fluffy, like a kitten. "What's your room number, please?"

"Eleven. We'll go straight up, shall we?" Johnny said. "Unless you'd fancy a drink."

"Let's have them sent up. It isn't eleven, though. It's thirty-seven."

"What is?"

"The room number."

But the receptionist could have been dealing with crazy mixed-up kids like Fedora all her life. She had the key to thirty-seven all ready on the desk. "Sorry," Johnny said, as they got into the lift. "I'm not exactly in top form, as yet."

"I can see that."

"I don't know why I thought . . . Oh, never mind."

The room, when they got there, was all black and white. Black and white tiled floor, black armchairs, white walls, and a black-and-white bedspread covering the essentials. There was a bathroom, and Laura went into it. Fedora bounced on the bed. It seemed to be just right.

His suitcase, which she'd opened, stood on the rack; and there was another, of steel-grey samsonite, in the corner by the window. That would be Laura's, no doubt. Fedora didn't remember it; she'd left Villafranca with only a weekend bag. But since then she'd done some shopping, which would account for it. There was a smaller vanity case on the dressing-table, and most of its former contents seemed to be littered over the table's glass surface; Fedora wandered absently across and tried a lipstick on the back of his hand. Everything was still mildly odd. It was only a hotel room, but it had a very definite air of occupancy; Fedora's hotel rooms never seemed to get that way and, even though this particular occupancy he shared with Laura, he still felt himself something of an intruder. That was understandable. He didn't know Laura all that well. Or it was as if he didn't. So this was her lipstick; fascinating. Fedora wiped off the smear with a handkerchief, moved across to open the door of the built-in wardrobe.

The wardrobe contained dresses. *Her* dresses. And things. A surprising number of them, too, all to have come out of one suitcase. Perhaps she had another one somewhere. He couldn't spot it, though. Or perhaps she was a very skilful packer. Perhaps, perhaps. God, Fedora, why don't you *know?*

"What are you doing, darling?"

"Just mucking about," Fedora said.

He opened the dressing-table drawer. A couple of light wool sweaters, a folder of nylon stockings from Galerias Preciados, quite a lot of lingerie. All very neat. He shook out a pair of bikini briefs; black nylon with red silk ribbons; *surely* if he'd ever . . . ? But no. No, not memory. Just imagination. Very nice, indeed delightful, but not the same thing. He shook his head, screwed the flimsy nylon into a tiny ball symbolic of nicely mingled concupiscence, irritation and frustration. No good. Nothing there.

Back in action. That was a laugh. A one-handed man with a one-track mind, and nothing much moving down it, either. He sat down on the bed again and fingered the bandage that swathed his wrist. Laura came in.

". . . That can come off tonight."

"Oddly enough, my mind was just dwelling on that subject," Fedora said. "On things that can come off tonight. And the bandage too, you say? Splendid, splendid."

"Not the one on your head. Just the, er . . . hand."

"Couldn't be better. Come over here, why don't you."

She sat down on the bed beside him. Fedora continued his research. Under the biege-coloured blouse she wore a bra of white flowered cotton and of satisfactorily dangerous cut. "That's nice," Fedora said.

"Yes, I hoped you'd like it."

"*Now* I know what I can talk to the psychiatrist about."

"Oh, shut up."

Johnny continued his researches in an unfurtive manner for a minute or so longer; at the end of which time Laura fell back on the bed and reached for, of all things, the telephone. "What are you . . .?"

"I'm ordering the drinks."

"No, don't do that."

"I think I'd better."

Fedora, who could take a hint, regretfully withdrew; so that after panting for a while into the receiver she was able to establish a claim on one John Collins and one Cuba Libre. "At once, madame," said the receptionist. She sounded sympathetic. Laura sat up and buttoned everything up again.

"I haven't spoilt anything, have I?"

"Of course not," Johnny said. "Don't be silly."

"I don't mean to make a habit of it. I promise. It's just that . . ."

"Yes, I know."

"Shall we take our drinks out on to the verandah?" She stood up, smoothing her skirt. "There's a lovely view."

"I think I'll prowl," Johnny said, "if you don't mind. You know. Go through my things. There may be something that'll . . . You never know."

"That's a good idea. I'll be out there if you want me."

"There's no *if* about that," Fedora said.

He stared at his reflection in the dressing-table mirror. A thin, brown, triangular face under a Sikh's turban of folded bandages; brown, but not as brown as usual. It was quite true; he *was* losing his tan. Probably the dent in his napper had something to do with it. As thin, though, and as triangular as ever. It wasn't a young man's face, exactly; some people would indeed have maintained that Fedora's face had never been young; there was a certain quality in the eyes that prevented it. But certainly not an old man's face, either. It just happened to be at least twenty-two days older than it had been the last time its owner had looked at it. Not a long time; nothing like a long enough time to make any difference to it; Fedora stared, all the same, at his reflection, as though seeking to discover, in some minuscular change, a clue to where he had been, to what he had done, in that brief but inalienably missing period. Hopeless, of course. There was a face there, and a bandage, and nothing else. Well, not *literally* nothing else, of course. There was a white shirt (one of its buttons still unfastened) and there was the top half of a grey-blue worsted suit by Pierre Cardin and there was a black silk tie with a grey and white diagrammatic design, Diva of Italy, fifty-seven shillings and sixpence. None of that was of any use. More to the point, visible not in the mirror but on the luggage rack, was his suitcase.

I'm not optimistic.

He opened it, though, and started to unpack.

Two more suits and a black dinner-jacket, all pockets empty except for fluff. Black dress trousers, pockets ditto. There would be room for these in the wardrobe, alongside Laura's dresses. He took time off to hang them there.

Back then to the suitcase. Walther PP 7.65 mm. pistol, as worn this year in a soft leather spring-clip shoulder holster; eight rounds in magazine, present and correct. Extra ammunition in wooden cigar-box, snitched from Colonel Cartwright, sixty rounds . . . all there. Half a dozen shirts, ditto pairs of socks; belt and springknife, custom built by Franz Rosenberg of Lillehammer; two pairs of rolled-gold cufflinks. Ties, various. Clothes brush. Three face towels, spongebag, shaving tackle. Electric razor. At the bottom of the case now; two pairs of shoes, one brown, one black. Underwear. Pyjamas. Slippers in a travelling case. Cigarette-case in brown pig-skin. Notepad, unused, and Parker Flighter pen in a white plastic zip-up holdall, also containing: six five-peseta stamps, two one-peseta stamps, two sixty-centimo stamps, air mail envelopes, a pocket calendar, unmarked. Zip-up case, zipped down again. Thrown on bed. Cigarette-case opened, cigarette taken. King-size Chesterfield, badly needed. Also inside cigarette-case, and now revealed; clip of transparent plastic, of the kind sometimes attached to office files; inside it, a slip of stiff white paper on which words have been typewritten in black. As follows: *Badajoz (Camera 11)*. Cigarette is being lit by Ronson lighter held in left hand (right hand being out of action); flame goes on burning for several seconds after the initial inhalation. Why? . . . Left index finger has forgotten to release the spring lever. That's why. *Badajoz* . . . Was that . . .?

Yes. That was it.

And in the silence of the room, a voice (Fedora's voice) saying in his own ear,

Room eleven . . .

Badajoz, camera 11 . . . Room eleven . . . What the hell did *that* mean?

It meant *something*. That was for goddam sure.

A place with a B in it. Badajoz, it was Badajoz all right. I remembered it, there was *something* that I remembered. And since it was the only thing that I *could* remember . . . even partially . . . then it has to be important. I haven't been to Badajoz, though, have I? Not according to Laura. Nowhere near. How would you get to Badajoz, from Sevilla? Straight to the north, surely, through Extremadura. What I need is a map. Some kind of a map. Johnny reached for the telephone.

". . . Yes, sir. I'll try and find one, sir. For the whole of Spain?"

"Please."

"I'll send it up at once, sir."

. . . And *that's* why I thought my room number was eleven. It came up from my subconscious or wherever, when I wasn't really thinking. That's the way it happens, according to Freud, oh, good old Freud. And maybe the rest of it's hidden away there somewhere, too, and all we need is a winkle-picker to get it out. A winkle-picker, like Laura's champion head-shrinker. If I can give him something to get started on. . . .

Owwww. Ooooo.

Johnny dropped his cigarette on the floor, sucked his burned middle finger; then stooped to pick the cigarette up again. Dangerous things, cigarettes. Very painful, that. But useful to bring one back into the world of reality. The subconscious may be all very well in its way, but there still ought to be room for the application of a little old-fashioned logic. Where, for example, could this peculiar thing have come from?

Half of his Cuba Libre still stood on the dressing-table. He went across to it, swallowed it. I haven't been to Badajoz, have it? . . . I've been to Alicante. . . .

Pussycat, pussycat, where have you been? To Alicante to see the Queen. And what did she say to you when you got there? . . . Yes, that was the crux of the matter. Wasn't it?

Feramontov had gone aboard Ortiz's yacht, and had very obviously got off it again. Durand had known exactly how and when. That was why Johnny had wanted to find Durand, and that was why—if Laura was right—Durand was now dead. But, if Laura was right again, Johnny had got there first. And what had Durand said to him?

Yes. *What,* damn it?

A clip of transparent plastic, of the kind sometimes attached to office files. And sometimes unattached . . . sometimes, indeed, pulled off by accident. Especially by people in a hurry. The last time Johnny remembered seeing Feramontov, he had been in a hurry all right; mounting the swaying ladder of the yacht, the Moscow file in the little holdall swinging from his left hand. Feramontov had gone to Villafranca to fetch that file; what was in it, no one seemed to know. But it had to be important.

The clip had come off, then, and Durand had found it later. Say, on the stateroom floor. Feramontov wasn't usually that careless, but a man in haste makes mistakes. He'd made one, all right, somewhere. Otherwise, Durand wouldn't be dead.

But Badajoz. Why Badajoz?... Well, why not? It was a frontier town, for one thing. And something of a trouble spot, historically speaking. General Delgado had been killed near there, though it certainly wouldn't have anything to do with *that*. Surely not?... Political murders were in Feramontov's line all right, very much so; but that one seemed rather small beer by his exalted standards. A lead-in, though, to something bigger? . . . Well, it was possible.

The real question was rather different. If Badajoz, then why Sevilla? Why three weeks in another town? Presumably because of something that Durand had said. Presumably Durand had . . . It was all so *frustrating*. The most frustrating situation imaginable.

Fedora walked out on to the balcony. Laura sat there in a black-and-white deckchair reading the *Gaceta Ilustrada*, her bare brown feet resting on the parapet. ". . . What did you mean," Fedora asked her, "when you said that you thought my job was finished?"

She put up a hand to take off her sun-glasses. "Why, you said so yourself. Practically."

"But *what* did I say?"

"You said we could go on holiday. That was . . . about a week ago." For some peculiar reason, she now seemed a trifle uncomfortable. "You said your business was finished, in Sevilla."

"Ah," Johnny said. "In *Sevilla?*"

"Yes."

"But then why did we go on to Cordoba?"

"You said you wanted to."

"Oh, hell," Johnny said, raising both hands in a gesture of near-despair. "Didn't I . . . No. I suppose I wouldn't have."

There was a knock on the door. They'd brought up the map. It was in fact the official effort of the Ministerio de Obras Publicas, a big blue-covered book about the size of a small telephone directory; just what Johnny wanted. He sat down on the bed once more and studied its pages in silence. Things seemed to be pretty much as he'd supposed them to be. Portugal was to the left, Extremadura to the right and Badajoz in the middle, right on the frontier and straddling the Guadiana river. Highway 5 ran east to Merida and then up to Madrid; there were two routes from Sevilla to Badajoz, one through Zafra and the other through Jerez de los Caballeros, but neither went anywhere near Cordoba. Cordoba was on another road altogether, on highway 4. It didn't make sense, that part of it. Not at all.

Unless the job *was* over.

But then the thing got puzzlinger and puzzlinger. He'd had good reason—apart from the obvious one—for getting Laura away from Villafranca. She'd been a good deal more than a material witness to all kinds of shenannigans, and the police —had they been able to get hold of her—would certainly have found her account of them extremely interesting. To have kept tight hold of her for three weeks still made excellent sense, metaphorically and still more so literally. But to have taken her with him on an actual manhunt—most of all, on a Feramontov-hunt—*that* could only have been called complete lunacy. Appallingly risky and totally unnecessary. Not even in a state of concussion could he have done such a thing. No, it didn't make sense.

Nothing did.

The morning's discoveries had at least had one definite result. Fedora now felt able to face the proposed head-shrinking session with relative tranquillity. He knew quite well what Colonel Cartwright's response would be to the idea that any of his employees—even temporary ones—should submit to the polite inquiries of any but the Department's own tame trick-cyclists; he would, in a phrase, blow his top. And very understandably. The Colonel, though, happened to be well over a thousand miles away. With Boyd and Granger both struck off the roster, Fedora had been left alone, without contacts and without assistants; and that was how, after all, he was used to playing it. Whatever mess he had organised had to be cleaned up entirely by himself, and pretty damned quickly; PDQ, as the Colonel would have said, PDQ. So this time—and once again—the Department's book of unwritten rules could be torn up and thrown out of the window. Fedora didn't want rules. He wanted help.

Cardenas was the headshrinker's name. Luis Cardenas. It said so on the little card he gave Fedora to hold: *Luis Cardenas, psiquiatro,* and an address in Madrid. No letters after the name; he probably thought they were vulgar. He looked on the youngish side to be a top man in the profession, but the appearance of Spaniards is often deceptive in that respect; frequently they seem to be younger than they are. Anyway, he appeared to be confident. Quietly confident. "Well, now," he said, when Fedora had read what was on the card; an opening which struck Fedora as being as good as any.

"There are things, doctor," he said, "that I can't remember."

"Uh-huh."

"It seems that I had this accident, and I woke up in hospital—"

"Yes, I've a note of the *material* details of your case." He didn't explain what he meant, exactly, by this. "As I understand it, you're suffering from total amnesia, is that right?... extending over a period of some three weeks. This, associated with some form or other of minor concussion. *Is* that right? *Total* amnesia?"

"Virtually total, yes."

"What do you mean by virtually total?"

A good question. "I mean there are two or three things that seem to... you know. Ring a bell. It'll take a few minutes to explain—"

"No, no, no," Cardenas said, waving his arm to and fro like an umpire signalling a boundary. "I don't want explanations. Not at this stage. Before I do anything else, I'll have to have a word with Dr. Baez here. Firstly because it's profess-ional etiquette... *that* old thing... and secondly because I want to see the X-rays for myself. I want to be satisfied there's no question of organic disturbance. Because if there is, I'm the wrong kind of expert. I've already spoken to Baez over the telephone and he seemed to be as sure about it as one very well can be. Nevertheless, I have to check."

"Yes," Johnny said. "I follow that."

"Now what about the urgency? I take it that the urgency's genuine?"

"Very genuine."

"The best treatment of all, you see, is that provided by time. Sometimes it's the only treatment that's at all effective. It's true that the process *can* be hurried along a little. But I don't actively recommend treatment, *any* course of treatment, unless the patient fully realises that that's about all I can hope to do.... Give things a little nudge. Push them along. No miracles. No wonder drugs. Just several hours—or sometimes several days—of rather tedious probing, with no absolute guarantee of success at the end of it. Have I made my point quite clear?"

"Yes," Johnny said. "Have we started?"

"You mean I'm being tedious already?" Cardenas, rather to his credit, smiled. "You're right, of course. Just professional patter, to put you at your ease. Go on and chalk it up. Mis-take number one. No—we won't really *start* until tomorrow; but I'd like you to answer a few initial questions, if you'd be so good."

"I'll try," Fedora said. "Go ahead."

"When is your birthday?"

"February the sixteenth."

"Where were you last February the sixteenth?"

"In London."

"Did you celebrate the event?"

"Not really. No."

"Do you remember what you did the following day?"

"In the afternoon I drove down to Brighton. That's about

fifty miles from London, on the South Coast. I had to see a man in a pub. Business. Then I drove back again."

"And in the morning?"

"I stayed home and did my homework."

"Homework?"

"Reading newspapers. Reports."

"That being part of your business?"

"I work for an Intelligence Department of the British Government. On a temporary basis."

"An official or an unofficial department?"

Another good question. "Unofficial, in the sense you mean."

"I meant that in case of inquiry, they wouldn't acknowledge you."

"Exactly."

"And in Spain. . . . You're here on unofficial business?"

"Yes."

"Yes." Cardenas took from his breast pocket a neatly folded white handkerchief, dabbed with it at the corner of his right eye. "With that aspect of things I'm hardly concerned at all. I don't say I suffer myself from amnesia, but I do have a highly developed capacity for forgetting things which come to my notice in—so to speak—the confessional. It's very important that you should feel yourself able to speak to me without reservations. . . . I imagine this difficulty will already have occurred to you, though."

"It has," Johnny said. "My position is that I can't do otherwise. Time's too important."

"Good. Splendid. I, for my part, don't anticipate at the moment any need to press you on any point that may affect your, er . . . professional career. I take it, though, that yours is a profession in which a good memory is more than ordinarily important?"

"Yes, it is."

"In fact, you need an exceptionally good memory to be in that profession at all?"

"Yes."

"So that your memory, under normal conditions, is excellent. You'd agree?"

"For most things, yes."

"... You're aware of any particular lines of weakness?"

"No. I'm good at numbers and fairly sound at names. I don't miss appointments and I don't forget dates. I think I—"

"Granada. 700412. Vigo. 997848. Salamanca. 112447. Repeat those names and numbers."

Fedora did so.

"Did I say four-four-*seven*?"

"You did."

"Oh. Well, I expect you're right. You say you're good at appointments?"

"Yes."

"Let's say you're supposed to meet me here every day at noon. Today I show up at 12.30, next day at 1.20, next day at half past two, next day at four o'clock. What time would you expect me for the following day?"

"Ten to six."

"Not bad," Cardenas said slowly. "Not bad at all." He got to his feet.

"I hope you're not—"

"No, no. An exercise, merely. I pride myself, I assure you, on my punctuality. So I'll call on you again at nine o'clock tomorrow morning ... and we'll see what we shall see."

"Good," Fedora said. "Thanks very much."

"How did it go?"

"All right," Fedora said. "We don't really start until tomorrow morning."

"You don't seem very optimistic."

"I told you. I'm not."

"He's very good. In fact, they say he's the best."

"I believe you."

"I tried to do the right thing."

"You did."

Laura had come in to change for dinner. The grey silk

dress was draped over the foot of the bed; Johnny sat beside it, fingering the hem. She watched him, thoughtfully, for a moment before unzipping the beige skirt and stepping out of it. "Johnny?"

"What?"

"I don't *really* seem like . . . a stranger, do I?"

"In a way you do. Yes."

"Oh God," Laura said. "That's what I thought."

"This thing takes some getting used to. That's all."

"But you weren't like this before."

"At Villafranca? I was . . . all there, then."

"I meant this morning."

"I seem to have sort of started worrying. Since."

"But what *about*?"

"About us."

"Oh don't," Laura said. "Darling, don't."

Fedora looked up as she moved round the bed. Slim brown body, white cotton panties. Her breasts moving out a little as she stooped to kiss his cheek. "Oh, there's still no 'if' about *that*," Fedora said, his fingertips touching very lightly the firm rounded flesh at the swelling of her hip. "It's just that I can't understand what I've been up to."

"Up to no good," Laura said, mumbling rather. "What did you tell the doc? That we were just good friends?"

"He didn't ask me."

"How very odd."

That morning, Johnny had felt good; and now he didn't. That was the truth of the matter. No aches or pains or physical malfunctionings; just a general unsteadiness, a queaziness. When it came to the point, how could he hope to tangle with Feramontov, of all people, under present conditions? It was absurd. He had been *all there* at Villafranca, in peak condition, and he still hadn't been quite good enough. And since then, what? . . . What Baez had said. Eye strain, fogged vision, headaches. Three weeks hanging about Sevilla, to no apparent purpose. Then the car accident. The hospital. And Cardenas. Maybe in Alicante he'd done something, had found out something, but it hadn't been enough; it couldn't have been. That was the trouble with Feramontov. Nothing ever seemed to be enough. ". . . Should we go down to dinner?" Laura said.

"Whenever you like."

"Okay. I'll have a quick shower, then."

She went to take the big bath towel from the hook beside the dressing-table; slung it over one shoulder and, seemingly as an afterthought, stooped again to hook her thumbs in the briefs and drop them to the floor. Johnny glimpsed again, this time in the mirror, that gentle forward tilting of her heavy breasts and the hairline crease across the whiteness of her belly, disappearing as she straightened up; watched her pad silently across the cool tiles, naked but for the towel and her low-heeled brown shoes. There was a self-consciousness about her that, in his present mood, he much appreciated; he couldn't imagine Laura ever having to consult a psychiatrist, even of the fashionable kind. He watched her until the bathroom door closed behind her, then swallowed. His mouth seemed to be fuller of saliva than usual.

He looked sadly down at the bandage around his right hand and wrist. *That* at least could come off. The doctor had said so. And before dinner, too; he didn't like having his meat cut up into little pieces for him, not even by Laura. He got the nail-scissors from the dressing-table and commenced operations. The bandage unrolled easily enough at first, but its inner folds were stiff and sticky with dried blood. Soak it off, then. That was the answer.

Across the shower compartment, the curtain had been half drawn; Laura sang there quietly, her voice hardly audible above the hiss of the water. Leaning over the washbasin, Johnny saturated the bandage under the warm tap, began to cut the innermost strips away. He felt uneasy about the blood. Fedora often worried about his hands: no doubt because of his passion for the piano and his more reprehensible liking for nasty little pistols with filed-down trigger mechanisms. The first thing he did on waking up every morning (according to his old friend Adriana Tocino, who should have known), was to check up on his fingers to see if they were all there. The second thing, to check up on Adriana. That had been a long time ago and a long way away. But Adriana... No. *This* wasn't the time to start thinking about Adriana. He had more than enough on his plate the way things were.

Anyway, everything was jakers. All four fingers and thumb, positively present. A half-healed scar running across the palm, another at the base of the index finger: long cuts, but not deep; nothing to worry about. A raw patch inside the wrist, and what looked like gravel sores. He flexed all four fingers experimentally. Around the third finger was a gold ring. A plain gold ring. A plain gold ring. Fedora stared at it for what seemed to be a very long time. He'd never worn a ring in his life, much less a... On his right hand, too. But, yes. That's where men *do* wear them, in Spain.

"Laura?"

"I've nearly finished."

"What in hell's name is this?"

He rasped the curtain back along its rail; Laura, smothered in sexy soapsuds, squeaked plaintively. He had raised his ring finger admonitorily into the air, and possibly she had misinterpreted the gesture.

"Oh, *that*. I've... I've got one. Too."

"A *wedding* ring?"

"Yes."

"Not you and me?"

Laura opened her mouth and a large dollop of soap disappeared therein. She sputtered, in some anguish. Fedora sat down heavily on the bathroom stool.

"We're MARRIED?"

Laura still said nothing. Realisation dawned on Fedora that his reaction to this latest intelligence was not, perhaps, particularly flattering to her. "Not," he said, "that I meant it *that* way. I'm awfully sorry."

"You're sorry? Already?"

"I mean I'm sorry I... It's a bit of a surprise, that's all. Why didn't you *tell* me?"

He handed the bath towel to her absently, and Laura wrapped it feverishly round her person. "But it was so awkward, darling. I mean, if you couldn't remember . . . I didn't see how I could *tell* you. Just like that."

"But how did this happen? I mean, when?"

"Eight days ago. Well, you had a friend at the Consulate, you see, and you said—"

"Googie Withers?"

"Yes, that was the name. Withers. He was nice."

"But I've known Googie Withers for years," Fedora wailed. "He couldn't have done *this* to me. I must have been . . ."

"Yes?"

"Well, I mean. Obviously. I must have . . . I've never been married before. Like, *never*."

Laura seated herself suddenly and adroitly on his lap, the towel slipping downwards from her shoulders. "It's like you said. It takes a little getting used to. That's all."

Fedora got used to it rather rapidly, the process taking him approximately thirty seconds. The towel finally fell all the way to the floor; steam rose from Laura's damp and writhing body and also, apparently, from Fedora's ears. "No, wait," Laura said. "I'm all *wet*."

"That's because," Fedora said acutely, "you've just had a shower."

"Clever boy."

"Well, I don't know."

"What don't you know?"

"I must have . . ."

"Must have? You *did*."

". . . Been barmy," Johnny said. "Absolutely barmy."

"Of course. I thought so, too. But it was so nice to be made an—"

"Hey."

". . . An honest woman."

"Hey. You're wet."

"I know," Laura said. "I don't care."

Her back arching luxuriously into the crook of Johnny's

arm. Gleaming drops of water, freed by the movement, ran down her neck and coursed round the curves of her lifted breasts, the channels separating as they approached the sudden tilt of the nipples; like pearls, Johnny thought, on a necklace. He followed their parabola with his mouth, from the collarbone downwards, until her body stiffened and then went limp. Her hand came up, began to unbutton his shirt. Which was, unquestionably, getting very damp; to take it off certainly seemed the best way of avoiding incipient pneumonia. She did it very competently. While Fedora, having nothing to unbutton or otherwise despoil (poor old Fedora), carried her through the bathroom door and over to the bed.

"What d'you ... think of ... married life so far?" She sounded breathless; which, perhaps, was not to be wondered at.

"Oh yes," Fedora said. Not the most coherent of answers, but one that she seemed to find satisfying.

"Well, what about a spot of consummation?"

"*Oof*," Fedora said, dumping her on to the mattress.

He lay, some fifteen minutes later, with his bandaged head on the pillow and with Laura's damp head resting on his shoulder. He felt, oddly enough, a great deal better. Undoddery. Less weighed down by saucy doubts and fears. It must have been those clothes that he'd been wearing. All those shirts and trousers and things. A great mistake. He felt much better off without them.

"Maybe," Laura said dreamily, "maybe we ought to go and turn off that goddam shower."

Fedora thought about this for a while.

"Yes," he said eventually. "You could be right."

He turned his head and looked at her. There was no doubt about it. *Much* better off. Her body moved a little on the crumpled sheets, turning towards him.

"... Later," he decided.

4

Fedora had, from one point of view, very little cause for complaint. That was obvious, or had *become* obvious by the following morning. But that didn't alter, or seemed not to alter, the unaccountable oddity of his past behaviour. Getting *married*, gawdstrewth. Given as fact one that he was a cagey so-and-so, given as fact two that in any case he had been, as the saying goes, getting it regular, fact three—that he was *married*—constituted a positive outsize in *non sequiturs*. There had to be more to the situation than met the eye. But then what met the eye was, in Laura's case, so singularly agreeable that one hesitated to pursue the matter further. Or one did, if one were Fedora. At any rate, at the outset.

Motives, other than those inspired by lechery, could of course have existed. He could think of several. None of them, though, were particularly pleasant. Marriage can be, in some circumstances, an effective means of silencing a material witness; a wife, in Spain as in England, can not be compelled to give evidence against her husband. Not even, say, in a case of murder. Fedora didn't think that he had murdered anybody —at least, not lately—but he couldn't be sure.

"If you had killed somebody," Cardenas said, "if you had performed any *really* unusual or violent action, I think we can assume that some traces of recollection would remain in your conscious memory. I don't say we can completely discard the possibility. But it seems most unlikely."

"It wouldn't be all that unusual, though. Not for me."

"What wouldn't?"

"Killing someone," Johnny said. "It's my profession, in a way."

"You mean you've killed *many* people?"

"Too many. One is too many, really. But . . . too many, anyway."

Cardenas wrote something down in a small notebook, a small black notebook, he held on his knee. "And this man you tell me you are looking for?"

"I'm looking for him with that aim in mind."

"Yes," Cardenas said, and looked at him thoughtfully. Delusions of this kind were not infrequent, but still . . . Yes. Very interesting. "You would call yourself a professional killer, then?"

"In a way. Except that I don't kill just anyone."

"Only certain people? Or certain *kinds* of people?"

"I kill people who kill other people. Or try to kill other people. It's not a *kind*, exactly.."

"And you work for the British government. You mean you kill *spies*?"

"That's an old-fashioned name for it."

"And . . . this man you're looking for is then a spy?"

"Not exactly. Nowadays we talk about agents. He's an agent. He's a *free* agent. That's the trickiest kind."

"Goldfinger?"

"What?"

"Like the man in that film? Goldfinger?"

A faint shadow of expression crossed Fedora's face; it wasn't a smile, but it might have become a smile, if given encouragement. "He's not like a man in any film *I* ever saw."

"But he does exist?"

"Oh, certainly."

"How do you *know* he exists? Tell me something about him."

The smile at last took definite shape as such. "You're assuming, are you, that I've gone right off my rocker?. . . If you find it useful, I don't much mind. I'd just like to know."

Cardenas looked obstinate. "Tell me about him."

"All right. His name is Feramontov. He was born in Odessa around 1920. Height, five foot eleven inches. Complexion, swarthy. Eyes, blue. Hair, normally fair. Distinguishing marks. . . . Deep scars around both ankles, he once worked in a chain-gang. Left forearm broken in 1944 and badly set. Present associates, not known. Present whereabouts—"

"Stop."

Fedora stopped.

"You've been looking for this man for some time?"

"For some time, yes. Off and on."

"And he knows that you're looking for him?"

"Oh, yes."

"Then tell me something *about* him. You know what I mean."

Fedora's eyes turned upwards to stare at the ceiling. His face remained expressionless. "I think so."

"Go on, then."

"The important thing about him," Fedora said, "is that he's an exceptionally gifted man. Intellectually gifted. With a more formal sort of an education, or maybe with a different kind of ambition, he could have done almost anything and got almost anywhere. He speaks ten languages, according to our records, and probably has a few more on the side. English, French, Spanish, German, Arabic, Persian, he's got the lot. And he's travelled so much he doesn't just speak them, he *lives* them. He never uses disguise. He doesn't have to. He just becomes somebody else. He's at home anywhere in the world, just about, and in another sense he isn't at home anywhere. Feramontov's only home is inside himself. You could call that his tragedy."

A match flared in Cardenas' hand as he lit a cigarette; his eyes remained, however, fixed on Fedora's face. "He seems an interesting character."

"Oh, that's not all. He's physically gifted, too. He could have made some kind of an athlete when he was younger— if he'd cared to. He can navigate a ship as well as most professionals and he can fly aeroplanes, too. Probably even four-jet jobs, for all I know. Anything with an engine in it is meat to him. He's got mechanical aptitude, as they call it." Fedora was watching the whorls of cigarette-smoke rise placidly in the still air. "None of all that is really important, though. Those are just the things that make it hard to get hold of him, that make what happened to him rather a pity. What matters is just *that* . . . What *happened* to him. What matters is why we *want* to get hold of him. What matters is his mind."

"That's what always matters," Cardenas said. "Though of course, I'm maybe biased. Tell me about his mind."

"Well, you could say that he has, or had, a certain form of creative genius. Except that instead of working in words or in paint or in music . . . he worked with people. He built patterns, and he worked them out with people. That's very difficult. Because," Fedora said, "people don't usually have much sense of pattern, of design; they don't see that at certain points in any pattern, the motifs that they themselves represent have to come to an end . . . if the pattern is to be perfect. That's where Feramontov was something of a genius. At ending his motifs in exactly the right place. Murder and assassination and suicide are usually untidy things . . . but not when Feramontov handled them. He made them fit into sequences, like moves in a game of chess. One job he did in Iran, in the late '40s. . . . The Agitprop boys quote it in all their advanced courses. It's a textbook thing, if you follow me. About as near as you can get to sheer perfection. Then he left, and Stalin wouldn't back his play, and Mossadeq made nine wrong moves one after another . . . and a damned good thing it was for the British that he did."

"A long time ago," Cardenas said.

"It was, yes. In those days, Feramontov was part of what you might call a greater pattern, weaving his pretty little figures in the dark corners. He worked for Soviet Russia. That's to say he had a peculiar kind of political object which you could agree with or disagree with but anyway was *there*. Then gradually, through the '50s, that object got its edges worn off—things cooled down—techniques got different. Feramontov's methods stopped fitting in. He didn't get on well with Khrushchev, for a start; Khrushchev liked to set things out his own way, over the conference table, not in such-and-such a back street. But by then Feramontov had become ... well, obsessed is the word ... obsessed with the game itself, with the beauty of these patterns of his and the excitement of working them out; he *couldn't* change. That can happen quite easily. He tried to work out one of his classic opening gambits here in Spain and it went wrong on him. So they said, come home, Bill Bailey. Pick up the *dacha* you've earned and go into retirement. *That's* what they said. But he wouldn't or he couldn't. He got Committee backing and went right on with the game and in that way committed himself, once and for all. But the next move blew up in his face, as well. They kicked him out. And some of his friends in Moscow got themselves shot. That was early this year. Before they got shot, his friends sent a new set of pieces out here for him to finish the game with, and the new pieces were Soviet property. That made him a traitor, a renegade. Moscow sent someone out here to kill him—a man called Retzow. Retzow's dead." Fedora shrugged. "They'll send someone else."

There was a few seconds' silence.

Then Cardenas said,

"I see now what you mean by a free agent. The way you see it, he's entirely on his own?"

"In one way, yes. In another, no. Feramontov's never on his own, because there are always people who can be made to see things his way—who'll help him build a nice new pattern. Why that's so, I can't say. But it's a fact. I assume he understands the techniques of persuasion."

"Yes. I see. And your job, then, is the same as ... that Russian you mentioned? To find him and to kill him?"

"Where Feramontov's concerned, the British and the Russians think alike. And the French. *And*, for that matter, the Spanish. We're all in it together. And yet, *not* together. That's the awkward thing. That's what gives Feramontov his best chance."

Cardenas flipped his notebook shut, put it away in an inside pocket. It held no further additions. "Well," he said. "It's certainly an extraordinary story. But I believe every word of it. I'm sorry if—"

"That's all right."

"When all is said and done, though . . . you're just one man, aren't you? And since this fellow's here in Spain, why can't you let the Spanish police look after him?"

"You can't have been listening," Fedora said, and sighed. ". . . Or only to the words."

Cardenas nodded. "There's a personal rivalry. Is that it?"

"Of an odd kind, yes. I've never met him. But then, I don't *have* to have."

"It'd be interesting—wouldn't it?—to hear what Feramontov thinks about *you*."

"I know what he thinks," Fedora said. Cardenas didn't press the point.

"What would happen, though, if you *did* catch up with him? I realise that you've been correctly modest about your own part in all these goings-on . . . but then you make him sound like some kind of a Superman. Can you do *anything* better than he does?"

"Yes," Fedora said. ". . . Shoot."

. . . And smiled, for the second time that morning. But it wasn't the same kind of smile at all.

". . . Techniques of persuasion," Feramontov said. And then, "Not that I'm a great believer in gimmicks. . . ."

He smiled pleasantly. He hadn't spoken for the past five or six minutes, and three of the four persons who constituted his audience at once registered respectful attention. Young Rivas, however, went on staring at the opposite wall; there was a thread of dried blood at the corner of his open mouth.

". . . But it's necessary," Feramontov said, watching him impassively, no longer smiling, ". . . it's necessary to move with the times. The device that we have here employs the Monichev method, which was developed by agents of the DST in Algeria. You'll have heard of the DST, Captain Bujas?"

Bujas. A flat brown face, fair close-cropped hair under a Field Service cap. "Yes, sir, yes indeed. By reputation."

"And just what do you know about them?"

"They're our ... You might call them our opposite numbers, sir, in France. *Direction de Securité de la Territoire* ... except of course that they're non-military. More of a Special Branch, that is, of the Security police."

"We've much to learn from them, Bujas. Remember that, too."

"Yes, sir. Yes, colonel."

"You'll notice," Feramontov said, "that the wooden framework of the rack takes the form of a cross. A form that within Christian societies takes on symbolical importance. Some people deny the importance of such interpretations, but in my own experience the effect of them on the mind of the subject can be considerable."

He tapped the crossarm of the crucifix lightly. It was a short crossarm, supporting Rivas' arms only up to the elbows; the wood was dark and slippery with sweat. Around Rivas' outheld wrists were twin six-inch rings of twisted wire; each encircled an ordinary electric-light cable from which the insulation had been stripped.

"... You'll see that any unconsidered movement of the wrists brings the wire rings into contact with the naked cable. The secondary cables, connected to the rings, can be attached to different parts of the subject's body. The armpits, for example. The genitals. The nostrils. Or, as in the present case, to the outer channels of the ears. So the Monichev method involves a kind of self-service technique." A joke, maybe, but he didn't smile; so Bujas didn't, either. The sergeant standing a little to Bujas' left didn't smile, but then sergeants aren't expected to. "The subject participates, so to speak, in his own inquisition. It's his own movements which bring the elements of persuasion into play. He persuades *himself*. So in some circumstances, the Monichev method is superior to those techniques in which the subject plays a purely passive role. On the other hand ..."

He turned towards the trestle table that stood in the corner, and the third member of his military audience—a technical corporal in loose khaki shirt and baggy pants—stepped smartly out of his way. "Through a simple reconnection at the control panel," he said, "we can revert to more conventional, activist methods. In that case the charge is fed direct to the subject by depressing this switch. . . . It shouldn't normally be held for more than three seconds. But you know that already."

The cell was not large and there were five men in it and, anyway, the temperature was well up in the thirties. The collar of Bujas' shirt was sopping wet. "And the flow of current, sir? Can that be controlled?"

"Certainly. By the use of this lever. Normally, we increase the voltage by slow degrees, and where the points of contact are relatively close to the brain it's not desirable to move much beyond a nominal eighty volts." Feramontov's hand on the lever inched forwards gently, and behind a small glass panel a red-tipped needle swung. "Otherwise, permanent brain damage can result." He released his hold, wiped his hand on his handkerchief. "In my view, this is something of a needless refinement. But—"

"The voltmeter, sir," Bujas said, "goes up to fifteen thousand. Surely that's not—"

"It's psychologically helpful, captain. Psychologically helpful. We can fry him to cinders whenever we want to, and the subject knows it. Oh, yes. He knows it." Feramontov moved back to face Rivas, his fingers still crumpling the linen handkerchief mechanically, blindly. "We connect to a high-voltage cable. We throw the switch. And . . . *pfffttt*."

Rivas stared still at the opposite wall. The ribs stood out almost painfully in his brown and naked body, and beneath them his diaphragm moved slowly in time to his laboured breathing; but his wrists didn't move. Didn't move at all.

"It's interesting," Feramontov said, "to notice the persistence, under the Monichev treatment, of the normal reflex actions. They remain noticeable even in the second and third stages of this form of treatment, long after the point at which

—you would imagine—the nerves and muscles have been trained not to respond. However. . . . Observe."

He brought his knee up sharply in the direction of Rivas' groin. The kick didn't reach its target. It didn't have to. Rivas' hands twitched and jerked; there was a sharp flash, a hiss of breath. Rivas' head lolled forwards. Fresh blood began to trickle downwards; he had bitten through his lower lip. "You saw the galvanic jerk of the shoulder and thigh muscles? Characteristic. Highly characteristic."

"At what point, colonel, does the subject usually . . . begin to talk?"

"To *talk*, you say? It's not a matter of getting the subject to *talk*, exactly. For that, there are better methods than Monichev's. Much better."

"But then—"

"It's particularly apt for cases such as this, in which the subject has—as you say—*talked* already. He's been with us, after all, for three weeks now; and I feel that what little he has to say has already been said. But of course . . . subjects don't invariably tell the truth. Or *all* of the truth. Indeed, it's most unusual for them to do so. And some of them go so far as to tell *lies*. That's why, you see, a period of reflection . . . in which, if they should *wish* to change their minds . . ."

For a lieutenant-colonel, Feramontov sounded unbearably arch. "Yes, I understand, sir," Bujas said.

"This is one thing we've learnt from the DST. No waste of time, no waste of personnel. All we have to do is leave the subject alone with Monichev's ingenious device and a tape-recorder. And get right on with our own jobs."

"Leave the subject alone . . . for how long?"

"Until he's dead," Feramontov said. "Or until he no longer has any mind to change. A good deal of research needs to be done, of course, as to the precise conditions under which madness results. We need more test cases, like this one. Research scientists have a phrase . . . don't they? . . . *to test to destruction* . . . which I think might apply to the present instance. But right now, as it's getting late, I feel we may as well adjourn for lunch."

He stepped towards the metal-barred door, which the watchful Sergeant Gris swung open for him. It had in fact been a tiring morning. He felt quite hungry.

One o'clock, on Fedora's wristwatch. A four-hour session, less a fifteen-minute break for coffee. He had felt pretty tired to start with; now his brain seemed to be mainly composed of chewed-up string and cotton-wool. If Cardenas was tired, too, he didn't show it. Whatever his fee was going to be, it was clear that he was setting out to earn it.

"... Tired?"

"A little."

"Well, that's what we want."

The black and white tiles on the floor; a pattern, a chessboard. Johnny was sick of the sight of them. Everything in the room was black and white. He'd have it changed.

"You'll be very tired indeed," Cardenas said, "by the end of the day. The tireder you are, the less resistance your conscious mind will be able to put up to our explorations. You must realise that you are in all probability actually *seeking* to repress your memories of the past three weeks. Even though that may seem to you absurd."

"I know about repression theory," Fedora said.

"Well, that knowledge may make our task a little easier. Or it may not. It's difficult to be sure."

"But why should I *want* to ...?" Fedora checked himself. "I suppose that's just what we have to find out."

"Exactly. There is, of course, an obvious possibility that presents itself. ... But maybe *too* obvious. We'll see."

"What's that?"

"The rejection of physical danger," Cardenas said. "A defence mechanism, as we say. It's very frequent."

Johnny closed his eyes, listened for a while to the hum of the air-conditioner. Under the rolls of bandage, his scalp itched. One o'clock. He wasn't hungry. Mostly, he wanted to go to sleep.

"This rivalry between yourself and Feramontov. There is, as you say, a personal element involved."

"Yes," Johnny said vaguely.

"You've been after him for a long time, and so far he has always escaped you; recently, according to what you tell me, you've suffered what could be called a serious defeat at his hands. And you speak of him with great respect, although he's your present enemy. You agree with all this?"

"Yes, yes."

"It's possible that you're secretly afraid of him."

"*Secretly?*" Fedora opened his eyes. "You have to be joking. He scares me stiff."

"No. No. Please. No." Cardenas waved one nicely manicured hard to and fro. "You must face up to this. Don't retreat into mock-modesty. When I say that you're afraid of him, I mean that you are really afraid of *yourself*. You're afraid that if it comes to another confrontation, you'll come off second best once again. So you're trying to avoid that confrontation by . . . You see? *Forgetting*. Simply that."

Fedora stared down at the floor. Black squares, white squares. His hands hung down limply at the sides of his chair.

"Courage," Cardenas said, "is a very strange thing. So strange that we psychiatrists often prefer to take no stock of its existence. You certainly shouldn't think that a failure of this kind—if you can call it a failure—you shouldn't think that it's anything to be ashamed of. I don't believe that you're afraid of death as such. Afraid of his killing you. Even though that's what another defeat might mean. It's just that you think of yourself as a professional in your field, and you have professional pride. *That's* what you have at stake. Your pride. If I can use that word to describe the intangible thing that keeps people like you going. . . . You'll know what I mean."

"I know just what you mean," Fedora said.

"Well. It's only one of a number of possibilities. It's too early yet to say. We just have to go on digging. By the way, I should like to bring along a tape recorder to this afternoon's session, if you've no objection."

"I don't mind," Fedora said.

"Tapes are useful. Yes. They're often useful."

Cardenas was now on his feet; but walked not, as Fedora had expected, towards the door, but towards the open french window giving on to the verandah. He stood there for a few moments, silhouetted against the light; a big, bulky man looking towards the hills.

"There's one thing," he said, "that to my mind supports that theory."

"What?"

He turned round; came to stand directly in front of Fedora, looking straight down at him. "You remember I asked you if you had done anything unusual during your... missing period?"

"Yes."

"And it later emerged that you had?"

"I got married."

"Yes. Quite so. You got married. Let me make it clear that, having met your delightful wife, I see nothing there but cause for congratulation, I find it *perfectly* comprehensible. On the other hand.... It might be said that in getting married, you *conceded* something to Feramontov. In a sense, you conceded defeat."

"I don't," Fedora said, "see it quite that way."

"Marriage involves... How shall I put it?... An impulse towards stability. At worst it *symbolises* a hunger for permanence, even when the external conditions are unfavourable; that's why you get a significant rise in the marriage rate in times of war. And of course... before getting married, you told her that your search for Feramontov was concluded. Or at least, called off. I find that interesting."

"That's what *she* says," Johnny said. "But——"

"But you don't believe her?"

Johnny closed his mouth tightly. Then,

"I suppose I have to."

"Why should she tell you that, if it weren't true?"

"Exactly," Johnny said. "Why, indeed."

"And there again. This other girl you mentioned. With whom you had this . . . previous understanding."

"Adriana."

"Adriana. Yes. You say that you broke off your relations some time ago because you were afraid that Feramontov would take some action against her if you didn't. He made, in fact, some kind of a direct threat. Against her life. That *is* what you told me?"

"Yes," Johnny said. "That's what I told you."

". . . You'll agree that *afraid* is the operative word?"

"If you insist."

"I don't *insist* on anything," Cardenas said. "I never insist. All I'm suggesting is that in getting married to someone else, you've conceded that particular point to Feramontov. You've told him, indirectly, that the game's over. You've given up. Of course you won't, perhaps, have realised at the time the implications of what you were doing. . . . You won't have *consciously* realised it. But deep down. . . . Yes. I think so. There's been a conflict, a tremendous conflict between your desire to opt out of the struggle and your . . . well, your pride, as we agreed to call it. And then, as the saying goes—something had to go."

Fedora nodded. "Something went."

"As I say, it's a working assumption. An initial *point d'appui*. No more than that. We'll see how things go this afternoon. I'll call again at three." Cardenas extended his hand, patted Fedora lightly on the shoulder. "I feel we're making progress. Excellent progress. And I want you, in the meantime, to have a really good lunch. The mind matters, yes. But so does the stomach."

"I'm not all that hungry," Fedora said.

So he stayed where he was, slumped bonelessly in the armchair, hands dangling, long legs stretched out in front of him. Relaxed, completely relaxed. But his scalp still itched, and his right hand and forearm, too; his lungs seemed deflated, to be hardly moving. As for his stomach, to hell with that. His stomach was the only part of him that didn't seem involved in his present mood of near-manic depression. His stomach was all right, Jack. The rest of him wasn't.

Of course it can happen like that, he thought. Just like that. We all know it. We have to live with that knowledge, all the time. It had happened once before, come to that. A long, long time ago. Just after the war. The crack-up, we called it in those days; now it had a fancier name, but whatever you called it made very little difference. Nightmares. Hallucinations. Long shadowy walls of stone, stretching out through the darkness into infinity. Johnny really *had* been young, then; a boy, in fact; with no idea of what was really involved, no idea of how to fight it. That might even have been his salvation; youth and inexperience give you a chance, if only a shadow of a chance. And there'd been a woman, of course; Davida Kane; Davida had helped. Yes, she'd certainly helped. Now Laura would try to help, but it wouldn't be the same. Laura was part of it. Cardenas had put his finger right on the spot.

It made sense. He could see now why he'd done it. You could say that it hadn't been his fault. In a way it hadn't. What a pity, though, about old Fedora. What, hadn't you heard? . . . Oh, he's had to give it up. His nerves, of course. Started playing him up. He's gone in for amateur neurotics. Could happen to anyone, of course. Not really his fault. . . .

Am I really afraid? Am I really *that* afraid?

Well, yes, I am. I have been.

Like that time in Madrid. With Hammerhead poised to strike, and nobody there to stop it. Nobody but me. *That* was fear all right. Tension, bowel-clenching tension; a taste of brassy vomit on tongue and throat. Being one man, alone; that is terrifying. And before that, on the Undertow caper. The smothering darkness inside the sunken U-boat, and Moreno part of that darkness, moving in; a glint of torch-light on the diving-mask, on the knife in his lowered right hand. The blood beating in your head, the muscles of your belly contracting in expectation of the screaming steel; *that's* fear. That's what it's like. Courage is going to the bank; each time you draw some out, there's less in the kitty. And I've been running for years on an overdraft. So here's the manager's letter; four or five pages in a little black notebook. *Dear Sir, I regret to inform you . . .*

And there's no way back into the real world, the world of action; leaving hospital doesn't mean a thing. You're still a prisoner, pegged down on a board of black-and-white squares. If you feel good, that doesn't mean a thing. You're still alone. Like Feramontov, yes, but he can do it. He can live alone; he can stand it; he's made that way. I'm not. I'm different. I can't, I can't, I can't. . . .

Fedora's face crumpled; he turned it sideways on the cushion. From the corner of one eye, a dampness spread; formed into a tear; rolled down his cheek. Fedora, professional killer, was up against it. And he knew it.

"You have assumed that this word, *camera,* means, *room.*"

"Room eleven."

Eleven, eleven, eleven.

"Play around with it. Try translating it into English. Into other languages."

"Room. Chamber. Cell. Chambre. Zimmer. Habitacion. Celula. Cuarto. Kvartera. Komnata. . . ."

"Try the associations. Just once more."

"Camera . . . oscura. Oh . . . Photographs. Light. Microfilm."

"You use them a lot, in your profession?"

"What?"

"Microfilms. Miniature cameras."

"No. Not a lot. I've come across them."

"All right. Go on."

"It's not *that* kind of a camera."

"How can you be sure?"

"Because the word doesn't mean that in Spanish."

"*Badajoz. Camera 11.* That could be in any one of several languages."

"All right. I'm assuming it's Spanish."

"Go on, then."

"Where from?"

"Microfilm. . . ."

"Oh yes. Microfilm. Camera, camera. Film. Estelle."

"Estelle?"

"She worked for Feramontov. She's dead."

"How recently?"

"A month. Nearly. Just before all this happened."

"Why her? What's the connection?"

"She stole my cine-camera. That's all. No connection, really."

"We'll come back to that. Go on."

"Camera."

"Camera."

"Pain."

"Why pain?"

"I'm feeling it. That's why."

"Pain where?"

"Headache. And my arm hurts. It's nothing. Sorry I mentioned it."

"This man you went to see."

"Durand."

"Yes. Durand. He was in a hotel."

"In Alicante."

"In a hotel. What was the number of his room?"

"I don't remember."

"You talked to him?"

"I think so."

"In his room?"

"I don't remember."

"Could it have been number eleven?"

"I don't remember."

"All right. In that case, we'll start again."

On the table, the portable tape recorder; its spools turning silently, meaninglessly.

5

CUARTEL GENERAL DE LA POLICIA DE SEGURIDAD
CENTRO DE COMUNICACIONES (Recoletos)

> From: C.C. 3 (Madrid)
> To: Reserve List (Inf)
> Time: 1832 26 de mayo

HIGHLY SECRET

Copy of report of Dr. Eustacio CARDENAS as telephoned verbatim by Captain RIVAS (Barcelona Division)

Time of origin: 1808 26 de mayo
Teleoperator: JSB

MESSAGE BEGINS

Sr. D. John O'Neill Fox (real name withheld)
Case history number: 744
    Initial report

Subject is a man in the late thirties claiming British nationality. General physical condition, excellent. Reported as suffering from total amnesia over a period of twenty-one days, 4th to 25th of May. Medical evidence of minor contusions previous to amnesia, but no indications of organic damage. (See files of Cruz Roja, Cordoba, 1174/12 Baez.)

Subject claims to be by profession a counter-espionage agent, working for the British government and currently engaged in searching for a hostile agent, named as FERAMONTOV, somewhere in Spain. In spite of the frequency among MD's of delusions of this general type (tabulated by

Schenk q.v. as inversion of persecution complex), his account carries instant conviction and in the absence of contradicting evidence must be considered acceptable. A measure of confirmation is forthcoming from his wife LAURA, whose statement has been recorded for files. (Tape G-119.)

It should be remarked that the marriage of the subject took place within the period in question, at the British Consulate in Sevilla.

Our initial observations postulate a marked withdrawal syndrome in which the above-mentioned marriage may be considered a relevant factor. The fear/hatred dichotomy (de Valois' integer) is evidently unstable. A group of somewhat similar cases has been recorded by Menninger, his case number 94.3 providing a particularly interesting parallel. Menninger's subject, like Sr. Fox, had some familiarity with psychotherapeutic theory, an exceptionally high intelligence quotient and considerable linguistic ability. The association with a porromaniac tendency we consider significant.

The evidence therefore indicates a temporary fugue, unassociated with hallucinatory responses, which we attribute to a period of intense nervous strain linked to a physical concussion. We perceive also a characteristic conflict between the subject's highly-developed sense of duty (associated with an intense awareness of professional skill, the which is conceived to be endangered), and a normal intimidation reaction, in the circumstances fully justifiable. There are similarities to the so-called Othello complex (loss of occupation/loss of support). The prospects of a swift and complete recovery of the normal memory-patterns are hence optimistic, Menninger's case 94.3 responding to sodium amytal/benzedrine treatment in a matter of hours.

Since in the present case we have partial amnesiac hiatus, we propose to postpone drug treatment until the fourth or fifth session. The principal hiatus appear to evolve around the remembered word-sequence BADAJOZ: CAMERA 11, and to an interview (morning of May 5th) in Alicante with one M. DURAND. Further examination in our third session may well expand this hiatus on lines demonstrated by Jimenez, Clostermann, et al., and a complete recovery immediately ensue.

MESSAGE ENDS

. . . The bald man read this with care, then picked up the telephone.

"I want a translation," he said.

"Sir?"

"You heard me. What's an MD supposed to be?"

"A mentally disturbed person, sir. It's a convenient abbreviation."

"And porromania?"

"Means running away, sir. Escaping, so to speak. Though not from any logically conceived danger, it's an irrational act."

"Fugue?"

"Very much the same thing, sir."

A pause. "Right. That doesn't matter so much. The important part would appear to come at the end." The voice on the telephone was soft and furry; relaxed, completely relaxed. He didn't make it *sound* important. He didn't have to. "What does he mean by the fourth or fifth session?"

"They're probably three or four-hour sessions, sir. That's normal practice. Morning and afternoon. Since they started this morning . . . they may be moving on to the drugs tomorrow afternoon."

"I can manage the calculations for myself. He seems to feel he may manage to get through in the morning, though."

"Well, yes, sir. That's quite possible."

"Thank you," said the bald man. "Thank you."

Click.

The bald man dialled another number.

"Get me Santa Ana," he said. "You know who to ask for."

Laura hadn't seen the report, naturally; but seemed to be satisfied with what Cardenas had told her, after the second session had ended. It had been a briefer one, anyway, of just over two hours. "He says he feels quite optimistic. Maybe it'll even be tomorrow. And if not tomorrow, then almost certainly the day after. Well, that's quick."

"The question is," Johnny said, "whether it'll be quick enough."

He didn't really think that it was the most important question. It was just something to say.

"I suppose you're fed up with talking," Laura said. "No need to talk now, if you don't feel like it. No need at all."

That was intuitive of her, anyway. Fedora's hand rested on the cool flat surface of the table, with Laura's smaller hand nestling comfortably inside his palm; they sat in the hotel garden, beside a row of rather desiccated shrubs and under a canvas shade—a shade that would become a necessity in the heat of the summer but which now, in the early evening, served mainly to create for them a pleasant illusion of privacy. All the other tables along the pathway, however, were occupied, and the sound of high-pitched Spanish conversation was all around them; a sound punctuated at irregular intervals by resonant splashes from the neighbouring swimming-pool.

"I can imagine why I married you," Johnny said. "You understand things, don't you? You're good at it."

"I'm good at not asking questions. I suppose that's what you mean."

"It's not a common gift."

"Oh, I have my curiosity." She looked down at their hands, intertwined on the table; the shadow of her eyelashes fell across her cheeks. "Maybe even a lot of curiosity. But it relates to what you *are*, not what you do."

"And what am I?"

"Oh . . . You're nice."

"Mice are nice. Ask any pussy-cat."

"I didn't mean to eat. Though perhaps that as well, if I ever get around to it. No, sometimes you're exciting . . . and sometimes you're restful. Like now. And it's nice both ways."

"But why did you marry *me*?" Fedora asked.

"You don't mean that inanely, do you?... No, you don't go in for inanities. You really want to know."

"Yes, I really want to know."

"The trouble is that the only possible answer's an inane one."

"You're in love with me?"

"Yes."

"I wouldn't call that inane," Fedora said. "It's a word that can mean almost anything, but it always means *something*. Love. . . . It's almost the only word that always does."

"It means something, all right," Laura said. Speaking with more vehemence than Fedora had expected.

"You think Cardenas understands that?"

"Yes. I think so."

. . . What Cardenas understood. *That* was the important question.

He said that tomorrow, Fedora might be cured. Tomorrow, or perhaps the day after. That was nice to know, of course. Encouraging. *But . . .*

A doctor, a psychiatrist, what would he *mean* by "cured"? Returned to health, of course. Normalised. Enabled to carry on a meaningful existence. Made meaningful by what? . . . By the things that make existence meaningful for everyone, of course. Love. Hate. Ambition. Pride. Laura. In a day or in two days' time, Fedora might be made a normal person . . . but what would be the good of sending a normal person after Feramontov? Of sending anyone but the cold, the passionless, the mercilessly impersonal Fedora, the Fedora who some three weeks ago had disappeared? . . . No good at all. It'd be hopeless. Sit a *normal* person down at the piano and tell him to compose the Goldberg Variations. Give him a pen and ask him to write *The Waste Land*. Normality, for certain tasks, is useless.

This wasn't to say that Fedora had done the wrong thing. Not exactly. He'd been right to try Cardenas, because Cardenas had at least been able to show, indirectly but very clearly, where the wrong road lay. The right road was any road on which no one walked but Fedora. Fedora alone. Not Cardenas; not even Laura. *That* was the only road that in the end would lead to Feramontov.

"Cardenas understands a lot," he said. "The trouble is, there's such a difference between understanding a lot and understanding everything."

All right. In that case, we'll start again. And on another road altogether. Back to Alicante, back to Durand, back to a hotel room three weeks ago. "You remember how it all began with that Durand bloke?"

"Yes," Laura said. She, too, seemed to be deep in thought.

"You said you had a newspaper cutting. About that."

"Oh yes. I got it out to show you. And then I forgot."

She released Fedora's hand, opened her bag. Then began to riffle through the paper's in a man's leather wallet. "Here it is."

Johnny hadn't expected it to tell him much, and it didn't. It merely reported, succinctly enough, the demise of Jean Aloysius Durand (52), of Belgian nationality, at the Albuferete Hotel in Alicante. He had died of a bullet through the head and the circumstances were not indicative of suicide. The heading referred to the incident as a Mysterious Occurrence—*occurrencia misteriosa*—with which estimation Fedora found himself in agreement. It didn't help. It didn't help at all.

"There haven't been any other reports?"

"Not that I know of."

Johnny smoothed the creased paper between his fingers. The *ABC de Sevilla,* for the 6th of May. A twelve-line fill-in, between the weather report and the cases heard in court. A matter, obviously, of no importance. And maybe the police, in any case, had decided to sit on it. It wouldn't do to forget the police. They'd have been there.

And the 6th of May. . . . That was a long while back. But the road would be a long one anyway, without Cardenas. And far longer still, without Laura. Because she was quite right; the word *did* mean something. It meant a lot. There remained the big difference between *a lot* and *everything*. He folded the cutting again, returned it to the wallet.

". . . Why a man's wallet?" It looked new.

"I don't know," Laura said. "*You* gave it to me."

"Did I? Oh. I'm sorry."

Tomorrow morning (Johnny thought), tomorrow morning I'll be gone. Meanwhile, there's this evening. And tonight. A few more hours of normality. If happiness is normal. And if happiness is what we've got. And what else would you call it? . . . Whatever it was, it didn't make going any easier. Early tomorrow morning, with Laura lying beside him, it would be more difficult yet.

There were other papers in the wallet. Laura's identity card and driving permit. . . . It was the photograph in the former that struck his attention; it didn't look much like her at all. Well, she'd been eight years younger. Or so. Social Service documentation, marriage certificate. To John O'Neill Fox, of course; that was what his British passport said. He supposed it was legal. Well, of course it was.

"What are you smiling at?"

"A thought just struck me," Johnny said.

"Well, tell me."

"Until this moment I didn't know what your other name was."

Laura stared at him. "You're joking."

"I'm not. They asked me at the hospital and I couldn't tell them. Well, it *is* a bit comic."

"You've just forgotten it, that's all."

"It's a nice name," Johnny said. ". . . Alonso. Laura Alonso. Yes, I like it."

He put the papers back into the wallet.

The line to Santa Ana was giving trouble. There were cracklings. Oscillations. A whining noise, probably from the scrambler. Still, these were the least of Feramontov's worries.

"I don't see," he said, "how you can expect me to *act* on this. Not at this late stage."

"Something has to be done."

"He can't know enough to interfere."

The quiet, patient voice remained quiet and patient. "He knows about Cell Eleven."

"That's impossible."

"Impossible? I have it here in black and white." The voice said something else, lost in a sudden hum of atmospherics. ". . . when this accident occurred. But for that, it seems reasonably certain that the whistle would have been blown on us already. It's nice to feel that someone up there likes us."

Feramontov's fingers drummed on the table-top. "How *can* he have found out?"

"That's hardly the point, is it? . . . The Moscow file may have been copied. He may have had access somehow to the amended blueprints in Madrid. The indications are, though, that he got on to it through Durand. In which case there's little doubt where the responsibility lies."

"Durand had nothing—"

"It's no good underestimating British Intelligence—or Fedora himself. Though right now, fortunately, we can assume he's a long way below par. Well, something has to be done and you're at hand to do it. No more needs to be said."

"But this is absurd. They'll only send someone else."

"Someone else will be someone else. Fedora is Fedora." The carbon whispered a faint, ghostly chuckle into Feramontov's ear. "That's the trouble, isn't it?"

"How do you mean?"

"You haven't been lucky in the past—have you?—with Fedora? A bit of a *bête noir*—could I put it that way?"

"I respect him," Feramontov said.

"You can still respect him when he's dead."

"We're following a carefully arranged programme. You are asking me to disrupt it in order to carry out an unnecessary assassination. I protest."

"All right. You protest. You'll still do it."

In Feramontov's forehead, a vein throbbed very slowly. He said nothing more.

"You will act *now*. At once. Do you understand?"

"I understand that I have instructions to which I'm obliged to conform."

"Conform, then."

The line went dead. Feramontov put down the telephone.

Then flexed his fingers, as though they had just been relieved of a certain strain. There were cigarettes in the table drawer. He opened it and took one.

Respect was a good word. But not the right one. Feramontov respected nothing and no one. *Recognise* would have been more precise. Fedora was one of the few people whose existence on the planet, as an influence operative on his own, he was ready to concede. Fedora was his enemy, and Feramontov thought of his enemies as most people think of their friends; by their departures and deaths was his own life in some way diminished. Fedora wasn't a Department or a Unit or any kind of an organisation with a name and a number; Fedora, as the man had said, was Fedora; *er war anders*. He and Feramontov were themselves like two planets, at times convergent, at times in opposition; their rivalry was that of circling dancers in a cosmic *sevillana* orchestrated by Schönberg, their enmity something fundamental, like that of man and woman, cat and dog, Lucifer and Gabriel. Now a voice on the telephone gave instructions, and that was to be changed. Changed utterly. And Feramontov, the pattern-maker, the weaver of celestial carpets, disapproved. It wasn't in the equations. The theorem would have to be worked out all over again.

Departments, names, numbers. They stood for nothing. A voice on the telephone gave orders; nothing there for respect or for recognition. There was a bald man in Madrid, and a fat man called Acuña; circumstances had placed Feramontov within the orbit of the one, just as seemingly they had placed Fedora within the orbit of the other. There were obligations, therefore, to conform. But the bald man and the fat man weren't really men at all; they were organisations; it was yet possible that Feramontov and Fedora together might teach them the limitations of conformity. Feramontov frowned; blew out smoke; his eyes palely focused on infinity. In his brain, the patterns broke up and swiftly re-formed.

When he had finished his cigarette, he pressed the buzzer on the table. The orderly sergeant came in, saluted. It was Sergeant Gris.

"I am going to kill the prisoner, sergeant. You will accompany me. And later, you'll dispose of the body as I instruct you."

"Yes, sir," the sergeant said.

"You'll report to me at nine o'clock, together with Private Vargas. I have a special assignment for you both. You'll check with MT and take a Land Rover from the pool. Is that clear?"

"Nine o'clock, sir. With Private Vargas. Will this be another exercise? Or the real thing?"

"The real thing," Feramontov said. ". . . Oh, very much so."

6

The first thing she knew, when she woke up, was that Fedora wasn't there.

My God, Laura thought.

Then, *I should have guessed it. . . .*

She looked at her wrist-watch. Five to six. Then briefly, at the telephone; an idea no sooner conceived of than dismissed. She rolled off the bed and prowled, naked, across the tiled floor to the chair where her clothes were neatly folded. Swiftly, though without apparent haste, she began to dress.

In the shade of the bushes Private Vargas squatted, his eyes turned upwards to the façade of the hotel directly before him, the rifle propped across his khaki-trousered knees. His broad brown face in the dawn light seemed withdrawn, absolved from all worldly cares; his eyes were slitted chips of patient stone, watching from between narrowed lids. *He* had no worries. In a few moments, he would receive his instructions. He knew what those instructions would be. And then, all he had to do was act on them.

God, alias Sergeant Gris, was crouched at his side. Watching, as he was, the blank black windows of the hotel, though through the synchronised lenses of powerful night-glasses. That was all right, too. God naturally had certain privileges. God no doubt had his instructions, as well, but it didn't do to think about where they came from. It wasn't in Vargas' nature to aspire so high. If he tried, he'd only get confused. All he had to do was remember that God was a soldier like himself, but with stripes on his sleeve; that was how you could tell.

"One minute to six," the sergeant said. He had lowered the nightglasses now, was studying the slow sweep of the second hand around his wrist-watch. "Make ready, lad."

Vargas' gnarled right hand went into the satchel that lay on the dry earth beside him. The grenade clipped into the thrower with a soft click; the release pin flicked out at his finger's end, the springlever pressing in instant response against the retaining bolt. Vargas checked its pressure with the ball of his thumb, adjusted his grip to the new point of balance. "Ready, sarge."

"Fire two at will."

He lowered the butt to the ground, steadying it against his right boot. The barrel aligned itself through five degrees of arc, became motionless; first pressure moved into second through one slow, powerful, practised clenching of the fist. The grenade whipped in silence through the suddenly vivid air, speeded by the sharp deep-toned crack of the propellant. It was a beauty. Behind the verandah, one of the doors of the french window was open, the other shut; the grenade flipped through the open space without even a smashing of glass. Even before it had reached its target, Vargas' left hand was moving with calm efficiency, snapping a second grenade into place, jerking out the pin; *whump* went the butt against his boot again. The recoil had moved the barrel a fraction out of true, and the second grenade went through the closed window with a sharp splintering sound; broken glass fell downwards, tinkled on the balcony. Vargas broke the thrower from the rifle, pushing it into the satchel; on his face, a half-smile of satisfaction. No one could have done that better. It was only a minor ability, no doubt, but one not to be despised.

As, together with the sergeant, he rose to his feet, the open and the shattered window were merged abruptly together in a shooting stab of flame. A quivering, sucking blast, followed three short seconds later by another. The windows were black no longer; quite the contrary; they formed a rectangle of blazing, silvery light against which the frame of the walls seemed dark by contrast. The sergeant looked up as they walked away; once; briefly.

"*Está bien*," he said.

The echoes of the twin blast reverberated down the corridor; Laura, making for the lift, stopped dead, turning towards the door she had just closed behind her. But she didn't go back. She went on, changing her pace to a run, and instead of taking the lift diving down the staircase. She'd put on her low-heeled shoes again, and was glad of it. Otherwise, she could hardly have managed to take the steps three at a time.

On the landing, a man called Pinto. She only knew him slightly.

"What's happened?"

"I don't know," Laura said. "He's gone."

"He can't have."

"He has. You'd better wait here."

In the reception hall, no one but a startled-looking night porter speaking earnestly into the telephone; trying, no doubt, to find out who was letting bombs off upstairs. Laura, too, would have dearly liked to know; but there wasn't time. She changed direction, moving out of the porter's line of sight towards the garden exit; the door was locked, and she had to waste a few valuable seconds trying the bolt to find out how it worked. In the end it slid open easily enough, and she passed out into the dim coolness of the dawn air; running down the length of the swimming pool, along the path that led past the now-empty tables and through the bushes. Looking back as she ran, she saw the harsh-edged flames leaping through the skeleton of the window and almost stopped again. Not quite, though. First things came first. She had to find Fedora.

At the end of the path, a rustic bench, placed with its back to the high brick wall of the hotel garden and for the convenience, doubtless, of courting couples. No *novios* in evidence at the moment, of course; not at this hour of the morning. A man in a dark suit sat there alone. Unmoving. Unmoving?

. . . *Asleep*, damn him to hell. Laura, gasping for breath, managed at the same time to click her tongue.

"Hey. . . . Ortega. . . . Wake up. . . ."

This was just a bit too bloody much.

"Wake *up*, blast you," Laura said, catching him by the shoulder. The man in the dark suit moved in response, his head falling sluggishly forwards. He didn't wake up, though. He wouldn't, ever again. The narrow knife wound gaped at the base of his neck and the blood, released by his movement, began to well again. The spinal cord had been severed; he'd been *descabellado*, like a bull. Laura drew her hand away, bit at her lip.

Fedora?

No.

Never.

Not like *that*.

She looked up at the hotel some forty yards distant, at the dark matchbox-like façade and at the one window bright as an aircraft beacon with leaping flame. She was suddenly, intangibly, aware of danger. This was it. The opposition. They were here.

She took three or four paces back along the path; came to a halt as the two tall shapes materialised beside her. Uniformed shapes. The Army. The *Army*? . . . Thank heavens for that. She stayed motionless all the same, motionless as Ortega. A sergeant and a private. The sergeant had a Luger. It pointed at her stomach.

"Please, what's going *on*?"

The sergeant looked her over expressionlessly. There was that, nevertheless, to indicate that he enjoyed what he saw; she had dressed very quickly. "I'd say it was up to you to tell *us* that, miss. What are you doing out here?"

"I'm staying at the hotel. There was a sort of explosion. . . ."

"Yes?"

"Well, I came out to see what was going on." She glanced over her shoulder. "There's a dead man there."

"I know," the sergeant said. "A friend of yours?"

"No, not exactly. He's a policeman. I have to go and report . . ."

Her voice tailed away into silence. There was silence everywhere now. Except for, somewhere in the bushes, the anxious creaking of a cricket; woken up, maybe, by all the excitement. Silly little beast. Though not as silly, perhaps, as Laura had been. She hadn't woken up properly yet.

"A policeman, eh?"

"Special Branch."

"How would *you* know that? What's your name?"

"My name doesn't matter," Laura said.

The other soldier, the private, was at her side now. He took her handbag, snapped it open.

"She has a pistol, sarge." He seemed mildly surprised.

"Never mind that. What's her name."

A pause. Big brown hands opening the wallet, fumbling with flimsy papers. Laura standing still, recovering her breath. "Identity card says Laura Alonso, sarge. There's a marriage certificate as well. She's a Mrs. Fox."

"Well, now," the sergeant said. "I thought as much."

The pistol barrel tilted slightly upwards.

"We'll get into our car," he said, "and then we'll have a nice little talk. This way, miss. If you don't mind."

Acuña didn't have to get dressed. He'd been sleeping in his clothes; he often did. Ten seconds after taking the call he was on his way downstairs, yelling for Rivas.

"There's a fire at the hotel. Fire and some kind of an explosion. This has to be it."

"Ortega?"

"No. Pinto. He says Alonso just left, and . . . never mind that. Where's that bloody car?"

It was parked round the corner and under the eucalyptus trees, a battered grey Land Rover with a military registration. Laura looked at Vargas, then at the sergeant.

"Do I get in?"

"That's the general idea," the sergeant said.

"Where are you taking me?"

"Just get in," the sergeant said.

Laura got in, smoothing her short skirt down her thighs. The car lurched uneasily as Vargas got in behind her. He had her pistol now and it was loaded; only a .22, but at that range it would be good enough. The sergeant walked round the bonnet and climbed in beside her. Vargas waited, lounging back in the rear seat, the pistol inclined at an angle to the girl's dark-haired head. What was he waiting for? . . . Instructions, of course. No need to say, *Ready*. He was ready. There'd be just the one word, *Fire*. Or maybe even, *Right* . . . That was what God was there for; to make decisions. Then he 217711 Private Manuel Vargas would implement them. An ideal set-up. He liked it. *He* had no worries.

But the sergeant, in point of fact, had. Initiative is a risky business. Sometimes it's wise to use it, and sometimes it isn't. Here he had a woman who was supposed to be dead; carbonised; burnt to ashes. Since she obviously wasn't, the matter should be rectified. *Y pronto*. But against that, an equally obvious factor militated; if she wasn't dead, it was because she hadn't been in the bedroom when the grenades went in. And if she hadn't been in the bedroom, then maybe Fedora hadn't been either. So there were questions that had to be asked.

Asked, and answered.

And that of course could be a *pleasurable* procedure.

Yes. But then the obvious thing isn't always the right thing —especially not in the Army. The operations schedule had been perfectly clear. Scour the hotel garden and eliminate opposition; fire two grenades through a specific hotel window. Observe the results. Report. You obeyed instructions to the letter in Franco's army; then you were all right. Start playing around with your own think-box, and anything could happen. Anything at all.

Anyway, they couldn't hang around here for very much longer. He'd ponder on the problem while he was driving.

He switched on the ignition. Let out the clutch. Set off down the long grey Avenida. He hadn't looked at the girl since she'd got in; he didn't want distractions. That one brief glimpse of thigh had been enough, *more* than enough. And anyway, Vargas was watching her. If she tried anything . . .

No. Not the pistol. It wouldn't end for her *that* quickly.

The house was on the outskirts of town. There was a narrow gravel driveway, a brick wall; then the portico. The front hall was dilapidated and musty; the just-risen sun was sending a narrow ray through a crack in a boarded window, exposing where it fell the yellowish, powdery dust that lay on the floor. There was no furniture at all. The house was empty. Perhaps it had been at one time a military billet; it had that air. But not for many weeks; months, perhaps. To that, the dust was witness.

The sergeant kicked open a door and went through. Laura followed him. Here the windows had been boarded up more efficiently and no sun ray came through; until the sergeant touched a switch the room was pitch-dark, and the lowpower bulb that then glowed into life high up in the ceiling didn't seem to make very much difference. It was a big room, but completely bare; the plaster was peeling away from the naked walls.

"Turn round," the sergeant said.

Laura turned round. Vargas had followed them through the door and stood a little to the left. He held the pistol pointing now at the floor.

"Well, now," the sergeant said.

He had decided.

"Well, what?"

"It's like I said. We'll have a little talk."

"If I talk to anyone," Laura said, "it'll be to your commanding officer." Not that *saying* anything would help. But it filled in time, that most valuable commodity. She was pretty sure that what she had left could be counted in minutes— and not many of them, either. "Where is he?"

"He's not here," the sergeant said. "There's nobody else in this place. We're quite alone."

His tone gave the statement no particular significance. Laura didn't like his tone at all. That the sergeant would want to kill her, she had taken for granted; but it had also seemed to her very likely that he'd want to rape her first. That they *both* would. And if it was a question of a bullet or a rape, she'd settle for a rape any time; that, too, filled in the time. Not that time really made much difference to the eventual outcome; but while there was life, there was hope. *Dum spiro, spero* and all that jazz.

If my Latin mistress could see me now. . . .

"Do you really *have* a commanding officer? You're not *really* soldiers, are you?"

That was the right tone, anyway. Proper 'aughty. The Latin mistress herself could hardly have improved on it. And the sergeant seemed indeed to be duly hurt.

"O' course we are. Special Detachment. Fourteen years' service I got, five of 'em in Africa."

"In that case—"

"When I said a talk," the sergeant said, "I didn't mean a friendly chat. I meant I'll ask the questions. You'll answer them."

"Oh, but I can't agree to that."

A click. The flick-knife in the sergeant's hand now had a blade.

"Five years in Africa," the sergeant said, his voice as inflexionless as before. "You'll answer 'em."

Vargas closed the door. The rattle of the latch had, Laura felt, a certain finality about it. "What was it you wanted to know?"

"You've got papers that say you're married to a man called Fox. Real name, Fedora. I want to know where he is.'

"The last I saw of him, he was asleep in bed." Damn it, she thought, that's the truth.

"In your bedroom? Back at the hotel?"

"Yes."

"Then why weren't *you* there?"

"I had to report to that man down in the garden. He was a police agent. So am I."

"Your papers don't say *that*," the sergeant said.

"Of course not. What'd be the good . . ."

She stopped. Yes, what *was* the good, indeed. The knife had a very sharp point. The sergeant tested it absently on the ball of his thumb, and a red bead of blood swelled out from the skin. "I suppose," Laura said, "*you* killed Ortega."

"Yes," the sergeant said. Absently; still absently. "And if Fedora *was* in that bedroom, then we killed him as well. That leaves just you, the way I see it."

"But why?"

He didn't seem to have heard the question. His eyes were fixed on the base of her neck, on the loosely fitting vee of her linen dress. ". . . *Why* did you kill him?"

"I had my orders. Just as you had yours. *If* you're a police agent."

"Of course I am."

"Then why do your papers say you're Mrs. Fox?"

Better not to answer that one. Better not to answer at all. He wasn't a very intelligent man, and he was getting confused. She stared past him at the handle of the door, trying to make herself register every smallest detail of its outward appearance; the dim reflection of light on its upper surface, the scratches at its base. The great thing was not to look at the sergeant. Nor at his knife.

"Oh, I know about Fedora," the sergeant said. "And I know about *you*. I been told what to expect. So don't think I won't know how to deal with you. Reds in Morocco . . . Reds in Spain. . . . They're all the same to me. *I* know what to do with 'em. And I know what to do with their women when I catch 'em. It's old stuff to me. Don't think it isn't."

His tongue was running away with him now; he knew it, and he didn't care. It *was* old stuff; it was always the same. He got confused. Because these Red bastards were clever, because they always had some goddamned story or other;

you listened, you got confused. They tried to make you feel stupid. The women, they were even worse than the men. And yet it wasn't clever, what they did; they knew they'd be punished for it, they knew he'd take them and hurt them, and yet they still did it. Confused him. So they were stupider than he was. And in the end, he showed them they were stupid and they looked at the knife and they didn't argue and, in the end, when the knife went in and the life went out of them, they still looked surprised. *That* was how stupid they were.

Now his tongue had run away with him, as it often did. You showed them they were stupid, yes, but sometimes it helped to tell them, beforehand and in detail, exactly *how* you were going to show them; it got you in the right mood. It helped when you were feeling hatred as much as lust. And he hated this one, all right. This one was just the sort he hated the most. He even found himself using the wicked words, words that he *knew* were bad; in the ordinary way he never used words like that. An enlisted man might use them; Vargas might use them. But not a sergeant. No. A sergeant was God.

. . . Here again (as Laura knew), the thing was not to listen. See no evil, speak no evil, hear no evil. But it wasn't so easy. It went on and on and on, an interminable monotony of revolting obscenity, with one ice cold word punctuating the flow like a recurrent splash of iced water; she heard it every time, she couldn't *not* hear it. *Knife. Knife. Knife. Knife.* It awoke, unlike the other words, a reality she could imagine. The needle point passing gently across her skin, the razorline of blood springing up across her belly. A second and a third line, the pattern slowly growing. . . . No. It had to stop, it had to be stopped. A scream would stop it. But that couldn't be the way. That would be what he wanted. All he needed. She closed her eyes.

Her fingers moved to the front zipper of the linen dress. Ran it downwards. She pulled the dress up to her waist, then over her head. There was silence, a sudden silence. Gris had stopped talking. Her eyes were open again, wide open; she looked at him. The dress dropping lifeless to the dusty floor. ". . . Well?" Laura said.

The sergeant wiped his mouth with the back of his hand. Then looked from her towards Vargas. ". . . Whore," he said, almost in stupefaction. "This one's nothing but a . . . bloody little whore. . . ."

. . . Not the kind *you're* used to, though, Laura thought (almost with satisfaction). You won't find eight-guinea lined nylon bikini briefs in any house *I* know of on the Calle de la Feria. Or in Morocco, either. Why, goodness me, I've *shocked* you. Haven't I?

Gris now staring at her again, his lips pulled back in a grin that had nothing to do with pleasure. The knife blade had come up as in a gesture of defence, horizontal to the floor and level with her navel. It had stopped him, certainly; it could still turn out to have been a mistake. "The bra," Laura said quickly. "Should I take off the bra?"

No good. No flicker of recognition in the sergeant's eyes of a question to be answered, a decision to be made. The imagination wasn't answering. Nothing there but a cold grey soldier's hunger, a hunger to kill. The knife moved forwards slowly, its point touching, pricking, the soft suntanned flesh beneath her throat. She unhooked the white plastic clasp; black half-moons of nylon slipped downwards. The knife point made no answering move. Only the sergeant's narrowed grey eyes followed the fall, then came back again.

No flicker. No question. No problem. Still, nothing but the hunger. The knife point, like his eyes, moved away and came back, settling, painlessly now, on the ridge of tautened muscle just below the ribcage, on the diaphragm that barely controlled her deep and shuddering breaths. It would go in two inches, no more. Then suddenly instead of breathing air she'd be breathing molten lead, and her whole body would contract around intolerable pain; would double up, twist in unutterable agony. The rest would be a dream. A dream of contorted face and limbs, of dust in the mouth. She looked down between her lifted breasts, and the dream was there.

Clenched in a hard brown hand. Waiting.

". . . *Sarge*," Vargas said.

The sergeant took no notice. Understandably, perhaps. But that was *his* mistake.

The door creaked loudly as it jerked open. Then there was the sharp, commanding crack of a pistol and, in the dimness of the room, a white-hot point of flame. Laura didn't see it. She saw nothing but the sergeant's eyes; his eyes as his head rocked to the impact of the bullet; they stayed open, they went on looking at her, but something was differen. Vargas saw it, though, as he jumped for the corner, his boots scuttering on the floor, his pistol hand swerving up and sideways with cold and unconscious efficiency. Cold, unconscious, but —with the squeezing of the trigger—a wave of sheer pleasure, or near orgasmic release. He knew, all the same, that for this, for *this*, the little .22 wouldn't be good enough. He, too, had seen what had happened to the sergeant. The pistol wasn't good enough, and neither was he.

He squeezed the trigger, which was more than many men could have managed in the circumstances. But he never got to see where the bullet went. It hit, as a matter of interest, the door. Then his boots scuttered once again as he collapsed, trying to hold himself up against the wall and abandoning the effort as soon as commenced; though not consciously, since the bullet had taken him just above the nose. Laura stooped to pick up from the floor the sergeant's knife.

"This is nice," Fedora said. "What are *you* rehearsing for?"

Laura looked at him, experiencing nothing so much as an intense desire to scream. *Desire* was hardly the word. Her apparent outward calm represented, in fact, a veneer of about a millimetre in depth, pasted miraculously over one tremendous, reverberating howl, a scream to end *all* screams. Yet somehow, nothing happened. Except that, as she looked at him, her lower lip began to quiver.

". . . Looks like quite a promising act," Fedora said, putting away his pistol. "It'll go down big, I should think, at the Pigalle."

"It's nice to know *you* haven't lost your touch," Laura said bitterly. "Through the head and all—both of them. Oh, quite astonishing. You might damn well have got here a little bit earlier, though."

"I've been here very nearly as long as you have." He seemed a trifle cold this morning. Or distant. Colder, anyway, than you'd have expected him to be to a girl dressed only in fetching nylon panties. "I was just off to the station in my little taxi when I saw *you* walking by. With your military friends. So I followed you instead. That's all."

"You weren't . . . listening? Outside?"

"For quite a while."

"Then why didn't you . . . ?"

"Yes," Johnny said, and shook his head. "I left it a bit late, I know. I was cross, *that* was why. You bloody well deserved it, was what I felt. Besides . . ."

He stopped, and left it at that. He went for a little walk round the room, frowning at the corpses. Laura looked at the sergeant's knife, which was still in her hands. She didn't *really* want it. She threw it away.

"You mean that about my working for the police?"

"Yes."

"You'd guessed it already. Hadn't you?"

"No," Johnny said. "You fooled me there. All ends up."

"But then why did you . . .? What *happened* to you this morning? I mean, did you *know* they were going to bomb the place?"

"If I'd known, I wouldn't have left you there to be fried. Now would I?" Fedora, in his turn, picked up the knife and examined it; but he didn't seem to want it, either. "We seem to have a low opinion of each other this morning."

"Johnny."

"What?"

"I suppose I ought to explain it."

"I suppose you ought to try."

She stooped again, abruptly, for the discarded bra. "Let me get my clothes on first. I just want to get out of this beastly place. And then—"

"No chance."

"What do you mean?"

"I mean, no chance," Fedora said. "You don't think we can get *out* of here, do you? . . . This is the trap, this is. And I've just had to walk into it."

By eight a.m. the fire was out and the *bomberos* had driven away. Apart from a blackened window frame and badly cracked paintwork, there was little external evidence of serious damage and nobody, it seemed, had been badly hurt. Except, of course, for Ortega; who now lay on his back beside the bench, under a white cotton sheet. The area around him had been roped off; the photographers and the fingerprint men had been and gone, but a Civil Guard still strolled to and fro by the wall. And Acuña was still there, too.

Acuña, smoking one of his black cigars and surveying the scene with that air of fatalistic bitterness that sits so naturally, so inevitably, on senior police officers of all forces in the world. The trap, such as it was, had been sprung. He had lost Ortega. Now life was going on as if nothing. Splashes from the bathing pool, where the early swimmers were taking their pre-breakfast dips; other guests were taking their coffee on the open-air parquet, discussing the events of the morning in voices that didn't seem to be particularly hushed. No reason why they should be, of course; the guests didn't know about Ortega. Who lay prone at Acuña's feet and said, of course, nothing.

Rivas, hands thrust deep into his pockets, came round the edge of the pool and along the path, the corners of his mouth drawn down in a near-caricature of despondency. Once clear of the overhanging palm fronds, he took sunglasses from his pocket and put them on; already the sun was beginning to take on its usual sharp brilliance. They didn't alter his expression much, though. He still looked right chocker.

"No trace," he said, halting alongside Acuña and staring back at the hotel. "They weren't there. Our friend checked

4—T

out at five forty-five this morning. . . . Paid his bills and then just quietly scarpered. No sign at all of Alonso. She's disappeared, too."

"She wasn't in the room, then, when it happened?"

"If she was, there's nothing left to show for it. And the Fire Chief thinks there would have been. Bones, buttons, something. There's nothing."

"It happened at six o'clock," Acuña said. "And our friend left at five forty-five. Incredible, that."

"Some kind of a tip-off, you think?"

"No. It's just that he earned his reputation that way. By staying alive. Don't ask me how he does it. A sixth sense, maybe."

Rivas pulled sceptically at the tip of his nose. "Ortega should have seen him leave."

"Yes. But Ortega was probably dead already. It's pretty clear as to how they worked it. They just lobbed a couple of grenades through that damned french window from down here in the garden . . . using a thrower, of course. Or some such device. They'd have had to get rid of Ortega first. Obviously."

"Obviously. How many of them?"

"Two. Maybe three."

". . . We'll hope that Alonso's managed to do a bit better," Rivas said lugubriously. "Maybe Fedora took her with him. Or maybe she went after him. There has to be still a chance she'll be calling us in."

"I doubt it," Acuña said.

And after a pause.

"A pity about Alonso. She was doing rather well."

He mooched off down the path, a thin trailer of cigar smoke drifting behind him. Rivas followed. At the side gate they met Lieutenant Pinto. Pinto was another of Acuña's bright young men. Two years ago, he had been an ice-cream salesman. Now he was the organisation's Liaison Officer with the regular police and, in Acuña's opinion, right on the ball. "What have we got?" Acuña asked briefly.

"Not much in the way of physical evidence, sir. The two

grenade pins you've already seen. I'd say they came from the usual PO2s, but the charges must have been . . . Anyway I've sent them to Ballistics to see if they've any comments. I've also had casts taken of two sets of footprints, though the ground's too hard for them to be really useful. They're booted feet, though. That much is definite."

"What about the firing cartridge cases?"

"We haven't found them, sir. They probably remembered to pick them up."

"They forgot about the pins."

"Maybe they thought the pins wouldn't tell us anything, sir. And they probably won't. Anyway, I've also spoken to the Duty Captain at the Comisaria. . . . He's fully prepared to leave the whole thing to us."

Acuña grunted. "I'll bet he is. You made the mess—you clear it up."

"Yes, sir. That's about it."

Acuña started to move away.

". . . There's one other thing, sir."

"Yes?"

For some strange reason, Pinto seemed hesitant. "I'm sure you'll want to see it, sir, for yourself."

"All right. What is it?"

"This way, sir." But Pinto didn't move. "If I may say so, sir, with all respect. . . ."

Acuña regarded him with no very marked air of forbearance. "What the hell is the *matter* with you, Pinto?"

". . . Not Captain Rivas, sir."

". . . Not. . . . ?"

"Not the Coordinator, sir. He'd . . . better stay here."

There was quite a long silence. Acuña's pebbly gaze moved from Pinto to Rivas; from Rivas to Pinto; and finally back to Rivas again.

". . . Stay here."

"If you say so, sir."

Pinto, making what almost amounted to a parade-ground about turn, marched off at a parallel to the wall. Acuña followed him. They passed a clump of waist-high bushes; beyond, there were flowerbeds bright with rose trees. A little to the left, a eucalyptus tree with spreading roots. At the foot of the tree, something lay. Pinto came smartly to a halt, while Acuña went forward and looked at it. There was a strange smell in the air, mingling rather horribly with the scent of the roses.

Acuña returned almost at once, wiping his nose with a handkerchief.

"I hope I acted rightly, sir."

"Certainly you did."

"It *is* . . .?"

"Yes, it is. Or rather, it was."

They walked back towards the side gate, where Rivas stood waiting. Pinto's gait was not quite as rigidly military as before.

"What exactly . . . happened to him, sir?"

"And what do *you* think happened, Pinto?"

"I don't know, sir. They look like burns. But I've never seen anything quite . . . I mean, it's . . ."

"Go on," Acuña said. "Say it."

"It's horrible."

"Yes. It is. You've called for the doctor?"

"Of course, sir."

"Well. No doubt the doctor will tell us what did it. At a guess, I'd say that he'd been electrocuted."

"He'll have to be told, sir."

He didn't mean the doctor, of course. Acuña knew who he meant.

"Yes," he said, "I'll tell him."

They went back to the side gate, where Rivas was waiting. And Acuña told him.

The news, after all, wasn't unexpected. Young Rivas had been three weeks missing; that made him dead. So the elder Rivas didn't burst into inconsolable floods of tears. He went with Acuña to the bar of the hotel and there he drank two straight whiskies, one after the other. They had some effect, because normally he didn't drink at all.

"But why *here*?"

"I don't know, Acuña said.

And a little later,

". . . It's the Feramontov touch."

And having lit his second cigar of the morning,

"We've poked him into making a move. At least that's something."

No one could have called Acuña a sympathetic man. This remark, however, was not as tactless as it appeared to be; it was designed to take Rivas' mind off the unpleasant topic on which it was brooding, and possibly Rivas accepted it as such. At any rate, he nodded in agreement. "We could even say that our idea's working out."

"Well, they went in at six o'clock," Acuña said. "And although it depends to some extent on his starting-point, we've got to assume that not even Feramontov could set up an operation like this one in much under eight hours. Which means that your report on Fedora must have got through to him by ten o'clock last night or before. You see anything wrong with that calculation?"

"No," Rivas said. "I'd worked that out for myself."

"The idea's come off *too* damned well," Acuña said. "That's the trouble."

The whisky bottle still stood on the table. He poured out a third glass for Rivas and, after a moment's hesitation, one for himself. It wasn't that he felt he'd earned it. He bloody well *needed* it.

"You weren't expecting trouble this early," Rivas said. "Not till this evening."

"That's how they caught us with our pants down. My own fault, that. But you can see what it means. By eight o'clock this morning . . . by *now* . . . that report of yours would have gone to something like forty people, to everyone on the Classified Reserve List. And almost any one of them could have acted on it. But to have got that report and to have acted on it by *ten o'clock last night*. . . ." Acuña chewed his lower lip.

"That's quite another matter."

"How many . . .?"

"I make it nine."

"Nine?"

". . . And three of those are right here on the job. You. Myself. And Alonso. There's the teleoperator at Recoletos who recorded the report and there's the Duty Officer. That'd be Bruno. They'd both have stayed on duty till midnight. And *then . . .*"

He ticked the names off dramatically on his fingers.

"Copy to files. That's Bruno. Copy to Central Control. That's Muñoz, *one.* . . . Copy to Field Security. That's Lain Perez, *two.* . . . Copy to the Minister's PPS, which means in effect to Riveda. *Three.* And . . . Copy to Chief of Military Intelligence. That's General Capdevila, Carlos Capdevila. *Four.* And out."

"Lain Perez and Muñoz are definitely negative."

"Definitely. And as for Riveda . . ."

"Queer as a coot," Rivas said. "I suppose you could call him a suspect."

"Possible, yes. But absurd. We have to imagine a third party, that's tricky enough without having to worry about a fourth. No. I don't see it. But Capdevila . . ."

There was silence. Until Rivas began to whistle quietly, under his breath.

"This means trouble," Acuña said.

"Yes," Rivas said. "I can see that it does."

7

Fedora wandered up and down. Up and down. His third cigarette dangled dispiritedly from his lower lip. Laura sat in the only place of the room where sitting was possible, the windowsill, with her back to the boards, watching him; while the sergeant and Private Manuel Vargas lay where they had fallen on the floor. Vargas' posture was relaxed; he might have been asleep. Not so the sergeant. His blue eyes stared towards the window, rigidly glazed, and above his right ear a broken splinter of skull projected repulsively, like a nascent horn. His gaze, like that of most men who have died through violence, was quite inescapable. It was giving Laura the creeping willies.

"Can't we at least get out of this bloody *room*?"

"I wouldn't care to try it," Fedora said mildly. Up and down, up and down. A meaningless sort of pastime, in Laura's view.

"But there *can't* be anyone here. You can tell by the dust in the hall."

"There's a fire escape outside," Fedora said. "And a window open upstairs. And probably a lad sitting up there with a tommygun. No, I wouldn't care to try it. Just because they let me in doesn't mean they'll let us out."

"But what are we *waiting* for?"

"For Feramontov, of course."

He seemed even to be mildly surprised at the question. Laura found his air of complete omniscience remarkably trying.

". . . Johnny, we've got to *talk*."

"Not now."

"What d'you mean, not now?"

"Not now," Johnny said. "I'm all shook up. I'm not think-ing straight. It wouldn't be a very good idea to talk about it now. That's all."

He wandered back towards her, stopping finally in front of her and at some two paces' distance. His face, as before, was preoccupied and dismal; but she saw, for the first time that morning, a faint glint of the old recognisable humour at the back of his eyes. "I never knew a girl like you for taking your clothes off, I never *did*."

Ridiculously, she pulled the hem of her dress down over her knees. "I thought it'd *stop* them. I couldn't..."

"Stop them? I should dam' well think so. You'd stop the Boston Philharmonic halfway through the *Bolero*. That's not the point."

"Then what *is* the point?"

"Well, I don't have to like it."

"You don't think—"

"How do I know what I think? That's the trouble. It's like I said. I *don't*."

Oh God, Laura thought. Ridiculous was the word. Having what to all intents and purposes amounted to a lover's tiff, in *this* of all places. Standing knee-deep in corpses. But there you are, that was Johnny all over. He just *had* to be different.

"Look, if there's someone up there . . . why don't they come down?"

"Why should they?" Fedora said. "They don't want to kill us. Not yet, anyway."

Laura looked down at the sergeant. "*He* certainly did."

"Oh, them, they were just the fall boys. They didn't know anything. Feramontov couldn't really have thought that a couple of thick-headed hard boys could hang *me* out to dry," Fedora said, with evident and insufferable conceit. "I was probably supposed to get out and after *them*, to see what they'd tell me. And they'd lead me into a nice little ring of machine-guns. Of course, it's tough on *you*, in a way. By rights you shouldn't be here."

"But haven't you done exactly what he wanted, then?"

"Of course I have." Fedora's rather unpractised pose of *sabelotodo* was broken by a genuine irritation. "What else *could* I have done? Just stand outside and let that crummy bastard carve you to pieces?... I couldn't wear *that*."

"No," Laura said. "You couldn't." He was standing just too far away from her to reach him. A pity, that.

"Anyway," Fedora said, retreating one pace further, "this is the way in to Feramontov. The quickest and the best. It could even be that there isn't any other. *That* could be why I did it."

"I like the first reason best. I think I'll stick with it."

"Okay. Stick with it. It may not be for long."

From outside the window, a sudden shaking rumble; the growl of a heavy lorry lumbering to a halt. Behind it, the higher, slightly asthmatic complaint of some other, much smaller vehicle; a jeep, maybe. Both engines died almost together. Gravel gritted under running feet.

"And there again," Fedora said, "... it may be."

The canvas flaps at the back of the three-tonner had been lowered and roped into place; one of the soldiers loosened the toggle, another nudged Fedora in the back with the business end of a CETME. Fedora put one foot on the mounting-plate and, with some difficulty, scrambled in. Difficulty, because he was wearing handcuffs. It was warm in the back of the lorry, very warm, and the light very dim; wooden benches ran the length of the cabin and at the far end of the offside bench an officer sat, his long legs stretched out in front of him, smoking. There was just enough light to catch the outline of the insignia that made him a lieutenant-colonel. He pointed to the bench opposite him.

For a few seconds, there was silence. Fedora looked down at the slatted floor, trying to accustom his eyes as quickly as might be possible to the near-darkness in which he now sat. The glow of the colonel's cigarette came at remarkably regular intervals, almost as exactly timed as a lighthouse flare; the effect was mildly hypnotic. Then the lorry's engine began to turn over; outside, someone shouted; wheels crunched on rough cinders and the lorry slowly began to move away. There was a great deal of vibration and the wooden seat was inordinately uncomfortable. There wasn't much point in complaining, though.

The colonel looked at his cigarette-end, then dropped it and crushed it out carefully under his left boot. "Should we shake hands?"

"Why not?" Fedora said.

The handcuffs again made things a little difficult. But that was what they were there for.

"Feramontov."

"Fedora."

"Something of an occasion, one might say."

"Yes," Fedora said. "Of course, we've seen each other before."

"Twice."

"But I doubt if I'd have recognised you. In uniform."

"Seeing people. . . . Oh, one *sees* so many people. It's not the same thing."

The lorry turned, rather abruptly; Fedora braced himself against the stanchion. Right turn, then left turn. They weren't on the road he'd come by, that was for sure. They were travelling north. Not very fast, either.

"I thought we might make this journey together," Feramontov said. "We may not have another opportunity for an uninterrupted chat. Like this. Alone. As for your wife . . ." He paused for a moment, apparently in reflection. "I don't understand that."

"What?"

"Your getting married. You're not usually so . . . inconsiderate."

He spoke English the way he spoke so many other languages; almost perfectly. If anything, it was his lack of an accent that sounded odd; it sounded like the English of an extraordinary machine, a computer's English. But it was very, very good. Very good indeed.

"She's travelling in another lorry, of course. For the time being, you've no cause to be concerned as to her safety." He smiled faintly. "I've noticed that your concern takes a rather violent form."

"I expect she's as safe as I am. That's not saying much."

"No—we don't really think in those terms, do we? Ours is a day-to-day business, at the best of times. And safety is always such a relative term. Am *I* safe?... No. Of course not."

"It's comparative, rather than relative. You'll be safer when I'm dead."

"Of course. One eliminates dangers whenever one can. But you're not particularly dangerous to me at the present moment."

"There'll be things," Fedora said, "that you want to know."

"That's quite true. There are. But as I understand it, you're a temporary victim of amnesia. You've been undergoing treatment."

Fedora nodded. Here we go, he thought; slow right turn, this'd be the roundabout. They were turning west down the Almodovar road, the old road to Sevilla. An *odd* choice of route. They'd committed themselves, in taking it. There were no turnings off, as he remembered it, until they were well past Medina Azahara. And if there were police cordons. ... He strained his ears against the all-pervading roar of the engine. Not just *one* other lorry, by the sound of it. There were several. The jeep in front, and at least two other lorries behind them. A flipping convoy.

"You're well informed already," he said. "Treatment. Yes, you could call it that. But not to very much effect."

"I want to know how you found out about Cell Eleven," Feramontov said. "And how *much* you know. I'd be interested. I really would. As a matter of fact, I've designed some treatments of my own, based on rather revolutionary new techniques. I think it quite possible that you'll respond to them."

"Unpleasant?"

"Well, yes. Unpleasant. Though that, again, is a purely relative term."

"So *that's* why you're taking the girl along with us," Fedora said. "There's nothing new about *that*, for heaven's sake, it's as old as the hills."

"We needn't go into it now. Not just yet. As you rightly say, it's an unpleasant topic. Cigarette?"

"Thank you."

"Black? Or American?"

"American, please."

Johnny leaned forwards, and Feramontov deftly slid a Philip Morris into his mouth. The flame of the little lighter burnt sharply in the dimness; Fedora inhaled slowly, breathed out smoke. ". . . Anyway," Feramontov said, lighting his own cigarette and flicking the Flaminaire shut, "that's not the *real* reason. That's just what you might call a by-product."

"The reason for what?"

"For taking you alive. I'm sure you'll have realised by now that I'm not, in the full sense of the word, a free agent. I'm an employee—just like yourself."

"And your instructions are that I'm not to be killed?" It seemed pretty unlikely.

"No," Feramontov said. "Just the opposite."

"You mean you're being difficult again?"

Feramontov laughed for a few moments in absolute silence. "Difficult?. . . You *could* put it that way. It's just that I don't really like working for someone else. It's not natural to me. I resent the necessity."

"People always ask for the wrong tunes."

"I beg your pardon?"

"It's an English saying. *He who pays the piper calls the tune.* You hadn't heard it?"

"I see. No. No, I hadn't heard it. There's a somewhat similar proverb, of course, in Russian, but Russian proverbs aren't very fashionable these days. Not since... *You* know. But yes, it sums up my position well enough. I prefer to... *whistle my native woodnotes wild.* ... Have I quoted correctly?"

"I wouldn't know," Johnny said. "Literature is one of my many weak spots."

"So it is. I was forgetting. You have," Fermamontov said diplomatically, "so few. But ... women, also, perhaps? In another sense?"

"In quite another sense, yes. Maybe. As you say, safety isn't everything."

"I'm quite fond of literature myself. I used to have some interesting discussions with Elsa. . . . You remember Elsa?"

"I do indeed."

"Shakespeare and so on. A very well-educated girl. How is she keeping?"

"Quiet," Fedora said. "In her place, so would I."

"Oh, no hard feelings, I assure you."

"No. No hard feelings."

Quite the contrary, Johnny thought. Very very soft ones. They'd been pleasant while they'd lasted. And at least he'd *known* Elsa was on the other side, was Feramontov's erstwhile playmate. *Erstwhile?* What am I doing with words like, *erstwhile?* The effect, perhaps, of my present cultured company. Laura. . . . Another matter. A big big surprise. Oh, well. He'd asked for it. And he'd certainly got it. The situation could do with a whole lot of looking into, that went without saying; but there'd be time for that later. And if there wasn't time, then it wouldn't matter. That's the way to take these things. Philosophically.

"... Be all that as it may," Feramontov said, "on these occasions, I like to choose my own music—to pursue your metaphor. Or as the Americans say, to call my own shots. My instructions were to have you killed, and I disagreed with them. Violently."

"Yes, I'll go along with you on that."

Feramontov rightly ignored the pleasantry. "You know how it is, Fedora. Or you ought to. One has a plan, a programme; one carries it out. If one allows one's attention to be distracted by the attainment of secondary objectives—no matter how desirable...." He shook his head. "No. It doesn't do. It doesn't do. It spoils the pattern. One things leads to another.... At first it's just an untidiness, then while you look at it it turns into a shambles—an utter shambles. But there." He raised his hands, palms turned upwards. "Given the commitment, one does what one can. I've tried to impose on this chaos a proper sense of order. I've left my ... visiting-card. At the hotel. To warn my own employer, as much as yours."

Fedora didn't understand very much of this. "*I* argue," he said. "Sometimes."

"And does that help?"

"No."

"Of course not. I never argue. I just ... misinterpret."

"That's not always possible."

"Well, but language is such an unsatisfactory mode of communication. When I say that my instructions were to kill you, that's not exactly true. That is simply what was *meant*. In actual fact, there was an element of ambiguity.... *Do* something about it, he said, *do* something about it. All right. I've obeyed. I've done something."

"Who *is* this nit?" Fedora asked idly.

"Oh, come now. Names are immaterial. He's my employer, that's all, my esteemed employer. Very capable. Very influential. But with—as you see—this leaning towards the ambiguous so common among our elder statesmen. Though you shouldn't think—"

The brakes squealed, throwing Fedora's weight forwards; he barely kept his position on the seat. The lorry ground to a halt. "We're not there yet," Feramontov said. "Stay where you are." He had unholstered his regulation Luger, was screwing a four-inch silencer on to the neat black barrel. "I'm not as skilful with pistols as you, but at this range I don't think I would miss."

"And if you didn't, your employer would be pleased."

"Screw him, too," Feramontov said pleasantly.

*   *   *

"You've never met Capdevila?"

"No," Rivas said.

"Big fellow. Six foot three or so. With a game leg. And a rather odd voice, sort of soft and effeminate. Nothing else effeminate about him, though, *caramba*."

"Head of Military Intelligence, too. It couldn't be more awkward."

Acuña clicked his tongue. "I wish that were all. He's only been in MI these last eighteen months, and God knows the post is a sinecure. What sort of Military Intelligence outfit can *we* hope to run, after all, in this damned country? The CIA look at our set-up and they don't know whether to laugh or cry. They only gave him the job to justify his seat in the Cabinet. *That's* what matters."

"Big fellow," Rivas said. "Big fish."

"Bigger than *me*, anyway. That's not to say we can't get him into the frying-pan. But it may take time, and time we haven't got. Besides . . . you know what he did before he went into MI, I suppose?"

"Commander of the Second Army Corps. Down in Sevilla."

"The Second Corps, yes. They know him and they like him. They like him a lot better than the sod they've got running the show now. Brentano. He's not with it."

"Bretano's is a temporary appointment, anyway."

"Exactly. So if Capdevila were to tell them to jump, I imagine they'd jump . . . without caring a lot if Brentano told 'em something different."

"When you say *jump* . . . you don't mean it literally?"

"What?"

"The parachute boys come under that command. Or most of them, anyway."

"Yes. So they do. Well, things *could* work out that way. The Army did it once, didn't they, with Franco? . . . If it came to the point, they could probably do it again."

"*Against* Franco?"

"You know the way things have been going lately."

Rivas shrugged.

"... Another thing."

"What?"

"Pinto said *boots*, didn't he? And a grenade-thrower?...
It all fits together."

"But with Feramontov?"

"Why not?"

Rivas ate a peanut.

The bar wasn't officially open yet, and the corner where
they sat was quiet and secluded. Beyond the plate-glass windows was the parquet, where people loafed on deck-chairs,
taking the sun. They were all well out of earshot. Which was
just as well.

"The question is," Rivas said, "how are we going to stop
him?"

"It won't be easy. No. It's not easy. Any of the ideas you
had at first... Egypt, Morocco, even Russia.... No trouble
there. No *real* trouble. But this is something else. This is high
treason. And just about as high as it can come."

"We could stop him," Rivas said, "by shooting him."

Acuña watched him for some little time.

"... Whoever did it would be caught."

"It might still be arranged."

"Yes, I'm sure it might. He killed your brother, didn't he?
... to your way of thinking?"

"Yes," Rivas said. "To my way of thinking."

"Then," Acuña said coldly, "you're not thinking straight.
In this kind of situation, people do get killed. And *everyone*
is somebody else's brother... or father... or son. That's got
nothing to do with it. I'm responsible for a Special Department of the Spanish State—not for this or that individual.
I'm the Chief of the Secret Police, and you—right now—are
my second-in-command. So either you start thinking straight,
or you go back to Barcelona. Do I make myself clear?"

"Yes, sir. You do."

"Right. Then let's see what the *real* question is. It isn't, how
are we going to stop him. It's, *are* we going to stop him? Bear-
ing in mind we're responsible for the whole of our Depart-

ment...."

The sharp scratch of a match. He was lighting yet another of his cigars.

"Maybe we can stamp out the fire and maybe we can't. And we want to be sure either way. Because *if* we can't ..."

The used match. Dropping from his fingers into the ashtray.

"... Capdevila can use the Secret Police as well as the present government can. He can use us as well, and he'll need us a whole lot more. But he'll need us *before*. Not after."

The bar was something other than quiet now. It was downright silent. Rivas had even heard the *ping* of the match in the ashtray. He pressed his tongue, meditatively, against the back of his teeth; a blasted fragment of nut had got under his plate. "... So," he said, "we talk?"

"We talk when we're found out more. We negotiate from strength. Meanwhile ... we think straight. No emotions. No vendettas. We just find out the odds. Odds are statistics. Impersonal. Objective. You follow me?"

"Yes, sir," Rivas said. "I follow you."

And after another pause.

"What would you say the odds are, at the moment?"

"Not good."

"No?"

"Not good."

... But then, neither had the question been. Had the odds been anything else, Acuña would never be talking in this way. He didn't otherwise show it, but he had to be worried. Yes. Badly worried.

"It's what Feramontov wanted from the beginning," Acuña said. "To know about *us*. That's what the Undertow caper was all about. But that one fell through, so he went straight on with the main assignment; and because he didn't have the information he needed, *that* fell through, too. Now it looks as though he's starting out again. And if he's really in with Capdevila ..."

"He'll *have* the information."

"Most of it, yes. It's not the sort of alliance I'd feel happy about.”

“. . . And Fedora?”

Acuña detached ash from his cigar with the tip of his little finger. “Well, what did *you* make of Fedora?”

A sudden gust of air from the swing door, lifting the ash as it fell and scattering it over Rivas’ sober grey flannel suit. Pinto came in, walked quickly towards them. “There’s been a phone call, sir. . . .”

“Yes?”

“From the police checkpoint on the Almodovar Road. They’ve had an Army convoy just gone by. And since their orders were to report anything unusual . . .”

“They didn’t hold it up?”

“No, sir. They couldn’t, very well. The transit papers were perfectly in order.”

“Whose authorisation?”

“HQ 21st Division, sir, at Sevilla. Colonel Gutierrez in charge of the convoy.”

“A colonel, eh? And who was in charge of the roadblock?”

“He gave his name, sir, as Lieutenant Sandaval.”

“Then he did the right thing. It’s awkward when you’re outranked. . . . Isn’t it, Rivas?”

“I’d say it was wise, in such circumstances, to act with caution.”

“*That’s* my boy,” Acuña said. “*That’s* straight thinking.” He stood up, wheeling his huge stomach around the table. “I fancy this is it. So all right. Let’s *go*.”

Fedora hadn’t been given time for more than a hurried glance at the outside of the aircraft, but the few brief seconds of the take-off convinced him that the motor had power of a kind that he wasn’t familiar with. They were airborne, by his watch, in under half a minute, which by any non-jet standard meant a packet of thrust; but in the passengers’ cabin the kick went unaccompanied by any propeller racket or sidewash. There was just that steady thrum, a barely perceptible vibration. Perhaps more to the immediate point, the cabin’s accoutrements were notably luxurious; he had practically disappeared into the ice-blue foam-rubber seat, and he found this pneumaticity—after the buttock-bruising agony of the lorry bench—extremely pleasing. His handcuffs hadn't been taken off, but that was a minor inconvenience.

Laura, also handcuffed, sat beside him; and directly opposite, an Army captain with sunbleached hair and a flat brown face. In front was Feramontov. Piloting. There were huge observation windows at each side of the cabin; in fact, the walls seemed to be made of mica; but dark grey curtains had been clipped across them to hold off the sun. And cooler tubes, overhead, kept the air temperature pleasant. Wherever it was they were going, this was clearly a damned good way of getting there. Better, far better than in an army lorry.

The changeover, of course, had been nicely timed. Even if Laura's policeman pals rumbled the convoy and checked on its route, it wouldn't help them; it certainly wouldn't lead them to Feramontov. Not now. Johnny didn't even know in which direction they were flying. It was anyone's guess. Though it seemed a safe bet that their course would take them comfortably clear of the radar screens at Cordoba and Sevilla. And if, which was most likely, they were headed north-west, they wouldn't run into anything else until they were on the Lisbon approach. Which they probably wouldn't reach; the odds were a hundred to one against their crossing the frontier. North-west, thought Fedora; what price Badajoz? It seemed as likely a destination as any other.

"... Coffee?"

"Thank you," Laura said, since the question had been addressed to her. The brown-faced captain nodded, pressed down a red plastic switch projecting from the bulkhead to his right. "It won't take a moment," he said.

Fedora went on thinking about Badajoz. Laura would have passed on the clue—if you could call it that—to the police; that was virtually certain. Yes, and how much else?... That was the question. He wouldn't have told her much, presumably, but with tabs as close as those she'd been keeping on him and a sharp native intelligence ... Well, of all the goddam things to do. Marry a Secret Police agent. And the most peculiar thing of all was that he didn't feel particularly surprised. Overhearing her talking to that scruffy sergeant bastard, that had been like ... Um. *What* had it been like? Hearing yourself on tape, maybe, for the first time. The immediate reaction is that it can't be true, that voice isn't *mine*. Yet you know all the time it is, you don't seriously doubt it. Yes, it had been something like that.

Because that, when you thought about it, had been the oddball in the Villafranca operation—the absence of the Spanish undercover boys. They'd known about Ortiz, of course, and by rights they should have dug their own little listening post; Johnny had expected it, had looked for it. But hadn't found it. No wonder. They'd been lurking behind Laura's big brown eyes all the time. It wasn't so very odd that he hadn't rumbled her; she'd had an exceptionally good cover and, in any case, everyone knew about the traditional Spanish aversion to woman operatives. Everyone except, apparently, Acuña. So there it was. She'd *infiltrated* him. Confound it. And so very expertly that he'd hardly suspected it. Well, *hardly*. It was just that story of hers about how she'd killed Donizetti, the man with the big black sock, that had seemed a little weird—and even that she'd managed to pass off. Fedora, when all was said and done, couldn't have been over-critical on that one point. Because she'd saved his life. And that mark still remained on the ledger, whatever had happened since.

All the same, though ... Women. *Blasted* women. Feramontov had been absolutely right. A weakness, that was what it was. A chink in the armour. And a gaping chink, at that. Why, even now there'd be room for two or three more to wiggle through a hole that size. *That* was a cheering thought.

Cheering? ... Downright over-optimistic. Feramontov clearly had other plans. Involving, as he'd said, techniques of persuasion. Johnny didn't want to think about them at all —still less consider the possibility of their having effect. He'd laid himself open all right. But then, so had Laura.

... He watched Bujas turn round in his seat, open a bulk-head panel beneath the switch; then draw from it, one by one, three plastic disposable cups of steaming black coffee. Very acceptable. He hadn't had any breakfast. He held his cup in both hands and sipped at it gratefully.

"Johnny?"

"Yes?" he said.

"Didn't he come?"

"Who?"

"You know. Feramontov."

"He came all right. He's piloting the plane. No doubt he'll introduce himself in due course."

Bujas watched them closely over the rim of his coffee-cup, but said nothing. There was no objection, apparently, to their conversing. Bujas, of course, could hear what they said, but it was hard to see how that could make any difference.

"Have you talked to him?"

"Oh, at length," Johnny said. "At length. We rode together in the back of a lorry."

"I was with this one." Nodding at Bujas. "What did he ... What did you talk about?"

"Well, he's worried, very worried about my amnesia. He's going to put me on a course of treatment."

"But—"

"But what?"

"That doesn't sound very pleasant."

"I don't know that Cardenas' system was, either. But I'll grant you that Feramontov's is certain to be worse."

"So that's why they brought me along. I wondered about that."

Certainly, she was no fool. But that, Fedora knew already. "I'm sorry," he said. "I might have done better, really, to leave you to the sergeant. I suppose I knew that at the time. But I just couldn't."

"There's no need to apologise."

"I wasn't. Just making a point, that's all. We're still not

quits."

"Quits?"

"You saved my life once, didn't you?... I haven't really saved yours. All I did was hold back the execution. That's the way it goes."

Laura pursed her lips to drink more coffee. Bujas, who had finished his already, was leaning back in his seat and watching them idly. When she looked up, it was towards him; and yet, not seeing him at all.

"... I wanted to *tell* you, Johnny."

"There's nothing to tell."

"But there is. It's all such a mess. I wish you'd found out some other way, that's all. I had it all worked out, in a vague sort of way, I mean I would've told you what had happened, and ... and I'd've stayed with you, of course, if you'd wanted. And we'd ... Well, we'd've been ..."

"Happy."

"Yes. Happy," she said, as though it were a swearword. "It all seemed quite forgivable, when I thought about it. I've only just got around to realising that maybe it isn't."

"We don't live," Johnny said, "in that kind of a world."

"How do you mean?"

"A *forgiving* kind of a world. To forgive someone, you have to make moral judgements. We don't do that. There are jobs that have to be done, and we respect the people who do them well. That's all."

"You *respect* me?"

"Yes. I do."

"But is that all?"

"... No," Fedora said. Sadly, almost. "That isn't all."

"It *could* be for us, too. Forgiving ... and all that. Why not?"

"Perhaps it could have been. A simple matter of tense. ... It makes a difference."

She had finished her coffee. Now she crumpled up the container, slowly, in her hands. "I had it right the first time."

"You think so?"

"Yes. Even if it's only to . . . wherever it is they're taking us. Half an hour . . . or even if it's less . . . it's *something*." She lolled her head sideways, so that it almost touched Johnny's shoulder. He could smell her hair. Not her perfume; she wasn't wearing any. Just her hair.

"Yes. It's something," Johnny said. ". . . It's nice."

"What is?"

"This amnesia business. You wake up and there's someone there you don't really know. So you can fall in love all over again. It's very pleasant."

"Christ," Laura said, lifting her head again. "You're such a *sentimental* cow."

"I'm not, really. I was thinking about how much more difficult it's going to make things . . . when we get there."

"Well, don't," Laura said. "Let's not think about it. In fact, let's not think at all."

Fedora's vague calculations with regard to their ultimate destination had been based, not unnaturally, on the premise that the aircraft, having taken off, would at some time come down to land once more. But—in a precise sense—it didn't. To that extent, Johnny had underestimated the ingenuity of Feramontov yet again. Curtained in as he was within the cabin, he was aware of no preliminary bankings or circlings, nor even of any apparent loss of height. He heard the motor throttle down, and that was all. Some forty seconds later he, like Laura and Bujas, was being joggled to and fro in alarming fashion as the aeroplane went through a series of skidding, grinding bumps unlike any that he—in his limited flying experience—had ever undergone before. He felt rather frightened. "Hell," he said. "What's going on?"

"Keep your seat, please," Bujas said, like some kind of bloody bus conductor.

Fedora had no intention of doing anything else; the question was whether his good intentions were sufficient. But things were now, in any case, steadying down; the plane was proceeding in a series of smooth, bouncing rushes and its speed had fallen so far below stall velocity that it was quite obvious they were no longer airborne. Equally obviously, they hadn't landed, either. That left just one alternative, and Fedora—who had been, perhaps, a bit slow—had by now caught on to it.

They had slackened speed, indeed, to the point where the movement and impact of the waves beneath the hull was clearly discernible; they seemed alarmingly solid. The hum of the propeller had taken on a curious whining note, due probably to some variation of pitch; and finally, as the aircraft came to a near-halt, no other sound than this could be heard. There was no sea movement, no pitch and toss. Fedora turned his head, looked at Laura.

"An amphibian," he said. "I should have realised that."

"A what?"

"It can land on the water. It just has."

"Well, I knew *that*," Laura said.

Of course, Johnny thought; she'd have recognised the symptoms. She was a powerboat fiend. "You might have told *me*," he said. "I nearly did my nut."

The hull was beginning to rock now, though only slightly, as the pilot began to swing her towards the starboard; the whining note faded as they began to taxi confidently forwards. Fedora said nothing more. He was thinking. He was thinking, precisely, that he could now maybe guess how Feramontov had left Ortiz's yacht. And since the aircraft presumably had a civil registration number that could be traced, and since its interior appointments suggested a proprietor of some influence and wealth . . . yes, he could also guess now why Durand's death had been thought necessary. And if Durand had told him *that* much on the occasion of their famous interview . . .

Yes, indeed. *That* could have been a reason for going to Sevilla. . . .

He looked up. The aircraft had stopped; and Feramontov, stripping off his gloves, had turned in his seat to look back at them. ". . . Captain Bujas?"

"Sir?"

"You'll find transport waiting at the pontoon, and an armed

escort. You'll conduct the prisoners to the Punishment Block and report thereafter to the Orderly Room."

"Very good, sir," Bujas said.

". . . Have a good trip, Fedora?"

"The end part startled me, rather."

"Yes, I forgot to warn you about that. It's rather a difficult touchdown here. But the plane flies herself, really—a beautiful piece of machinery. Really beautiful. I'm sorry there's no time for me to show you the refinements."

He drew down the safety lock, and the curtained perspex swung effortlessly upwards and outwards. He turned back once more to nod to Laura. "*Señora*," he said. Then clambered agilely out. "He's polite," Laura said, impressed. "Isn't he a bit *shy*?"

"He loses his timidity," Fedora said, "as he gets to know you better."

Bujas was standing up now, his pistol out of its holster. It wasn't necessary for him to motion with it; Fedora was also on his feet. Through the exit hatch he could see, directly beneath him, a pontoon erection leading to an improvised quay; behind the quay, low flat land, a group of army vehicles peacefully parked upon it and, behind them, two or three grey and impersonal-looking huts. There were hills in the far distance and nothing much else anywhere. It was dry, dusty and hot. It was anywhere in Spain south of the Ebro.

Feramontov was mounting a shiny black Mercedes which drew away the second its door was closed, sending up a smoke-like trailer of feathery dust. Another black Mercedes stood waiting, two soldiers in sloppy uniforms standing watchfully beside it. The escort, no doubt. ". . . Come on," Bujas said, his pistol nudging Fedora gently in the back. "Let's go. Hup, hup."

Fedora hup-hupped obediently; Laura likewise. On to the lurching platform, and from there up to the quay. Bujas followed them closely, but not too closely. One of the waiting soldiers drew his automatic rifle down to the ready position; the other opened the rear door of the car.

"Punishment Block," Laura said. "Orderly Room. It all

sounds horribly *organised*."

"Why shouldn't it be? Regular Armies are always horribly organised."

"Are they really . . .? It's like that sergeant this morning. I can't believe that they really know what they're doing."

"No Regular Army ever does."

They stopped in front of the car; Johnny looked back at Bujas. "We get in?"

"You get in."

They got in.

The view from the rear seat of the car was still of somewhere nondescript in the middle of nowhere. They had landed on a wide lake, on the far side of which were steep sand-coloured cliffs and rocks like crouching lions; farther to the west there was a fringe of young pine trees, *pinos tiernos*, but otherwise no vegetation at all. Spain? . . . It looked more like Africa. Johnny said softly to Laura,

"You know where we are?"

"Sorry. I'm a stranger here myself."

"Doesn't look like much of a place for a honeymoon."

"No," Laura said. "Too much company."

She had a point there, Johnny thought. Though the aeroplane, resting now at its moorings, could have provided in other circumstances an admirable answer to that little problem. A twin-boom job with a pusher prop mounted behind and above the passenger cabin, which helped to explain its quietness of flight; smartly painted in scarlet and brilliant white. A beautiful bit of machinery, Feramontov had called it. Yes. It was. And Johnny knew now the registration number, though it probably wouldn't help. It hadn't helped Durand over-much.

"You know anything about aeroplanes?"

"Well, I know what it *is*, if that's what you mean. It's a Riviera. They make it in Milan. Custom-built, probably."

"Italian," Fedora said. With deep sagacity.

"Siai-Marchetti."

"You're a mine of information."

"We'll stop talking now," Bujas said amiably, sitting heavily down at Laura's side and placing a hand, no less amiably, upon her right knee. The hand with the pistol in it rested, however, in his lap. "I shall have to shoot the lady," he said, "if you do anything ... you know. Ill-advised."

He probably didn't mean it seriously; Feramontov would have been *very* cross. Johnny, however, didn't feel like arguing the toss. He nodded acknowledgement of the intelligence and went on staring out of the window. The view of the lake was there, for what it was worth, and he had the feeling that he'd better make the most of it. Punishment blocks rarely offer much in the way of stunning panoramic vistas, and he didn't suppose that those of the Spanish Army would provide any exceptions.

The road down which they drove paralleled, at first, the near bank of the lake, though rising slightly, so that the water-level began to drop away beneath them and to their right. It remained, however, nothing but a large stretch of water; no boats, no birds, no atomic submarine bases. Just before the road turned away, however, Fedora had the impression, in the extreme distance, of some kind of an erection. ... It was as vague as that. ... Of sharp concrete-like lines, made hazy by the distance and the rising water vapour, crossing and rising high above the lake level at the point where the two banks of the lake perspectived together and were joined, almost at the horizon. .. But it could just as easily have been an optical illusion. The road, which was a reasonably good one, then ran for some five miles due east (or so Fedora judged by the position of the sun), through the usual rocky, sharply un-dulating ground of the low sierras; there was scrub, sage, clumps of Spanish oak and everywhere, the dry red earth. Suddenly—and incredibly, since they had seemed to be travel-ling more or less in a straight line—the lake was in front of them again, running a narrow blue ribbon between the sun-torn hills; they headed down towards it, then turned away again, and the rocky slopes closed in on them once more. It was damned confusing country in which to get one's bearings.

They drove on for some twenty minutes, by Fedora's watch, and at no time did the lake appear again. They seemed still, on the whole, to be travelling east, though the road twisted and turned so much it was difficult to be sure. In the end there was a longish valley, flattening to a trough; and in the trough there were huts, houses, long grey-painted sheds, all crouching behind high barbed-wire fences. There were signs along the road, painted in red on a white background; the nearest, and the only one immediately legible, said,

ZONA MILITAR—ENTRADA PROHIBIDA

which seemed only to clarify the already obvious. The Mercedes drove on, though, its engine purring softly, towards the main gate, where another and larger sign said,

PANTANO DE Sta. ANA
DEPARTMENTO
8
GUARDIA CENTRAL

which didn't help matters much, either. But then, signs aren't put there to *help* you, in the Spanish Army; or, for that matter, in any other. The St. Ana dam, Fedora thought; Department Eight. No. No bells were ringing.

Either the guard at the main gate was unusually lazy, or he'd been warned of their arrival; probably the latter. At any rate, he waved them straight through. The car drove fast across the parade ground; crawled more cautiously round a block of huts; skirted what looked like a group of transformer units; came at last to the main building, a large though not especially imposing structure of red brick and glass. For an army camp, the place seemed unusually deserted; hardly anybody seemed to be about. The car passed one, two, three entrances, each of which was marked confusingly with red and with yellow painted lines; came to a stop at the fourth. Smaller. A little green-painted door above four wooden steps. Bujas leaned forwards, looked at Fedora.

"All right," Fedora said. "I know. Hup, hup."

There were tiles on the cell floor and the walls were of roughly plastered masonry. There was no electric light, no furniture, no fitments other than a metal pail in the far corner. There were two narrow windows, placed high up in the wall and heavily barred. Throughout the afternoon and early evening, the light in the cell had seemed dim in comparison with the hot white brightness beyond those windows; but now that the sun was near to setting, the light poured in past the bars in smoking rays. The door was thick and of unvarnished oak, with an observation slit at eye level; Fedora, peering through it, could see nothing but the opposite wall of the corridor beyond, whitewashed and blank. There was no key; only solid iron bolts on the other side of the door. He had just heard them rattle back into place. He rubbed the spot above his elbow where the hypodermic syringe had gone in, and felt the first wave of dizziness come up at him from the rubber soles of his shoes. His legs, too, felt as though they were of rubber. He sat down on the floor, back to the wall.

It helps a little to know what kind of a drug you've been subjected to. Not much, but yes, it helps. Fedora didn't, though. The fluid in the syringe had been colourless and there had to have been well over an ounce of it. The medical orderly had worn a white jacket and bifiocal glasses, but that wasn't relevant. It was anybody's guess, then. Not pentothal, though. Pentothal would have hit by now. *I'd* have used pentothal if I'd used anything, but I'm not Feramontov. One of the barbiturates, though, surely? What else could it have been?. . . Fedora looked at his wrist-watch. They hadn't taken it away, which was odd but didn't have to be significant. Time was rushing by now. Fourteen minutes odd since the shot had gone in. And as yet no reactions. Apart from the dizziness. He checked his pulse rate; awkwardly, because of the handcuffs, but finding his own wrist without difficulty.

What was odd was having nothing, well, nothing *really*, to worry about. That was odd again. He'd go into the speech-phase, if ever he did, with nothing at all to tell them. There was nothing he knew. Or more exactly, nothing he remembered. Except of course about Laura. And the police. He'd try not to tell them, but if he did it wouldn't make very much difference. It'd mean no change from plan. They'd' go on from there just the same, with her, too bad. Too bad. And that about Cell Eleven, as Feramontov called it, which didn't mean anything. Here he was, and this was funny, in the cell. Which could be Cell Eleven, for all he knew. A cell with a bee in it. Cells. Bees build cells. Don't they? It begins with a bee, they build cells. And they hum. He could hear the humming, but that was all right, too, because he'd heard it all the time, all the time he'd been here. Hours and hours. Somewhere near there was a generator, a high-power generator. Something like that. And naturally hearing a humming you think of bees. That was all right, too. But then, why was he holding on to his wrist?

Oh, yes. The pulse. Tick tick.

He let go; tried to focus his eyes again on the dial of his wrist-watch. Eighteen, no, nineteen minutes. Time going slower now. And visual references going. The dial, coming nearer then moving away; narcosis developing. What takes twenty minutes? Sodium amytal, yes, but *that'd* do no good. *Nothing* would do no good. Nothing, he had nothing to tell them. All the same . . .

All the same, we have to fight it. Don't we? Yes. Slow, deep breaths. The chest, rising and falling. The lungs pumping in the oxygen, feeding, refreshing the bloodstream. If only you could stop your blood flowing, that'd be the answer. Stop the poison circulating. Could a fakir maybe do it? There ought to be a way. Focus on the wall, on the far wall. Nothing there to check on; just blank plaster; they thought of *that* all right. Uniform texture, uniform light, dark behind the golden sunrays; no way of measuring relative sizes or distances. Nothing moves. There's just the wall. Except over there, in the far corner, just there where the eyes can't quite see them. . . .

Fedora watched the spiders building their webs. Golden spiders, shining in the sunlight. The web grew fast, spreading out from the corner of the ceiling across the bars of the window; the sticky threads black, then gleaming silver, then seizing all the colours of the spectrum as they floated downwards. A great multicoloured web, swelling out like an expanding balloon. *Hallucinogenic, then,* said a small voice at the back of Johnny's brain; small, almost inaudible. *One of the psychedelics. LSD, even?. . . Maybe?. . .* It was too small a voice to have any effect; it faltered and was lost in the ramifications of something far, far larger, something swelling up inside him as the web was swelling towards him, something horrible; fear; more than fear; terror; panic. He tried to brush the web away with his hand. But a weight held it down. His hands were linked together. He lifted them both.

And saw them also swelling, hideously swollen; then suddenly contracting; expanding and contracting like lungs. His fingers were held together by webs of skin; they were frog's fingers; flippers. He stared at them for a while, then closed his eyes. Then round his bared forearm he could feel the constrictor, tight red rubber around the arteries, with a tube that led to the blood pressure gauge; the gauge that would give him warning of the approaching syncope. It was coming. It was coming. The needle turned. His legs were beneath the white sheets, the heavy white sheets that held him down. His lips moved fervently, but made no sound.

The face of Cardenas, frowning, preoccupied, emerging from the filmy strands of the web. Peering down at him. Cardenas and not-Cardenas. Someone else; somewhere else; and the small voice insistently seeking utterance from deep inside him. *Cell Eleven,* it said. *It's important you remember this. Cell Eleven. You must remember this . . . a kiss is still a kiss. . . .* The face now that of Laura, a big round tear rolling down her cheek, or perhaps a raindrop. *Sevilla. The British Consulate. Sevilla. The British Consulate. Sevilla. Married married married.* The voice no longer his but weirdly distorted, a voice on a tape recording, manic in its insistency, *married buried buried. Buried bride, bride buried. Fedora?* it said now. *Fedora? Fedora?* And Johnny's dry lips moved again, saying,

"Fedora. That's me."

Anxiety in his voice. An overwhelming anxiety. Because this at least he must never forget; Fedora. That's me.

Cell Eleven. Cell Eleven. Remember Cell Eleven.

Yes, of course. "You must . . . remember this. . . ."

Yes. You must remember. Where is Cell Eleven? Where is it?

A bee. A bee. "With a bee."

A bee? Now, listen. You must try to remember. Where is Cell Eleven? You must tell me all about Cell Eleven. . . .

"Badajoz. Badajoz?"

Feramontov's face. Peering downwards, like the others. But somehow different. This face was real. This was the spider's face, at the centre of the web. The breath was labouring in Fedora's chest; something was changing, was taking a new shape. Was coming back. If only he could move his legs, he'd have it all. His legs. Or his arms. If it weren't for the sheets.

Badajoz. Yes. Tell me more. Tell me where Cell Eleven is.

"They didn't tell me that."

Who didn't? . . . Who didn't tell you? . . .

Yes, a notice board, there had been. Big red letters. "Santa Ana," Fedora said. "At Santa Ana."

Now who told you that, Fedora? About Santa Ana?

Yes, he knew. That was the crazy thing. He knew. It was coming back now, it was almost there. He was on the down-phase now, or was that just another trick? No, he was almost out. He knew where he was. The hospital. The hospital in Cordoba.

Who told you? Yes, it's coming back now. Who told you?

A name now, coming out of nowhere. He'd remembered it. A name without a face to it. ". . . Durand."

That's it. It's coming back now. You'll feel better when it's back. Better, better. Just tell me all about it. That's all. You saw Durand. Yes. Where was it?

"Sevilla. The British Consulate. Sevilla."

No, that's not true. You're guessing. Aren't you?

"It's what they told me. The British Consulate. Sevilla. Married."

You're married, yes. We know about that. The web thinning now, disappearing. Just Feramontov's image now, swaying to and fro on the back of the retina; behind it, the whiteness of the ceiling. The hospital. "I'm coming out now," Fedora said cheerfully. "I'm fine. I feel fine."

Was it Alicante?

"Yes," Fedora said obediently. "Alicante."

But Durand is dead now. He died because you talked to him. It was all your fault. You must have talked about a lot of things. Why not talk to him now, Fedora? . . . As though he were still alive. Then it won't be your fault. What did he say about Santa Ana?

. . . Puzzlement growing now in Fedora's mind. He licked his lips. That was no good. His tongue was drier than his lips were.

Tell me. You'll feel better, much better. What did Durand tell you? What did—

"He said I'd remember it all when I woke up. Cell Eleven, Badajoz. Though that came later. And that about Laura. Then I woke up and felt better and that was in the hospital and the nurse was there. And Laura. Later. She knew about it of course because she was there when it happened. You see. Hit my head on the bumper. Of the car." Confidence now; complete confidence; he was talking with a godlike ease and fluency. He *wanted* to talk. This was it. He knew now what it was that he had to remember. "And as for the drug, no, that was something else. I thought it was halluciogenic, but it was something different, it was in the syringe. I saw it

there. And Cardenas said . . . Except that it wasn't Cardenas.
. . ." He paused. Again, that inexplicable perplexity. Just
when at last he'd understood it all.

Let's get back to Durand. . . .

The urge to talk, tremendous, overwhelming. But something there to hold it back, to hold it in check even now. Yes,
but the urge, the *need*, like a physical need, urgent as the
incipience of orgasm. "I don't want to tell. I mustn't."

*I know. I know it. You're putting me on, aren't you? It
wasn't Durand who told you. He didn't know anything. I
want to know—*

"Laura. I told you about Laura. She was there."

The words were an act of betrayal. He couldn't help it.
They came out quite involuntarily, like the tears that were
streaming down his cheeks. He had to hold them back, hold
everything back. But he couldn't. Couldn't help it.

*That's an unpleasant topic. We won't talk about that.
That's why you want to tell me about Cell Eleven, isn't it?
Everything you know about Cell Eleven. That's what's important. I bet you don't know what's going into Cell Eleven. He
couldn't have told you that.*

"He did, he did."

I don't believe you.

"I want to tell you. Why shouldn't you believe me?"

All right. Maybe I will. Go on. Tell me.

But Feramontov had made a mistake. *An unpleasant topic.*
So unpleasant that, suddenly, it was real. And Fedora became
gradually aware of the existence of his own body, of the
smell of his own sweat, of the dampness of his own cheeks;
of the shirt sticking clammily to his back and chest. And with
the awareness, a certain degree of knowledge. He was coming
back, yes, he knew *that*. But coming back from where . . .?

From the drug. Yes, of course. What drug . . .?

*Fedora. Listen. This is your last chance. What's inside Cell
Eleven?*

The question just wasn't relevant any more. It didn't mean
anything. Fedora breathed in great, shuddering gulps, his

tongue lolling halfway out of his mouth; he was on the way down now and he knew it. He was out, it was almost over, the only thing left to beat was the reaction. Which would be pretty horrible. But the knowledge would help, the knowledge of what they'd done. The drug, yes. The old double-take. One of the lysergics, with a follow-up of benzedrine to give the kickback. The wild opium dream and the violent awakening; the benzedrine kicks you out of it and that's when you talk, that's when it all comes out of you. Dangerous, bloody dangerous, but he was out. He'd beaten it. Hadn't he? . . . Well, not to worry. Just lie still. And take the reaction when it comes, and it won't be long now. . . .

"This is the Colonel speaking," Feramontov said abruptly, incisively. "You hear me, Fedora?. . . It'll soon be too late. Make your report now. What has Capdevila got in Cell Eleven? "

Capdevila? Who the hell was Capdevila?

Feramontov, leaning forwards now. His eyes shielded by the palm of his hand, watchful, intent. "*Answer me. Answer me at once.*"

It *was* too late. He'd beaten it. He was out. The web, the faces had gone; he was alone in the room with Feramontov. "No good, Colonel," Johnny said. "This is Control. I'm in control."

Speaking, now, unbelievably difficult. His tongue swollen and heavy, gummed to his palate. How the devil had it been so easy before . . . ?

Feramontov said nothing. He went on watching Fedora; Fedora met his gaze stonily. Then he leaned back once more, stood up. Fedora followed the movement easily, perfectly. He fingered his chin. He said,

"So you're with us again."

"Yes," Johnny said. "Dad's back."

"I'm afraid you didn't tell me . . . quite enough."

"No," Johnny said. Now he felt sick.

"So we do it the hard way. I'll admit I'm disappointed."

"The hard way's no good, either. A . . . waste of time. . . ."

"I wouldn't say that," Feramontov said. "It's always entertaining and often instructive. We'll be ready for you in about an hour."

Now Johnny said nothing. Feramontov went out, and the bolts rattled into place behind him. Johnny lowered his head into his hands. And shook like a leaf.

. . . Out of the nightmare, two things that he'd dragged back with him into the light of day. Firstly, a name *Capdevila*. A name that could well be important, because Feramontov certainly hadn't really meant to impart it. He'd been nervous, he'd seen Fedora move away from the top and inexorably away from him, and in his anxiety he'd pressed a little too hard. *What has Capdevila got in Cell Eleven?* . . . Fedora didn't know; but he had the idea that, could he find his way through divine intervention out of the present jam, the answer mightn't be too difficult to discover.

Because he knew now where Cell Eleven was. Whatever it might be, it was right there in front of him; there at Santa Ana. *Santa Ana,* he'd said; and Feramontov had accepted that, hadn't pressed him any farther. So it looked as though by chance he had hit the target. He'd been brought—as indeed he'd hoped to be—to the centre of the web; this was Santa Ana, and Badajoz was probably close by. That was one thing; getting out of the web would be quite another. Divine intervention was just what he needed; he couldn't think of anything else that would do the trick.

There again. . . . The strange thing was that he'd *heard* of Santa Ana. Or had heard the name mentioned, in some connection or other. It wasn't one of his missing memories, or he didn't think so; it had a different *feel,* it was something that had slipped his mind simply because the name had arisen so casually or because he'd heard it a long time ago. How long ago? . . . Months, anyway. Maybe years. If his head didn't ache so much, maybe he could re-establish the lost link. But as it was . . .

As it was, he felt like nothing. *Think of anything else . . .?*

He found it almost impossible to think *at all*. A minimal dosage of LSD-25 is supposed to keep you higher than a kite for anything from five to eight hours; the stimulant—pervitine, benzedrine, whatever—kicks you out of it too damned quickly and the after-effects of the combination are murderous. The best antidote was milk and plenty of it, but there wasn't any in the cell and it was obvious that none would be supplied. So Fedora stood up with his back to the wall and his arms hanging loosely at his sides; stood up and began his deep-breathing exercises. Diagram A to diagram B; the proper textbook approach. In, out. In, out. It was hard work, though it didn't look it.

It wasn't by any means clear to him, either, what Feramontov had hoped for. Resistance techniques to most of the employable drugs are a standard part of home-based training for all field operatives, and have been since 1955; Fedora had been through the narcosis mill in the same way as everyone else, though with better results. His rejective capacity of narcotic and hypnotic suggestion—both post-treatment and normal—was high above the average, and his record-sheet said so; Dr. Bohr—the part-designer of the notorious Bohr-Schmidt scale—had gone so far as to say that Fedora's responsiveness to sodium succinate, even when intravenously injected, was about on a par statistically speaking with that of Table Mountain. Feramontov, of course, hadn't seen Fedora's record-sheet and hadn't even the dubious pleasure of Dr. Bohr's acquaintance . . . but it was still far from clear what he'd hoped for. Whatever it was, he'd got a great deal less. He'd given away a little and had gained nothing. In his present position, it was true, he could give away as much as he chose and it wouldn't much matter; but he couldn't give away time. No one ever can. Fedora looked down at his wristwatch. The hour was almost up.

And the sun was almost down. Its rays had long since gone; the cell was dark and shadowy. And very quiet. Except, of course, for the constant grumbling high-pitched hum of the generator; Fedora couldn't trace that noise to its source because the windows were set much too high, but he could see the conductor cables crossing the evening sky. . . . They were indeed the only things he *could* see. The cables, and the crosshead of a steel pylon. They looked pretty thick. An HC job, definitely; but why would they want a high-power generator in a place like this? . . .

Something in his brain went, *click*. The question—which had been idle—elicited a response as no other had done, a response disproportionately violent. Well, of course, he thought. That was *it*. Santa Ana. . . .

And his brain, computer-like, perhaps still under the influence of the stimulant, began to reel out a sudden string of once-recorded and never-quite-forgotten data. Six of them; there were six of them, altogether. Cijara, Garcia Sola and Orellana; those three the first to be completed. Zucar, finished late in '64. And still under construction, the Alange. Five dams, regulating the flow of the Guadiana, five dams with a total retention capacity of something like four million cubic metres. The component units of the so-called Badajoz plan, irrigating and industrialising one of the poorest regions of Spain. Franco's major economic success. It was famous, damn it. *Famous?* . . . It didn't *have* to be famous. It was all on file, in the Madrid office. A bloody great bulky folderful.

Yes, and then . . . Santa Ana. The village that no longer existed, was now under water. The keystone of the plan, the biggest of the lot, one of the biggest dams in Europe. The cost, by Spanish standards, astronomical. It tied together the waters of the Guadiana and the Tagus; later on it'd provide a network of interlaced canals over hundreds of sun-drenched square miles. Yes; he remembered it now. And *that* was what he'd seen from the road, that distant structure of concrete spanning the horizon. The Santa Ana dam. And the aeroplane had landed on the lake. It all fitted together. Perfectly.

. . . Except that for the life of him he couldn't see what there could be at Santa Ana to interest Feramontov. A minor point, doubtless. But a tricky one.

The beginnings of a hydroelectric system? . . . nothing in

that. Feramontov wasn't interested in minor sabotage. The dam itself, then? . . . No. That was preposterous. Not even 617 Squadron could have done more than scratch the surface of *this* baby; it had to be a real monster. The question was, in any case, a stupid one. Fedora knew already what there was at Santa Ana to interest Feramontov; it was indeed the only thing he *did* know.

Cell Eleven.

. . . Together with whatever it was Capdevila had put in it.

. . . Whoever *he* was.

Fedora held up his handcuffed wrists, clenched his fists slowly. He began to walk to and fro, to and fro. Slowly, but at a rhythmic pace. According to his watch, his hour was up.

The bolts rattled once more. The door came open. Bujas entered, and looked at him.

"How are you? Feeling the strain of modern life?"

"That's right," Fedora said. "I'm deafened by the traffic."

"Ah, well. We're sorry to keep you waiting." He looked round the cell with quiet enjoyment. "It won't be very long now. Or that's what I've been told to tell you. Maybe fifteen? . . . twenty minutes?"

Fedora sighed. *That* old gag. The waiting trick was so corny he hadn't expected it and consequently, had fallen. "Thirty minutes? Or even another hour?"

"Who knows?" Bujas said philosophically. At least, that kind of remark passes for philosophical, in Spain. He carried in his right hand a bundle of what looked like clothes; this he tossed casually down on to the floor. ". . . Amuse yourself with that. If you like."

"Thanks," Fedora said. And didn't move. Bujas looked round the cell once more and departed. He had that quality. He didn't come in and go out; he entered and departed. You could call it an *officer-like* quality, if you didn't think it a shade too theatrical. Fedora, who didn't much care either way, waited until the bolts had rattled yet again, then mooched across to pick up the bundle. He had to be careful how he stooped, but he managed it all right.

It was clothes all right. Laura's clothes. They seemed to be all there; she hadn't been wearing very much, as Johnny that morning had noted. Dress, shoes, bra and briefs. That was the lot. Cornier than the other, he thought. Cornier than the other. *Don't let it work*. A real surge of adrenalin now, that'll finish you off.

Corny. And yet he's not wrong. After this morning . . . this is the worst thing yet. That's right. Think about how bad it is. Not about what's happening to Laura. *No*. Not that. Because perhaps it isn't. He could be kidding you along. He could be. . . . .

No. You know he isn't. This is how it begins.

Fedora sat down, heavily, on the floor. One of the brown low-heeled shoes in his hand. Fifteen, twenty minutes; or even an hour. He found along the sole of the shoe the remnants of the warmth of her foot; his fingers moved inside, treasuring it. He stared up at the ceiling. Probably for an hour or more, the great thing now was not to think at all.

Someone else getting nowhere fast was Acuña.

"The more I look at it, the less I like it."

"The less you like exactly what, sir?"

"This Capdevila theory. It won't hold water."

Rivas sucked his lower lip. "Well, it's hard to believe. But it's not impossible."

"That idea of mine about the Second Corps, though. *That's* impossible. Whatever he's got up his sleeve, it's not an armed insurrection. That's for sure."

"What else could it be?"

"That's the question." Acuña's fingers rattled briefly on the table. "It's all down here in black and white, though. The Second Corps are on field service allocation, ammunition-wise. The supply dumps are right outside Madrid, with the Guadarrama Division sitting on top. And Capdevila's got no pull with *them*. Well, if he really thinks he can launch a revolt on a field service bloody allocation, he's about the biggest optimist since Hitler. It can't be done. The Generalissimo's still not a fool—he's taken care to *see* that it can't be done. And that's all there is to it."

"They'd have the factories at Sevilla, though, wouldn't they?"

"An' a bastard lot of use that'd be to them, with the Air Force bombers stationed right next door in Malaga. Even those crummy old One-Eleven's couldn't miss that lot, they'd go up like that dump in Cadiz did back in '47. No, the idea's just not on. There'd be no rhyme or reason to it at all."

"It still has to be Capdevila," Rivas said. "It *has* to be. It must be something . . . I don't know. . . . Deeper. Subtler."

A few moments' silence. Rivas' hand—though he wasn't aware of the fact—was resting on the telephone, his fingers rubbing its black smooth surface. "I wish to hell," Acuña said, "that Pinto would come through."

"You think he'll manage to trace Fedora?"

"He ought at least to find out what *happened*. Fedora can't have disappeared clean off the face of the earth."

"We may even hear something from Alonso."

"No," Acuña said, and shook his head. "It's been too long. Of course, it's a pity. The little bitch was really quite attractive."

9

After the darkness of Fedora's cell, the lights in the room at the end of the corridor seemed exceptionally bright; this was an illusion, though, to which the after-effect of the stimulants no doubt contributed something. The only source of ilumination was, in fact, a naked 60-watt bulb that dangled from the ceiling. Laura, also naked, stood by the far wall, strapped as young Rivas had been to the crucifix; she didn't see Fedora, because her eyes were closed and loose strands of her dark hair were curtaining them. There were fresh red bruises darkening her ribs and shoulders, and her lips seemed to be more than usually swollen. Fedora looked from her to Feramontov; and from Feramontov to the technical corporal who stood, unobtrusive in khaki, by the table, one hand on the control panel. He followed, almost absently, the barely-visible threads of the wires that ran from the panel across the floor to Laura's legs, terminated where they had been taped with sticking plaster to the insides of her parted thighs. His expression remained as it had been before. Cold; distant; withdrawn.

"You'll have seen this sort of thing before," Feramontov said. "I'll grant you it doesn't always work. But then, we don't *really* have to go through with it."

He sipped at the cup of coffee he held in his hands, looking the while at Laura. Reflectively. "Are you feeling all right now, Fedora?"

"That'd be an over-statement," Johnny said.

". . . *Dele al señor una tazita de cafe.*"

The percolator stood just clear of the control panel on an electric hotplate. The corporal poured out from it with a large tremorless hand and held out the cup to Fedora, who took it in both his own. A *real* cup, this time; of china, not of polymerised cardboard. The sharp smell of the coffee came up to his nostrils, but he tried to suppress the immediately consequent pleasure-response; he could allow himself no emotions now, none at all. The coffee was medicinal, and as medicine he drank it; slowly, not gulping at it; permitting no sense of flavour or of agreeable warmth to register. It was wet stuff with caffeine and sugar in it; caffeine and sugar he could use. And so he drank it. But no responses, no responses at all. He was a corpse.

Feramontov's pensive grey-green eyes were turned now in Johnny's direction. *Like a cat,* Elsa had once said; *he reminds you of a cat;* Johnny could see now the force of the comparison. It wasn't a physical resemblance. It was something else. As for Laura . . . She was a corpse, too. Motionless, impassive, though her eyes were open now and she had shaken the hair away from them. She was a corpse. Or as good as.

"You've seen how the thing's set up," Feramontov said. "The wires run to the cervix. Or, as the layman would put it, to the neck of the womb. The experts say that this is a convenient place to begin, because the impact of the initial electric charge is largely psychological. The nervous system isn't much involved and so the pain is by no means insupportable, but the mental distress. . . . That's considerable. Then there are convulsive contractions of the walls of the uterus that usually affect the subsequent functioning of the organ as a whole. She will not, as a result, be able to have children, nor is it probable that she'll be able to undertake normal sexual intercourse. All this you'll want to bear in mind, Fedora. She's *your* wife, after all."

Holding the cup in both hands, Fedora sipped at his coffee. The chain of the handcuffs clinked against the china; but only once.

"Then we'll go on, of course, to the breasts, the soles of the feet, the fingernails. Finally, the nose and ears. Women unfortunately have less inbuilt resistance to this technique,"

Feramontov said, "than most men. So we must face the possibility that some time in the latter stages she'll go completely mad. Oh, I know what you're thinking. Not a pleasant topic. But there you are. We may be here for some time . . . for quite some time. We're in no great hurry."

"You're not telling the truth," Fedora said.

"Or, come now. You'll be able to judge the results for yourself."

"I meant time," Fedora said, placing the empty cup down on the table. "Nobody has enough. Not in *this* business."

"Oh, we shan't *waste* it, certainly. Since you're a highly-trained operative, I'm assuming that the initial psychological assault isn't very likely to bring results. For this reason, I'm going to commence with the highest charge that the subject can take without losing her senses. Emilio. . . . *Por favor, las trescientas.*"

Fedora watched the electrician inch the control lever fractionally forwards; on the calibrated dial in the panel, the needle moved round. Something splashed on to his shirt front; a drop of sweat, fallen from his chin. Now, at last, Laura was looking at him. Not in hope, of course. There was nothing he could do. Why, then? . . . He couldn't think why. Unless it was to have something to take with her wherever it was she was going. But that sort of memory is the first thing to go. He couldn't meet her eyes, anyway. Not yet.

"*Estamos, Emilio?*"

"*Sí, señor.*"

". . . She's a very pretty girl, Fedora. A lovely girl, one might almost say. And beauty's sufficiently rare for it. . . . Ah, well. You'll realise there's nothing personal behind this, nothing personal at all. I'd do it to anyone else who happened to be your wife. No hard feelings?"

"None at all," Fedora said harshly. "The mistake was mine."

"You really have nothing to tell me?"

"There's nothing I remember."

"Ah, but as yet you've not received the necessary stimulus.

I'll try and provide that now, by counting to three. With *reasonable* slowness." He glanced towards the corporal, nodded. "One. Two . . ."

"No," Fedora said. The tone of his voice was completely conversational; but it was odd, because he hadn't meant to say anything at all. Feramontov looked at him, one eyebrow raised in mild surprise, then said to the electrician no less conversationally,

". . . Three. . . ."

The switch went down beneath the corporal's finger. The sweat seemed to pour from Fedora's forehead in a sudden surge; blood gleamed from the sudden crevice that his teeth had torn in his lower lip. Laura's head jerked back, became motionless as if turned to stone. Feramontov made a strange sound, remotely suggestive of enjoyment; he clicked his fingers, and the corporal cut the switch.

". . . Did you say something, Fedora?"

"Yes," Johnny said. "But I didn't mean to."

"That's exactly what I'd supposed. But before very long, you *will* mean to. This may not take so long as I'd supposed." Feramontov nodded, satisfiedly. ". . . Right, Emilio. That was fine. This time we'll try it with the current on."

"*Si, señor,*" Emilio said; and, smiling patiently, reached across to trip the connection to the cables.

Rivas. His elbows on the table; his chin cupped in his hands. His eyes opaque, despondent. He didn't raise his head as Acuña came in. "Nothing," he said. "Nothing doing."

"We're doing what we can," Acuña said.

"We set the trap. He walked in and out again. And all I've done since is sit here and wonder why it's empty."

Acuña's chins wobbled as he took his own seat. "We're doing what we can," he said again. "We're waiting. That's never easy."

"Waiting for what?"

The wax match flared in Acuña's fingers. He lowered his head, closed his eyes, inhaled smoke voluptuously; his fat little legs comfortably crossed, ankle to knee. . . . "It's like this very often," he said. "Waiting. And waiting. And waiting. And then quite suddenly, everything comes along all together. Like that. In a rush. And when it does . . . the great thing is to be ready."

"It gets rather warm in here," Feramontov said.

With a clean white handkerchief he wiped the perspiration from Fedora's forehead, cheeks and neck. Fedora stood still, unblinking. Feramontov, when he had finished, crumpled the handkerchief into his balled fist and walked away; took up his former position in front of Laura and a little to her left.

"I think perhaps we might now continue."

Johnny's eyes turned towards the electrician, who stood slouched, as before, over the control panel. A complicated machine, Johnny thought, but simple enough to handle. You could even say that it had a certain beauty, the beauty of the functional; though obviously it hadn't been built for this specific purpose. That was the Feramontov technique, almost the Feramontov trade-mark; to take the functional, the beautiful, and to divert it hideously away from its original design. He himself was in a sense a distortion of something beautiful, something superbly functional; was something that had been changed; a fallen angel. And he—like this machine—carried an infinitely higher voltage than the normal usages of life ever required; the difference was that he was human, could seek an outlet, a channel for that great and shattering surge of malevolent power. That was the real secret . . . the chosen channel. Fedora didn't now think that he would ever discover that secret; time had passed; it was already too late. All that remained was an eternity of silence, here in the electrocution chamber, while Laura was slowly jarred into babbling animality. Talking wouldn't help her. He knew that. The cat might play with its victims, but would never release them. But in so far as words distracted from reality, talking might help *him*.

"When I went to see Durand . . ." he said. Feramontov was ready to talk; he was sure of that. For words, too, Feramontov could make part of his purpose, part of the gentle cruelty of the Waiting Game. "Just what happened to Durand, exactly?"

"Durand is dead. I had him killed," Feramontov said. "You weren't the only one who went to see him. There was a policeman. . . . He arrived a little later."

"What sort of a policeman?"

"A Secret Policeman. He died, too." Feramontov nodded towards the crucifix. "He died of fifteen thousand volts. He hadn't very much to tell me, either."

Fifteen thousand volts, Johnny thought; he'd have curled up under the impact like a burning twig. He looked again at the control panel, the lever, the calibrated dial; the metal and the painted plastic. A beautiful job. ". . . That would have been in the end."

"In the end, yes. He resisted very well . . . as far as *anyone* can be said to resist it well. But it all has to do with what we were discussing before . . . with my relationship with my present employer."

"Capdevila," Johnny said; but got no reaction.

"Capdevila, yes. There are times when my resentment gets the better of my curiosity. And that was one such. So I . . . finished him off."

"Curiosity about what?"

"Oh, it was a matter simply of finding out what other people knew. About Cell Eleven, and so forth. The same things, in fact, that I'm hoping *you* will tell me. In your case as in his, though . . . and even if you *don't* tell me anything . . . there remains the scientific interest." He reached forwards with his right hand to pat Laura's flat brown stomach; gently, almost consolingly. ". . . Death fascinates me, Fedora. As you know already. Death, and the different means by which we achieve it. There's the question of why the death of certain beings means the life of others . . . and then, the *universality* of it. Men die, dogs die, plants die. In the end, even the rocks will die. I see it as an unanswerable force . . . like the force of gravity . . . and I like to consider myself a student of the one, as Newton was a student of the other. Of course I shan't publish a book as the fruit of my researches; there'll be no *Principia Mortis*. That would be illogical. Death doesn't recognise books. Death recognises nothing but itself. Death recognises nothing, because death *is* nothing. Death is the death of thought, as of everything else. Have we made the connections now?"

"*Si, señor*," the electrician said. He never seemed to say anything else.

". . . The real thing this time, Fedora. Not death itself, of course. That comes later. But, so to speak . . . the first caress. From that point on, the rest is inevitable. As an expert in seduction—"

"I wouldn't call myself that," Fedora said. No good, though. Feramontov went on as though he hadn't spoken.

". . . you'll appreciate the beauty of what the physicists name sequential logic. Death blinds, deafens, paralyses. Death is the impossibility of further life. Even—as Dante would say—halfway down the road of a woman's life, the imminence of death seals the womb. And now we're simulating the whole of the process, as it were, in miniature. How old is . . .? Twenty-five, maybe?"

"Twenty-three." That was what the marriage lines had said. Fedora's head drooped slightly forwards.

"Yes. Well, there you are. The biologists have it that we all begin to die at the age of twenty or so. Brain cells wear out and are no longer replaced. Thousands of them every day —thousands and thousands. So you see this experiment does no more, really, than foreshadow inevitability. You follow my reasoning?"

Johnny was getting tired of it. Of the Waiting Game. *Get on with it, why don't you get on with it?* . . . But no. He had resources yet of self-control, though they were wearing damned thin. "Yes," he said. "I follow your reasoning."

"It's strange, isn't it, how loss of memory invariably leaves the sense of logic unimpaired. But then, we've so much to learn about these things. How *is* your memory, by the way? Has nothing . . . returned?"

"No," Johnny said. "Nothing's returned."

And again he looked—as now did Feramontov—towards the electrician; who was lounged, three paces to his right, against the control panel table in the pose of one who has gone to sleep on his feet. He wasn't asleep, though. He was waiting.

"Right," Feramontov said. And sighed. "We have the subject prepared and the experiment designed. So let's embark on it."

The electrician raised his head. Rather, Johnny thought, as a dog might who hears a significant change of tone in the voice of its owner. At any moment now, it would be *walkies, boy*. But there'd be no more of that one-two-three stuff. No more of that. He looked at the panel, the control lever, the master switch.

"Play it again, Sam," Fedora said.

". . . In point of fact, Bogart never said that. You want to bet?"

"Bogart?" Feramontov seemed puzzled. But that was all right. That was the whole idea.

"The thing is it *wasn't* Bogart. It was Ingrid Bergman who said it. In *Casablanca*. I've won a lot of bets," Fedora said, "on that." Taking, as he spoke, two sidling paces to his right. His third pace brought his foot into contact with the electrician's buttocks; not in a kick, but in a purposeful shove that sprawled the other off his balance and down to the floor. Easy. The corporal hadn't even been looking in his direction. Feramontov—still predictably—went on looking puzzled; the pistol was in his hand now, but he didn't find it necessary to take the trouble to raise it. "I don't know what you hope to gain by *that*."

"Don't you?" Fedora said. The corporal was getting up again, looking not so much puzzled as annoyed. Well, that, too, was natural.

"Surely it was rather childish—"

Feramontov's brain was usually nothing if not quick; Johnny could only suppose it to have been briefly numbed by his recent excessive indulgence in philosophy. If that was what you called it. It wasn't until Fedora's handcuffed hands were moving, and very fast, that Feramontov seemed to realise what he was up to; and by then he was half a second too late. *Much* too late. By then Fedora's outstretched hands had stabbed the control lever right across the panel, and his finger was stabbing down the release switch even when the needle on the dial still span in desperate pursuit. From the high-voltage cables that fed the machine, some five to ten thousand volts imploded with a blue-edged flash and an ear-splitting bang; in the darkness—which was instant, as the lights fused—chains of leaping sparks chased at fantastic speeds down the walls, across the floor. Johnny felt a great surge of heat strike him full in the face, twist him sideways, even as the skin of his hands and wrists seemed to dissolve into numbness; he crouched for a moment on one knee, his bearings completely lost, then dived awkwardly to his right and collided with the hefty body of the corporal. Feramontov didn't shoot. He couldn't see anything. There was darkness in the cell, and a tingling silence.

". . . Fedora?"

Scufflings. But no reply.

"Effective," Feramontov said admiringly. "What a late distinguished statesman called, I believe, the Final Solution. Effective, yes. . . . But surely a little drastic?"

He, too, was crouching now, wrist resting on knee, pistol levelled. In the darkness, the scuffling continued; the electrician gave a strangled cry. To shoot or not to shoot? . . . He bit his lip. He only had Fedora left now. And he wanted Fedora alive, if only for a while.

"All right. You've made your point. I want you to keep—"

Drowning his voice, a rather horrible sound. A pause; then one even more horrible. A sharp snap, like that of a dry branch breaking. The sound of someone's neck giving way.

A pair of handcuffs, skilfully used, can be nearly as efficient as a garotte; and that, Feramontov felt with some irritation, a corporal in the Spanish Army ought to have known.

Ah, well.

He knew now.

Feramontov rose to his feet again, soundlessly. There was something wrong. It wasn't that he was *afraid*. He wasn't afraid of Fedora, even though the darkness had reduced his pistol to virtual ineffectiveness, even though Fedora was obviously in a killing mood; Feramontov wasn't normally afraid of anything or anyone. There was something wrong, that was all. Or something . . . not quite right. He moved back silently, until his left hand brushed the wall behind him. Fedora also was striving for silence, but not so successfully. There were sounds coming out of the darkness, sounds of furtive movement; suddenly, and with total unexpectedness, a jingling of coins. He came near, at that moment, to risking a shot.

Only Fedora left.

. . . Surely . . .?

But *that* was what was wrong. He was sure of it, now. There was no smell of burning. Rivas had taken a charge like that and had smelt of badly charred pork. The girl must have . . .

That was what was wrong.

He turned, cautiously, in the darkness, weight evenly balanced on the balls of his feet, bracketing, as best he could, the crucifix. The sound of the shots, the ricochet of the humming bullets reverberated from the low ceiling; he smelt the cordite. And felt a hand close, with an awful and ruthless intensity, over his right wrist.

Fedora had strong hands and the grip of his fingers was phenomenal. Feramontov should have known that. He knew now. Pain raced up his forearm as the grip tightened, became excruciating as the metal links of the handcuffs bit into his wrist; in a moment, his arm would go the same way as the corporal's neck. He threw his whole weight violently sideways, trying to cannon into Fedora, knock him off balance and fall with him to the floor; but it was the pistol, torn free by the movement, that fell, rattled. Fedora was not where he'd expected; the fingers of his free hand rasped on cloth, grabbed, missed. He knew, as he went head over heels, that Fedora had missed as well; he felt the wind of a savage kick, aimed probably at his crutch, whip past his face. Then, wrenched out of Fedora's grasp, he was on the floor, prone, face downwards. The pistol? . . . *The pistol?* . . . His right hand searched the darkness desperately, quartering the area where it had fallen. Nothing. Nothing. And Fedora? . . .

Was he searching, too?

He wriggled forwards a couple of feet, groped again. A sudden wild elation as his fingertips brushed the cold steel of the barrel . . . He had made a mistake, firing blindly. He wouldn't make the same mistake again. Next time he'd be completely sure; he'd fire at close quarters, hand to hand. His fingers, snatching at the barrel. And finding it suddenly, as though miraculously, twisting away from him, the foresight cutting his thumb as it was jerked into the blackness. His hand had been on the barrel . . .

But Fedora's on the butt. On the butt, and waiting. The clever cunning bastard. . . .

He was rolling even as the pistol was pulled away from him, rolling desperately and this time away from the wall. And knowing, as he rolled, that sheer speed of reaction wasn't going to save him . . . that *nothing* could. The icy white blast from the barrel opened out full into his face; blinded, he thrust his powder-burned forehead in agony on to the hard stone of the floor. His eyebrows were suddenly sticky with blood. His right foot, kicked out behind him, knocked against the wall. . . . Impossible, surely? . . . and the wall, even more impossibly, seemed to give way under the impact. How could it . . .?

The door. It had to be the door. And before the thought had fully dawned, he was rolling again towards it, moving in frantic evasion of a second shot. But there wasn't any second shot. Fedora had lost him.

He crouched, halfway out into the corridor, for a moment before getting to his feet. Fedora said, "Laura?"

And from somewhere in the darkness a quiet voice said, ". . . Yes?"

"What the hell happened, anyway?"

Yes, Fedora thought. A reasonable question.

"Well, I pushed the lever right across and gave you the works. Fifteen thousand volts or something like that. Well, just for the giggle."

Her voice in the darkness. Quiet enough, calm enough. "Then why aren't I frizzled?"

"You need special cables for that kind of a current. *These* wires wouldn't take it. They blew out and shorted where they touched the floor."

"But how could you be sure?"

Johnny grunted in relief. The third key on the corporal's keyring fitted; he turned it, heard the click as the locks of the crucifix came open. It would have been awkward—very—if Feramontov had had the only key. ". . . All right?"

"Yes. Thanks. How could you be sure?"

"Well, I wasn't *sure*."

"You weren't. . .?"

"How could I be? I'm not an electrician. I just thought I'd chance it."

"Charming," Laura said. "Oh, charming. You send fifteen thousand volts up me, near as a toucher, and then you . . . Who do you think I am? Eskimo Nell?"

Fedora gazed, open-mouthed, through the darkness at where he imagined her more or less to be. Even allowing for the resilience of youth, he hadn't expected to find her *quite* so chipper. Calm and quiet, yes, but this was ridiculous. "I didn't," he said, "have an awful lot to lose."

"Nor did I. They pinched the lot. What am I going to do about my clothes?"

"Clothes, this is a fine time to think about clothes. We've

got to get out of here, and fast."

"Where are you?"

"Here."

"... Where?"

"*Here.*"

"Ahhhhh." Her hand found his in the darkness, clasped it stickily. "... You're sweating."

"Aren't you?"

"What do you think?"

"If you won't tell me," Fedora said irritably, "I'm damned sure I don't have the time to find out. Come *on*, for God's sake."

"But I can't see a thing."

"And it's just as well. I've blown the lights all over the bloody camp. That gives us a chance. But not," Fedora said, "what you'd call a good one."

"Come on, then. What are we waiting for?"

Fedora sighed windily. Cautiously, they stepped forwards into the blackness.

Blackness. Total blackness.

Blindness, maybe. . .?

Maybe the one thing of which Feramontov *could* be afraid.

His face seemed to be aflame with the stinging powder grains. He stopped in the echoing corridor, knuckling at his eyes with his clenched fists. The breath sobbed in his throat. He lifted his head, staring through inflamed and blood-smeared eyelids into nothing. He needed light. Just one little flicker. A match. Anything. The lighter in his pocket. But he didn't dare. Fedora could be somewhere near, somewhere behind him, could be walking down the corridor, pistol at the ready. Not only that. What if the flint whirred, the spark leapt, the gas ignited. . . . What if he didn't, what if he couldn't see it *then*? He'd be blind. That would mean he was blind. It would mean . . .

What?

In the darkness, would he go mad?

... In the blackness, the total blackness, a muffled drumming. Feramontov, his teeth bared, beating with his closed fists on the roughly plastered wall. From his torn-open knuckles, blood welling invisibly.

Captain Bujas, Sergeant Corpas, coming to the rescue. Bujas with a pistol in his hand, Corpas with a smoking oil-lamp. The shadows, chasing up and down the corridor, throbbing to the sound of that strange drumming. They paused for a moment as Feramontov came in sight; he lowered his hands, turned warily towards them as again they moved forwards, their booted feet thumping on the solid floor.

"... Who's that?"

"Captain Bujas, sir. Are you all right?"

Corpas, halting, lifted the lamp head-high. Feramontov faced them, blood dripping from his savaged hands. His hair and forehead and eyebrows also smeared with blood, the bullet-crease standing out like a long purple welt from the centre of the left eyebrow to the right temple. The eyes screwed up, burning hot, focused nowhere.

"Can you see me, Captain Bujas?"

"Of course I can, sir. What. . .?"

Bujas stopped.

"You've got a lamp there?"

"Sergeant Corpas is with me, sir. He has a lamp."

"I can't see it," Feramontov said. "I'm blind."

Laura started to giggle.

Not very loudly. But too loudly. Fedora pushed her tear-streaked face hard into his shirt-front, and hoped for the best.

He had been expecting the reaction for the past five minutes; now it had come, and it was a real shocker. He lay as still as he could, his handcuffed arms encircling the girl's jerking, twisting body; its warm nakedness emphasised the horror of what was happening to it. She was throwing a wingdinger. He couldn't blame her. Sweating?... No. Steaming like a Derby winner. From head to toe; all over. And still without making any loud noise, other than that weird hysterical keening, so high pitched as to be almost inaudible. *Not* so chipper. But she'd held it back, somehow, for just long enough; Fedora wasn't any too sure that he himself could have gone much farther without blowing his nut.

They lay like a pair of courting yokels in the shadow of a clump of bushes, the earth hard, dry, and still very warm beneath them. Shadow, because here in the open there was light, a very little light; starlight, a sliver of moon, and all round them the orange-yellow rectangles of windows behind which oil-lamps were burning. The fusing of the lights had been a more successful operation than Fedora had expected; if they had any sort of emergency supply available, it was taking them a long time to get it working. . . . He winced, but said nothing, as Laura's teeth very nearly met in the soft flesh just beneath his collarbone. Biting was a good sign; it showed she was turning to the aggressive. Coming out of it. . . .

Her sharp nails now, raking at his shoulders. The thin cloth of the shirt ripping, though luckily without too much sound; it was still sopping wet with his perspiration, and perhaps also now with hers. The damp skin tearing, too, ploughing up into furrows. She had rolled him over from their original position, had writhed on top of him and pressed herself downwards so that now, squinting past his nose, all he could see of her was the loose tangle of her dark hair and, lower, the curved twin whiteness of her tight little buttocks, the muscles clenching and unclenching like fists. That's how the body helps the mind, Fedora thought (searching for rationalities to pit against the pain of his flayed back and shoulders); that's how it comes to life when the conscious self goes dead, goes through the motions of the act even while the mind most furiously rejects it. That rejection—even for Laura, even for Laura and himself—must be hovering on the very edge of finality: her brain had turned from the reality of sex, had turned away from it in disgust, and only her body was left to reassert its rights. This particular fight was hers and hers alone. Later on . . . Fedora thought . . . perhaps my turn will come; in the end, to lay this ghost she'll need my help. But right now, she's alone. All I can do is lie here and hold her tight and let her tear me to shreds—show me with her nails and teeth her present views on the male sex in general. I'm a man, after all. No getting away from that. Even now she has me feeling like a man, she has that effect on me. Always. Right now she hates me. She loves me. It's a mess. But it'll all work out.

We've got a chance to get away. But not what you'd call a good one. Every moment we stay here makes that chance smaller. I know we shouldn't have stopped. We should have gone on. But she has to do it *now*, to fight this thing *now*; if she doesn't, if she holds it in much longer, then it may stay with her for years. Feramontov would have sealed her, after all. And what does our getting away matter, if we can't take the other thing with us?. . . That's what's Feramontov's trying to destroy. Not her. Not me. Something between us. It can mean almost anything, but it always means *something*. Feramontov's logic had left it out; Feramontov didn't understand it and didn't allow for it. But he knew it was there, knew that it must in the end be destroyed before his patterns could be perfect. Whatever else happened was subservient to this. Here, under the prickly bushes, here in the shadows. . . . Here was where Feramontov lost the game.

"What the hell *can* we do?" the lieutenant asked.

Bujas shrugged. "I don't know. Nothing. Nothing, yet."

"Oughtn't we to sound the general alarm?"

"For God's sake. We've got chaos out there already. Sound the alarm on top of that, and before you know where you are they'll be shooting at each other. How long before we get the lights back?"

"An hour. Maybe more. Anyone's guess."

"I don't see what else we can do," Bujas said. "We've got the oil-lamps issued from store and lit. We've got torches to the perimeter guards. They know what to do, if they spot anyone near the fences. We've got—"

"But how are they going to see. . .? The fences ought to be

illuminated. But all the damned searchlights are u/s."

"I *had* noticed that," Bujas said.

The lieutenant, prudently, was silent. For a few seconds, though, no more. "Can't I take a patrol round the fence?"

"What, over ten square kilometres of scrub? In the pitch darkness? What bloody kind of use do you think *that* would be?"

"The colonel said—"

"Never you mind what the colonel said. I'm in charge now. Sit down there and shut your flaming cakehole, and that's an order."

"Yes, sir," the lieutenant said.

They'd have to find her some clothes. That was obvious. Travelling over the open sierra, she'd need protection; the bushes and the thorny scrub would lacerate her legs to ribbons, otherwise. At the very least, she'd need trousers and a good pair of shoes. And that made for something of a problem; the last place you'd normally choose to look for a rather small size in ladies' footwear is in an army camp. They'd probably have to pinch a ruddy great pair of regulation honky-tonks and settle for that. Her feet would be in a mess, any-way, before they'd finished.

"We've got to find you some clothes," Johnny said.

She lay motionless now, except for an occasional violent shiver. "I'm not cold."

"You will be. And we've go a lot of walking to do. I don't know exactly where we are, but it seems to be the hell of a long way from anywhere."

"We could maybe pinch a car."

"No," Johnny said. "Too risky."

"If we could get to where they moored that aeroplane..."

"Can you fly?"

"No. But there were motor-launches there. They'll have thought of the cars, but they may not have covered the boats. Or not so well."

Fedora sucked his lip. There were worse ideas than *that*

one. "It's still a long way."

"Well," Laura says. "If you knows of a better 'ole . . ."

"That's just the trouble. I don't."

. . . If you looked at her closely, there'd be signs. The pupils dilated, probably; a tremor of the lower lip. That kind of thing. But in the darkness, and judging mainly by her voice, you'd say that she'd gone back to normal. The fight was over. Maybe she'd won and maybe she'd lost; it was too early to say.

"First things first," she said. "We have to get some clothes, then. How?"

"Steal them," Johnny said. "How else?"

"From one of the huts?"

"No. *That's* too risky, too."

"Then how?"

Johnny told her. There was a pause. Then suddenly, she sat up.

"I don't think I can do it," she said.

Johnny said, "Yes, you can."

"Do I *have* to?"

"Yes. You have to."

". . . Then I will."

Johnny breathed out. Slowly, heavily. "Attaboy, girl," he said.

The torchbeam turned to the right, and there she was. Standing by the wall of the hut, her arms at her sides. Her white skin turning to pearl in the sharp light of the torch, to pearl and to marble, so that she looked more like a statue than a human being . . . one of those Greek statues, maybe, you saw in the museums. But undraped. Naked. And she was alive all right; her dark eyes glinted in the torchlight, her eyelids fluttered. She was close. Not more than six feet away. The sentry's mouth opened, closed again.

Escaped prisoners, they'd said. Nothing about *this*. So what do you do? . . . when Venus comes to you naked out of the night? You can't say, *Who goes there?* It seems ... inappropriate. And she might just disappear again, you don't want *that*. What you do is, you go opening and closing your mouth, with the rifle clutched uselessly in your hands, until something hits you very hard at the back of the neck and the goddess shoots off skywards, leaving behind her a sparkling wake like that of a falling star. After that, there's nothing but darkness; peaceful darkness.

And subdued bumpings. Gruntings. Ripping sounds. Laura picked the torch up, switched it off.

"These handcuffs," Fedora said. "They're a bit of a nuisance. You'll have to help."

Laura came forwards and helped.

... They'd been lucky with the boots. Lightweight night patrol boots, rubber soles and canvas uppers, lacing round the ankles; miles too big for her, of course, but they couldn't really have hoped for anything better. The shirt and trousers fitted her about as well as they had fitted the sentry; atrociously. The ammunition belt had in fact no ammunition in it at all; Fedora strapped it round his victim's extended legs, then tied up the limp, unresisting and somewhat skinny wrists with a strip torn from the tail of his own shirt. Laura, meanwhile, had improvised what appeared to be a rather effective gag; Johnny tested its tightness with the tip of his finger.

"... What did you put in his mouth?"

"One of his socks."

"Oof," Fedora said. "The poor bastard."

A neat job, all the same. Quick and efficient. They might have been working this way together for years. He humped the sentry on to his back, followed Laura away from the huts across the rough open ground to the west. At some eighty yards' distance, they found the fence. Fedora lowered his burden to the ground, crouched down beside it; Laura knelt at his shoulder. For a few moment they rested, talking in whispers.

"... The rifle?"

"Here. Do you want it?"

"I don't see how I can fire it with handcuffs on. I'll stick to the pistol. You'd better just check the magazine."

"I have. Fully loaded. And one up the spout."

"That's the way I like it. All right. Ready?"

"Yes," Laura said.

10

At a quarter past twelve, the lights came on.
But not for Feramontov.

Captain Bujas halted at the foot of the bed and saluted correctly, even though the action seemed somewhat pointless. He looked down with a certain curiosity at the dark head on the white pillow, the dark malevolent head with its swathings of bandage: "Captain Bujas, sir," he said.

"Yes, captain?"

"The circuit has been restored, sir. And things have gone back very much to normal. Except that one of our sentries has failed his twelve o'clock timecheck. . . . We assume he's missing. I've sent out a search party along the western perimeter."

"Which sector was he guarding?"

"BX sector. Boundary huts to fence."

"They've got away, then," Feramontov said. "That's rather unfortunate."

"I've alerted the outlying detachments, sir, and ordered a double guard on the motor transport pool. Patrols will be going out at first light. There's still a reasonable chance of our picking them up."

The dark head in the pool of light moved fractionally. Bujas wasn't sure if the colonel had shaken his head, or had merely chosen to adjust his position slightly. He waited, properly to attention, while the silence lengthened. In the end, Feramontov said,

"They shouldn't have got past the fences, Captain."

"No, sir. But we did our best."

". . . In the difficult circumstances," Feramontov said

sardonically. "Yes. I know."

"With respect, sir, our internal security design is related to stopping people getting *in*. It's not so effectve for stopping people getting *out*."

Feramontov sighed. "What you call a reasonable chance isn't good enough either, Captain. There'll be no patrols. Tell the ODs to cordon off the normal exit routes and leave it at that."

"I've told them already, sir."

Again that curious semi-negative movement of the head. ". . . As for the Holding Detachment. . . . All ranks will parade at first light in full marching order. The MT Officer will provide initial transport on an emergency petrol allocation. From now on, you'll act in accordance with the detailed instructions filed in the Top Security section of the office safe. Under the heading of TIMELOCK."

"Very good, sir. But—"

"You'll familiarise yourself with those orders now."

"But . . . TIMELOCK, sir, requires a prior authority from Divisional HQ."

"It'll be forthcoming, captain. That's *my* worry."

"You mean you'll be . . . ?"

"I'll be accompanying you. And I shall remain Officer in Command of this detachment until I'm formally relieved."

There was a moment's silence. Thoughtful silence.

". . . I'll need the safe keys, sir," the captain said.

Timelock.
One o'clock.
Nothing.

. . . Acuña, sifting slowly through the great sheaf of typewritten flimsies that had just been flown down from Madrid. Rivas, slumped in the armchair, his chin in his hands. The air, thick with cigar smoke. The Vent-Axis, for some reason, wasn't working.

The telephone rang. Rivas picked it up.

"Yes?"

. . . With one hand over the mouthpiece,

"It's Pinto. . . .

Stonily, Acuña went on reading. While Rivas listened, scribbling frantic notes with his free hand on a loose-leaf pad. When the receiver went back on the cradle . . . not till then did Acuña look up.

"He got the authority through. Brigade HQ are co-operating."

"About time, too," Acuña said.

"The convoy picked up four passengers in Cordoba, from a house in the Avenida de Linares. Two civilians, a man and a woman. A *young* woman. And two military—Colonel Gutierrez and Captain Bujas. Gutierrez assumed command of the convoy."

"On what authority?"

"All papers were stamped with the HQ seal of Military Intelligence, Madrid."

"Yes. So far it figures."

"All four disembarked at an emergency airstrip just south of Posadas. I have the map reference. There was an aircraft waiting there. Civil registration."

"What number?"

"No one seems to have noticed."

Acuña blew out his lips, bristling a non-existent moustache. "Hell and damnation."

"We've something to go on, though. There were eight wooden crates offloaded at the airstrip as well, under the same authorisation. Contents unknown. The thing is that Pinto has talked to the men who did the offloading, and one of them happened to see that the stencil markings . . . Well, they were consigned to a Special Intelligence unit with 405 Holding Company of the Second Army Corps. Four-oh-five. . . . So maybe if we find out where they're stationed . . ."

"Better than that," Acuña said.

"Better?"

"It just so happens that the number rings a bell. Almost literally."

Rivas shook his head. "I don't understand."

"We've been checking up on Capdevila's communications." Acuña tapped the pile of papers on his lap. "Seemed an obvious step." He began once more to riffle through them, this time at tremendous speed. "... Yes. Here we are. I thought it out of the ordinary when I read it. According to this, late last month the *Transmisiones* boys put down a direct cable connection between Military Intelligence HQ, Madrid, and 405 Holding Company. At Santa Ana. I like it, I *like* it."

"Where the hell's Santa Ana?"

"Don't you ever read the newspapers?... You'll find out soon enough, anyway," Acuña said, trundling himself on to his feet. "It so happens you're on the way there."

TIMELOCK.

... OPERATION TIMELOCK (Bujas read) *assumes the attempt of a hostile power or powers to capture and retain control of the SANTA ANA dam and pilot hydroelectric station, a complex of key strategic and economic importance. In this exercise, troops of the Holding Detachment and supporting units will occupy prepared positions in the vicinity of the dam and will defend them against all odds for a period of 72 seventy-two hours. In the later stages of the exercise, strike aircraft of the Spanish Air Force will simulate ground attacks and defensive manoeuvres will be practised. The 21st Twenty First Infantry Regiment ("Guzman el Bueno") will meantime execute a force-march northwards from Sevilla and will relieve the Holding Detachment through either of the following schemes of attack. ...*

Bujas looked up in perplexity, pushed his cap farther back on his head. The same old bumf as ever, and more complicated than most; pages and pages of it. Not for the first time, he wondered just what the hell he was getting into.

As for Johnny and Laura, they were lost.

Since from the start they had had no clear idea of where

they were or of where they were heading, it was arguable that they had never been anything else. Johnny's theory had been that, travelling north-west by the Pole Star, they would reach, within half an hour or so, the road by which they had arrived in the Mercedes, and from that point would be able to re-orientate themselves towards the lake; but they had walked over the rock-strewn hills for two hours and a half, and . . . No. No road. The theory had been wrong. Well, even people like Einstein had had it happen.

They had found a goatpath, though, and had followed it first northwards and then north-eastwards and then due west-wards, until it petered out completely among the boulders. The rocks around them, in the darkness, seemed almost high enough to be cliffs; there was shelter at their foot, a deeper darkness and, after a little while, a pleasant smell of sage crushed under their bodies. They lay there for a while, talk-ing, their legs aching from the exercise and from the super-ficial cuts and stabs of their passage through the scrub; Fedora's back and shoulders hurt him, too. Then for a while longer they lay there, saying nothing. Then Laura sat up and began to unbutton her shirt.

"Bloody shirt," Laura said. "Bloody boots. Bloody trousers."

"After all the trouble we took—"

"Oh, shut up."

"But what's the *matter* with you?"

"Fleas," Laura said. "Bloody fleas."

She rolled up bloody shirt and bloody boots and bloody trousers into a neat, competent ball and lay back again be-side him. After maybe a minute, she began to laugh; and this time it was the right kind of laughter. Her *usual* kind of laughter. A right old witch's cackle. She burrowed her head under Johnny's linked wrists, pressed herself up against his chest and went on laughing there. "Fleas," she said. "Fleas. That was *all* I needed."

"Well, don't give 'em to *me*," Fedora said.

"You're *so* sympathetic."

Quite suddenly everything was grand. She started crying

instead of laughing, her head tucked into Johnny's shoulder and the tears trickling wetly down his neck. He held her tightly. The tears didn't mean a thing. They were both very happy. Happier, in fact, than ever before; Johnny couldn't believe that in any of the places he couldn't remember, in Alicante or in Sevilla, or that in any of the place he *could* remember—Villafranca, Cordoba—he couldn't believe that *anywhere* it had been quite like this. He felt quite incoherent about it. "Darling,' Laura said. "Darling, darling."

"Yes?"

"Scratch me."

"Where?"

"There. . . . Oh, *yes*. Now lower down. . . ."

"There?"

"Oh, *yes*. Oh, *bliss*."

Her back arching in ecstacy, Fedora scratched away grimly; a temporary measure, of course; a good long scrub in a bath of carbolic, that was the only answer. Well. . . . More effective, yes. But not so enjoyable. "One good scratch," he said, "deserves another."

"What?"

". . . You ought to see my shoulders."

"I *know*, oh, God. I must have torn them to ribbons. I didn't mean it."

"Of course you didn't." His fingers following the line of her spine, up and down, up and down; but no longer scratching. Just touching lightly. "You're all right now?"

"I will be. No, I think I am. Already. The worst thing, really, was thinking . . . that you'd mind."

"That I'd *mind*?"

"That you'd hate me. Afterwards. After *that*."

"There very nearly wasn't any afterwards."

"But that's the crazy thing. I never doubted it for a moment, not even . . . when they put me in that crummy machine. I always thought there *would* be. Always."

"Well, now maybe there will," Johnny said. "Though we've got some way to go. Still, as long as you're—"

"You'll help me, won't you? You'll make love to me? Again?"

"Oh, yes, on that point I can set your doubts at rest. Why ever shouldn't I? We're married, aren't we?"

"No," Laura said. "Of course not."

The stars overhead, unnaturally bright and clear. The smell of the crushed sage stronger than ever. Such was the extent of Johnny's well-being that quite a few seconds went by before he became fully aware of the *oddness* of her reply. She should have said, *Yes, of course we are.* In fact she'd said, *No, of course not.* A reply that . . . deprived him of something. That jarred, damn it all, on his present mood. He didn't like it.

"What the hell d'you mean, *of course not?*"

"I thought you knew," Laura said. ". . . I thought you'd realised."

TIMELOCK

. . . Defence in depth will be established in all sectors and lines of communication kept open at all times. O Groups will normally be held at Detachment HQ, situated at ref 186399 one eight six three nine nine, and officers i/c forward observation posts will send POSITIVE or NEGATIVE sighting reports hourly. . . .

"You mean to say," Fedora said, "that I never lost my memory *at all?*"

"I drove you into the hospital at Barcelona that night," Laura said carefully, "and phoned my boss to tell him what had happened. He had you shifted to a private nursing home, and the doctors there kept you under sedation for three weeks. Then we ran you down to Cordoba in an ambulance . . . and that's where you woke up. From then on, I just had to tell you a string of lies. You never went to Alicante, you never saw Durand. We never went to Sevilla. *None* of it was true."

"All right," Fedora said. "Now tell me *why.*"

"You were the goat to catch the tiger—that's why. But it's

more flattering than it sounds. The way *el jefe* figures it, you're the only man who really worries Feramontov . . . enough to push him into making mistakes. So if Feramontov knew that you'd picked up some really important information, say, as to where he was hiding or something like that—"

"But I *didn't* have any information."

"No," Laura said. "We had to give you some."

". . . Badajoz, Cell Eleven?"

"Yes, exactly. One of our agents found it in Durand's hotel room, after he was murdered. As to what it means, we haven't a clue. It seemed to be the sort of thing we could pass on to you quite safely."

"Safely," Fedora said; and snorted. Of course, Feramontov had been quite right. Safety is a relative term.

"You see, while you were under sedation, they . . . well, not *hypnotised* exactly. Subliminal impression, I think they call it. But you gave them the hell of a lot of trouble, you really did. They wanted you to be persuaded, when you woke up, that you *could* remember things—under treatment. Talking to Durand and all that. They thought it'd be more convincing like that. But you weren't a good subject—not at all."

"Who's *they?*" Johnny asked. Then, "Your boss isn't called Cardenas, by any chance?"

"Yes. Except his real name is Rivas." Suddenly on the defensive. "But he really *is* a doctor. And a very good one."

"He's a very good-*looking* one."

"He's just my boss, that's all, you silly fool."

So that, Fedora thought, was who *they* were. *They* hadn't been altogether wrong. He'd remembered things under treatment, all right . . . under Feramontov's treatment. He'd remembered a bit too damned much. He could hear the echo of his own voice in the dimness of the old *Befragungszelle*, saying the most peculiar and inexplicable things . . . *You must remember this . . . Cell Eleven . . . They didn't tell me that. . . . That's what they told me; the British Consulate, Sevilla. . . . They, they, they. . . .* The drugs had returned him somehow to his previous period of sedation; to the hospital, the sheets weighing down on his legs; he had told Feramontov the whole truth, and Feramontov—quite predictably—hadn't understood a bloody word of it. He could even have understood it, and still not have believed it. It was all so incredible.

Well, and what about the Consulate in Sevilla? What *about* that?

"My getting married," Fedora said. "Why the hell would *that* have worried Feramontov?"

"I think the idea was more to worry *you.*"

"There are worse things to worry about than this," Fedora said, squeezing her.

"Ah, come on. It worked. You know it did."

"Only when he started getting *on* to me about it. Your bloody Cardenas."

"Well, and there was more to it than that. The thing with a goat," Laura said, "is that someone with a rifle has to keep pretty damned close to it. And when you've got a goat that can run away . . . the only thing to do is to chain it to someone. To *me.* I suppose he thought that marriage might be the sort of chain you'd . . . well. Recognise."

"He was wrong there, wasn't he? I hopped it, anyway."

"Yes, you did. Only he thought you were a *gentleman,* you see. Being English and all. *I* could have told him different, if only he'd asked me."

"He must have asked you. It's service beyond the call of duty, surely?"

Somewhere out in the darkness an owl called. Laura waited a while before replying.

"I *could* have said, no," she said in the end. "But he knew the way I felt about you. So he knew I wouldn't. He had the documents right there on the table in front of him. Oh, yes, he knew I'd jump at it. He knew I'd have fun—pretending."

I should have *known,* Fedora thought, that old Googie wouldn't have done that to me. That's what came of doubting one's old pals. If only I'd taken the trouble to check on it. . . .

But Cardenas, Rivas. *He knew I wouldn't.* Now *there* was

a thought. I was just like that poor bloody sentry back there; I hadn't wanted Laura to vanish. There was something, yes, there was certainly *something* in this psychology racket. . . .

". . . Can you say, *no*? To the Secret Police?"

"It seems to me I've started. Haven't I? I'm mentioning names and all. But if . . ."

"If what?"

"If you don't . . ."

". . . ?"

"The fact remains I sold you. Right up the river. I told you all those lies and I . . . It didn't seem so bad, at the beginning. But now things are different."

"Why? I wish you'd stop crying."

"Sn'f."

A few more moments of starlit silence. Then she went *sn'f* again. Yes, she'd been a naughty girl, She was sorry now. Fedora wondered how soon he could persuade her to do it again. He said,

"I don't see how at any time you could have done anything else. Except just the once."

"You mean right at the beginning? At Villafranca?"

"No. Just a few hours ago. You could have told Feramontov what you've just told me. Then he'd have known that I had nothing at all on him, or nothing that mattered. That any information worth having—*you* had it. You could have told him that."

"I could've, yes. But why should I have?"

"Well, if you had," Johnny said, "then *I'd* have been what you might call the expendable party. And *I'd* have been in that contraption, instead of you."

"I didn't think of that," Laura said.

"Oh, yes, you did."

"Well, if I—"

"What's more, you slipped up there. In the last resort, an agent's job is to stay alive, no matter what. They didn't spend all that time and money training you so that someone could strap you down and fry you in place of a blasted British agent, now did they? Rivas is going to love it when you tell him about *that*."

"I don't care."

"Well, you ought to."

"I don't care a damn about Rivas."

"It's not—"

"I've had enough of him to last me a lifetime. And of you as well, if it comes to that. Oh, screw you both."

"No, don't do that," Fedora said. "I'm nearer."

The sound of the helicopter woke them up.

Fedora hadn't intended to sleep; he'd decided deliberately to stay awake, for one reason or another. And—since his powers of self-discipline were normally considerable—he had a certain initial difficulty in realising that, on this occasion, they'd goofed. Or rather, had gone off duty and left him to snooze. There was a moment of unreality, of struggle towards wakefulness, in which yet again the sensation, the indescribable feel of the hospital surrounded and pervaded him; in which he felt again the fear and paradoxical need of the needle's prick, the slow peaceful flow of the sedative through his veins . . . then he was wide awake listening to the retreating hum of the whirling blades high overhead. It was still much too dark for the helicopter to be seen—even the pilot lights seemed hidden from view—but his impression was that it had passed directly above them. As the sound drifted away, the neighbouring bushes seemed to stir to the faintest of breezes, to the backwash of its passing; but that had to be imagination. It was flying too high for that to be possible.

Laura, at his side, also awake. At some time in the night she had taken her shirt and pulled it over her shoulders; Fedora's fingers, which had moved towards her, felt the rough texture of its weave in momentary puzzlement. And beneath, the slow rise and fall of her breath. ". . . Do you think they're looking for *us*?"

"In the dark?"

"No. I suppose not."

"They've probably sent out for one. Or two. Or three. It'll be another matter," Johnny said, "by daylight. We shouldn't have gone to sleep."

"What time is it?"

He tilted his imprisoned wrist, started at the luminous dial of his wrist-watch. "Nearly four o'clock."

"We can't have slept more than a couple of hours, then."

"No," Johnny said. "The point is we shouldn't have slept at all."

He sat up. He felt pretty ill. And what was more, hungry. His total intake yesterday, two cups of coffee. So it wasn't surprising. Hungry, ill, and tired, tired, tired.

"I'd like," he said abruptly, "to sleep for a month."

"That's just what you *have* done. You lazy devil."

"Yes. I suppose I have." His eyes seemed gummy; he rubbed at them. "I had in mind something rather different."

"I remember thinking you looked so *lonely* in there."

"Where?"

"In that damned nursing home. In that bed."

It was going to be awkward, Fedora thought, explaining all that to Colonel Cartwright. Even if he got out of the present brouhaha with a whole skin, they'd flay him alive back at Whitehall. Oh, *they'd* have no trouble in explaining it. Sexy old Fedora. At it again. He knew what *they'd* say. "Oh, God," he said. "I feel awful."

Movement in the darkness. Quiet, but not furtive. Laura, getting dressed. He sat up, and felt something hard under his hipbone; hard, but of a hardness so familiar as almost to pass unnoticed. He took the pistol in his hands; sniffed at the barrel absently; stroked the well-worn butt against his right palm. There were worse guns for open-air work than the old-fashioned Luger.

"I'm wondering . . ."

"Yes?" Laura, grunting softly with pain as she pulled on her boots.

". . . I'm wondering if I *hit* him."

"Feramontov?"

"Yes."

"It was dark," she said, tugging at the laces. "He didn't get very close to hitting *me*."

"You were the other side of the room," Johnny said. "I had him right in front of me. On the floor and about two feet away. I saw his face in the pistol-flash. And of course, if I *did* hit him . . . that accounts for it."

"For what?"

"For our having got this far."

"Or he may have reckoned that even if we did get clear of the camp, it wouldn't matter much. Had you thought of that?"

"Yes," Johnny said. "I'd thought of that."

The boots were now laced. She sat very still. "I don't know this part of the country at all. It's the first time I've been here. But I do know that to the north and the east there's an awful lot of nothing. Just the meseta—miles and miles of it. Wide open country. And if he's got troops . . . and helicopters . . ."

There was a silence. In both their minds, the sound high overhead of the whirling blades.

"South takes us straight back to the camp. And east, there's the lake. It seemed to stretch for an awful long way. And . . . how wide would you say?"

"A couple of miles," Johnny said. "Not more."

"It could be swum. But not by someone wearing handcuffs. If we'd got to those boats quick enough . . . but then we didn't. We'd never make it now. Not by day."

"Stop trying to cheer me up," Johnny said. "All right. So we have problems. *Everyone* has problems."

"Not everyone has helicopters, though."

"No."

"They scare me."

"Me, too."

". . . Sorry."

Silence again. Fedora's head ached, dully, interminably. Reaction, it had to be. The kickback. That was why he

hadn't wanted to go to sleep. The LSD and the benzedrine
. . . they could have worked *for* him, not against him. Maybe
for an hour or so, they had. Without them, perhaps, he could
never have found the willpower to throw that handle. The
cables *might* not have melted. And if they hadn't . . .

All that was in the past now. The drugs had turned against
him. Lassitude, migraine, enervation. Now the real fight was
due to begin. It would last all the morning; maybe all day.
Come on, Fedora. Stop trying to cheer yourself up. Get that
giant brain ticking over. Demonstrate the power of positive
thinking. . . .

"Where could he have got the helicopter *from?*"

"I don't know," Laura said. "Some air base or other."

"What I'm really asking is, just how much *power* has he
got? There's a Holding Detachment of the Spanish Army
back there, several hundred men and equipment, and Feramontov seems to be running the show. Well, who gave him
the authority? Who's *behind* him?"

"If we get away," Laura said, "we can probably find out.
And then the job will be over. My part of it, anyway."

"The thing is there's positive backing. And negative backing. I suppose I'd always thought he was getting the latter.
You want to disappear for a while . . . and Feramontov certainly did. . . . Well, then the Army'd be a good place to
disappear into. Protective coloration. I can quite see that.
You get someone with enough authority to forge you some
papers and plant you in a unit somewhere—then provided
your rank's high enough, no one's going to ask you any questions. Least of all in Spain. You can travel where you want
on a military permit, you can walk right through a police
cordon and all they'll do is stamp your pass and maybe salute.
That's how he got up to Catalonia when your people thought
you had him all sewn up down here in the south." The pistol
still in Johnny's hand, his finger very gently caressing the
trigger. "But it goes a lot farther than that, doesn't it? He
was getting too much help, up at Villafranca. And the wrong
kind of help. Like that girl Estelle. She was the one who set

everything to cock, because no one was expecting her. We thought Feramontov would be working on his own. And he wasn't. And then Estelle. . . . She was OAS. She didn't tell me that, it's a guess, but I'm sure of it. Well, in most ways they're a tricky crowd. They don't work for just anybody . . . or the *good* ones don't. And *she* was good. It'd have to be someone in with the gang . . . military or para-military. . . . So it all fits together."

Positive thinking, through the raging headache. The jigsaw, the scattered pieces. And a quiet voice on the hillside putting them together. Around it, the night; black; immense. And Laura, close by; listening.

"The file that Feramontov wanted, that he went to Villa-franca for. It was sent in from Russia. But that can still make sense. Because it originated from the people who saw Spain as the real centre of operations in Europe. Last year they tried Hammerhead . . . you know about that? . . . and it didn't work and, in trying it, they went in too far. A hydrogen bomb on a neutral capital—*that's* going too far, for the Russians nowadays. So that group got mopped up, by the Russians themselves. But they couldn't get hold of Feramontov. He was here in Spain."

"And now he's got the file."

"Yes. He's got the file. And nobody else seems to know exactly what's in it. But . . . Well, Hammerhead didn't work and they couldn't have been *sure*, at any time, that it'd work. It was kind of a far-fetched scheme, in a number of ways. My idea is that they had up their sleeves some sort of alternative. Of alternative operation. And that's what's in the Moscow file. Whatever Cell Eleven is, that's what it's all about."

"But the Russians? *They* must know."

"Maybe they do and maybe they don't. Either way they won't tell us because they daren't. They'll never admit to *that* kind of responsibility."

"To having been behind it, you mean?"

"Yes, to having been behind it. Of course, it won't be *only* Russians involved. There were plenty of Spaniards mixed up with Hammerhead. . . . Among them, a man called Pombo. He's dead, now, but before he died he was quite a distinguished figure in Madrid society. My guess is that there was some other distinguished figure that we never got on to . . . and that he's taken over. And that the alternative operation is under way."

"The trouble is," Laura said, "that you still don't know what it is."

"I know it has something to do with Santa Ana."

"That's just a guess."

"It's a bit more than that. The Pombo character I mentioned just now, he was the Pombo of *Chaval y Pombo*. . . . You've heard of them?"

"Yes, of course I have. They're the biggest electrical engineering firm in Spain. Or just about. That makes him a special high-class sort of Pombo, right, so what?"

"That infernal machine that you were tied to," Fedora said "was constructed by *Chaval y Pombo*. It said so on the side, in great big letters. Of course it wasn't made for that particular *purpose*. . . . But if they've been working on the Santa Ana installations in general, then it's going to be interesting. Because they worked on the H-bomber bases, too, and that's how the Hammerhead business started off. It's a little too much, to my mind, to pass for a coincidence."

"*Dios mio*," Laura said. "I don't think Rivas knows about that. You could *have* something there."

"I fancy we can do better than tell Rivas about it. I know Chaval quite well, as it happens. You could even call him an old friend of mine. And I'm wondering if *he's* ever heard of Cell Eleven."

Laura said nothing. Her silence had a quality that Johnny found very pleasing; of admiration, *awestruck* admiration. She had probably never realised he was quite so brilliant.

". . . Chaval's a millionaire, isn't he?"

"Many times over."

"Gosh, I'd no idea you knew any *millionaires*."

Johnny felt vaguely that she had somehow missed the essential point, but it didn't seem to matter; it's always nice to be admired, even for the wrong reasons. "Oh yes, indeed," he said. "Dozens 'n' dozens."

"I think you're wonderful. I really do."

"Oh, I don't know."

"No, no. You *are*. The way you work the whole thing out from really almost *nothing*, it's simply fantastic."

"Well, I wouldn't—"

"And after all the dreadful things you've been through. Those drugs an' all. You're jus' so *strong*, I thing you're the strongest man I've ever known."

"Well—"

"Do you think," Laura said coaxingly, "that now you've had a nice long rest, you could maybe manage to walk just a little *little* way? A hundred yards or so?. . . . Maybe?. . . . If I help you?"

Fedora closed his eyes.

"No," he said. "I couldn't possibly."

"Ah, come on. Don't be such a baby."

". . . Just five minutes more."

"No," Laura said. "Come on. Or I'll hit you."

TIMELOCK

SEALED ORDERS

TO BE OPENED AT 0600 HRS BY OFFICER I/C STA ANA DETAIL

. . . Bujas licked the envelope, sealed it, stamped it heavily with the office seal. Lastly, taking a pen from his tunic pocket, he initialled it. The despatch rider stood by the desk, alertly to attention, waiting patiently.

". . . Lieutenant Soto. At once."

"*A la orden, mi capitan.*"

Bujas wearily returned the rider's salute, watched him stamp his way to the office door. Then he stood up; flexed his arms and shoulders, but didn't yawn. Spanish officers do not yawn on duty. He turned and went through the door into the inner office. Feramontov sat at the Commanding Officer's desk, motionless, his arms resting on the pockmarked wooden surface. Beneath the flat stiff field officer's cap was nothing but bandage, turn after turn of neatly pinned bandage. He looked, thought Bujas, like the Invisible Man. Though that was too near the mark to be funny.

It wasn't funny, anyway. Anything but.

"Captain Bujas, sir." He didn't salute, this time. It seemed ridiculous.

"Yes, captain. Make your report."

"I've just sent off the last of the special instructions, sir, with the duty despatch rider. All officers at the encampment have received verbal orders and will be standing the men to at six hundred hours." A pause. He wetted his lips. "As yet, sir, no official authority for the exercise has arrived. That means we have only two hours left in which . . . to cancel the instructions. Should that be necessary."

"It won't be," the colonel said. "There'll be no cancellations. Is that all?"

"Yes, sir."

"Carry on."

Bujas turned and stepped smartly off towards the door. At the last moment, struck by something not quite definable about the bandaged man's . . . what? . . . posture, maybe? . . . he paused and looked back. Feramontov hadn't moved. Literally. Not so much as a finger.

"Colonel, sir?"

"What?"

"Are you . . . in pain?"

"That's a damfool question, if you like." Still no movement, or even hint of movement. "Yes, I'm in pain."

"Should I send for the MO again, sir? Maybe . . . morphine or something . . . ?"

"That will be all, captain."

Bujas shrugged, closed the door behind him. Seated once more at his own desk, he took the packet of Celtas from the drawer and, striking a match casually on the wall behind him, lit one. Fifteen minutes' relaxation; he felt that he'd earned it. He'd take a few quiet inhalations, a crafty drag or two; then he'd order coffee.

After maybe two minutes, with one finger resting on the bellpush, he became aware of the sounds coming from behind the closed door. Strange, stifled sounds; very strange indeed. It sounded almost as though the colonel were weeping.

"I hit him," Johnny said. "I know I did."

"I don't see how you can be sure."

"Well, I am."

"You can't—"

"My head," Johnny said. "It hurts so much."

Laura turned her head, for the first time with concern. To no real purpose, of course; he was no more than a still shape among the shadows. "I don't understand."

"It doesn't matter. I hit him, that's all."

"All right, darling. All right. You did if you say so. Let's try and get a little bit farther."

"It's no good," Johnny said.

"Just to the next crest."

"That's all there is. Just one crest after another. And then another. We're not getting anywhere."

"Just to the next one. We'll stop there."

"All right," Johnny said.

They walked, or stumbled, on. Through the darkness. That wasn't quite as dark as it had been before. It wasn't yet dawn, or nearly dawn; it was just less dark; that was all. The sky could now at times be distinguished from the horizon, only there wasn't really a horizon. Just crests, the crests of hills. One after another. Mile after mile of interlocking slopes. They worked their way upwards, over the rough stony ground, the rifle bumping awkwardly on Laura's back. She had one arm round Fedora's waist and was helping him as much as she could. His feet were wandering all over the place. In the end, though, they reached the crest. And stopped. But didn't sit down.

"What did I tell you?"

"Water," Johnny said. He didn't seem all that interested.

It was some way off, but not hard to see. It reflected such light as there was with a peculiar luminosity; it lay beneath them and—though distance was difficult to judge—not so *very* far away. "It's the lake," Laura said. "We're nearly there."

"It can't be the same lake. It *can't* be."

"We've come out at the wrong place, that's all. We're too far south. We're south of the dam, and we should have been north of it. Look."

Fedora's aching eyes probed the darkness to the north. Below the Great Bear there were other stars. Low stars, very low; reddish stars. He said,

"Lights."

"I think there's a line of them. A straight line. So that'll be the road that runs on top of the dam."

"There's a road there?"

"When you think about it, there *must* be."

"Yes," Johnny said. "I expect you're right. Well, that could be the way out, then. The only one left to us. If we can manage to get there before it's daybreak...."

"They'll be guarding it."

"Yes. But even so." Johnny sat down, looked at his watch. "We'll rest for five minutes. Then we'll go on."

"What time is it?"

"Just gone five."

"It gets light now about a quarter to six."

"Five minutes," Fedora said.

"All right."

Laura sat down beside him, began to unlace her boots. Her feet were so sore and swollen that now they very nearly fitted. But Johnny's trouble seemed to be rather worse. He appeared to be only just in touch with reality.

"Johnny?"

"Yes."

"Johnny, talk to me."

"What about?"

"Anything. Just talk to me. That's all."

His head was bowed down on to his chest. He said nothing. Laura wondered what on earth to do.

... There was only one thing she could do that would be of any use. And that was find the road. Johnny was half-doped still, and fresh from hospital; he was right out of training, and the hills and the scree and the rocks were killing him slowly. The dam could be only two miles distant, maybe even less; but they'd never get there walking cross-country. He wouldn't give up, but he'd give out. He'd die on the way. Unless...

No. She didn't know *what* to do.

"Johnny? Did you know that we have a file on *you*?"

"... Suppose you must have." The words hardly audible.

"A big fat file. And I've read it all. What I don't know about you isn't worth knowing." He didn't raise his head. He didn't move at all. "What about all those other girls of yours?"

"What girls?"

"That's a very good question. I'll tell you what girls. Someone called Elsa and someone called Carlotta, *that's* what girls for a start."

"I like girls," Johnny said indistinctly. "I'm funny that way."

"Yes, and they like *you*. That's the point. Yes, and what about Adriana?"

For a moment, no response. Then his head lifted. Well, so she'd got a reaction. Fine. But now she almost wished she hadn't. Still, she'd started it. She had to go on.

"You nearly married *her*, didn't you?"

"Yes," Johnny said. "Yes, I did."

"Well, why didn't you?"

"I expect the file will tell you why not."

"I don't need a file to tell me why not. I *know* why not. Because you're a lousy bastard, *that's* why not. You walked out on her, and you'll walk out on *me* if I give you half a chance. I know that perfectly well. You're such a bastard."

Her anger wasn't altogether simulated. She found it easy to

get that way, thinking about Adriana.

"... Well, I don't care. You know that? *I* don't care. You can play around with anyone you like, Adriana and all the rest of your ... private harem. But you've got to get me out of this jam first. For God's sake, you owe me *that* much."

The metal chain of the handcuffs, clinking on stone. Then the pressure of his fingers on her wrist. "What are you trying to do? Get me wild?"

"I'm here to tell you," Laura said, "that you make *me* wild. Every time I think about—"

"No need for it. You've got it all wrong. I only said I hit Feramontov. . . . That was all. Can't you take my word for it?"

His fingers on her wrist. Steady as a doctor's. ". . . Yes," Laura said. "Yes. I believe you."

"It doesn't make a lot of difference. I didn't kill him. But he's hurt and maybe badly." A pause. "I just *know* it, that's all. It doesn't mean I'm going round the bend."

"I didn't think—"

His hand now tightening almost painfully on her wrist, twisting it so that she was forced down to the ground. But by then, she had heard it, too. Her first thought was that the helicopter was returning; but then the sound was louder, nearer, was leaping towards her with a frightening rapidity, and the bushes around them were suddenly alive with a bright and searing light. The drumming roar of the engine, the hiss of the tyres, then the motor-cycle was past them and humming down the road ... the road. . . .

"*The road,*" Laura said. "My God, we're sitting almost on top of it."

An exaggeration, of course. At no point had the motor-cyclist been nearer than twenty yards away. But an acceptable one. They watched in silence as the bright cone of the head-lamp came once more into view as the rider rounded a corner; the road glittered grey and silver as he went on, now seemingly with painful slowness, due north towards the distant lights. "A despatch rider," Johnny said. "Going towards the dam."

"Where else?"

"To the dam. From the camp. Don't you see? . . . He'll be coming back."

They made their way down the steep slope to the road. It was easier going, of course, downhill; but probably it would have seemed easier going anyway. They had some idea of their bearings now, together with something that might have been called a chance. Enough of a chance, at any rate, to give their movements a definite objective. They clambered with some difficulty past the barbed-wire fence that bordered the road, descended the three-foot dip into the ditch, mounted the verge and stopped. They were there.

"How long do we have?"

"I don't know," Johnny said. "But we'd better be quick."

They followed the fence uphill, tracing the lowest of the barbed-wire strands to its linkpoint. Then Fedora prised it loose and Laura carried the free end across the road, to secure it to a post on the far side. They did the job hurriedly but efficiently; in ten minutes' time there were two strands of wire across the road just clear of the bend, taut but not too taut, one at a height of two feet and the other some eighteen inches higher. They risked a quick flash of the sentry's torch to check their position, and another to check the firmness of the posts; everything was satisfactory. Except that the handcuffs had yet again made Fedora's task unnecessarily difficult; his hands were bleeding by the time he'd finished, and rather badly.

They sat down amongst the bushes just above the curve. To wait.

While they were waiting, they talked.

". . . In that camp," Fedora said, "there are people who know something about what's happening, and there are a whole lot of others who sure as hell don't. This is probably one of the ones who don't."

"It's us or them," Laura said. "We've got no choice."

"Yes, that's true. But don't think I feel *good* about it, all the same."

"I know. If you weren't such a bastard, you'd be quite nice, sometimes. It's just that we *matter* more than this chap does—that's all."

"Who to?" Fedora said sadly.

There wasn't any answer to that one. At least, there was; but Laura didn't think there was much to be gained by giving it. She didn't feel *good* about it, either.

They sat there, waiting, for almost twenty minutes. So they needn't have hurried so much, after all. Then they heard the noise of the motor-cycle once more, saw the bright shaft of light returning down the road. They lay down flat. The Luger was in Fedora's hand, but he didn't think he'd need it.

As it turned out, it was over very quickly. The lower strand went, but the top one didn't. It took the motor-cyclist precisely where it was meant to take him, at the base of the neck, and the barbs tore his throat out as neatly as a razor. He was killed by them before he hit the ground.

". . . Stop thinking about it," Fedora said.

I I

There was now that in the sky which could pass for light, other than that emanating from the thorny stars; there was a faint palling to the east, behind the hills, and a corresponding darkening to the west, and the land between taking on at last discernible shape and contour. There were spurs running down to the long valley, to the pale mirror of the lake, and the occasional darker splodges of ilex clumps. There were trees to the right, five or six of them, with mist-like wraiths of Spanish moss hanging from the low black branches; to the left, a jumble of fallen rocks and of scree. And directly in front of them, the great hard-rimmed monostructure of the dam, picked out along its enormous length by pools of orange light; isolated, monstrous, against the still water and the dark slopes. There was a road across it all right, a big road; two lanes, maybe even three, though of its actual width it was impossible to be sure. At the near end, some kind of a building, hidden in the shadows. Nothing moved.

Only the bushes rustled gently in the dawn wind.

"I'd give a lot," Fedora said, "for a decent pair of night glasses."

"We can't get very much nearer."

"No. We can't."

The motor-cycle stood on its wheel-rest at the edge of the road. They went back to it; stood beside it for a few moments, looking at each other. Two dim, silhouetted figures in the cool stilness. There seemed to be nothing to be said.

"Remember that the trick is in the speed," Fedora said. "Thirty-five to forty. No faster. If it's a wooden barrier and we hit it right, then we'll break it. If it's iron, we'll kill ourselves as easily at forty as we would if we were doing seventy. We won't know any more about it than *he* did. It'll be over in a second. Just like that."

As always when there's nothing to be said, once you start talking it's difficult to stop. Laura said,

"I wish *you* could take it."

"Yes," Johnny said. "So do I."

He pushed the machine forwards off its rest, tapped the starter reflectively with his foot. Just wishful moving, that was all. He couldn't possibly drive it. Not with handcuffs.

"There'll probably be a barrier on the far side, too. But if we break the first, then we ought to break the other. Take her up to sixty across the dam, then throttle back and take the far barrier in just the same way." Say three miles across, at sixty miles an hour, three minutes or a little longer. A long, long time. "We may get past the first without any shooting, if we're lucky. But not the second. Don't lose your concentration, that's the main thing."

"What's the time?"

"Ten to six," Johnny said. He didn't have to look at his watch; the chronometer in his own mind had started ticking a few minutes back. "That's a good time. The guards'll be thinking about going off duty."

"There's no such thing as a good time. For *this*."

She swung a leg over the saddle, dropped her hands to the handlebars. She had no gloves or goggles. She could have taken the despatch rider's equipment, if she'd wanted to; but she hadn't wanted to .They had left the rider lying exactly as he had fallen. Fedora didn't think he had even seen so much blood before anywhere. He settled himself down on the pillion, the rifle slung over his left shoulder and nestled in the crook of his arm, the pistol in his right hand. "Ready?"

"Ready," Laura said.

"Let's go."

She kicked the starter and the engine woke first time; its roar seemed deafening. She accelerated slowly away down the slope. Fedora was impressed with the way she handled it; a

BSA M.20 is a whole lot of bike for an ordinary girl to handle, but then Laura wasn't ordinary in that respect. She and machinery clicked. She could take a screaming powerboat through a force six Mediterranean blow-up at thirty knots and over, with the whitecaps coming at the hull like blows from a mallet. She could heel-and-toe her way down from the Pyrenees with the ice lying in pools on the Andorra road, the snow spinning up from the wheels and blanketing the windows with slush, and still pin back an average mileage of fifty-odd kilometres an hour. She didn't just *like* speed; she understood it. In that way, she was a bit like Adriana. . . .

All she had to do now was to break one little barrier. One little *wooden* barrier. As they say in Liverpool . . . easy, easy. The road unwinding now, dark grey in the headlamp, like a ribbon; the dam maybe half a mile ahead. The trouble was the blood. It had shaken her up. If only it hadn't been for the blood; on the road, on his uniform, everywhere. And on his face, an expression of startled surprise. He'd have been about twenty. And you say, *Stop thinking about it.*

Easy, easy.

Only you can't.

Only we're coming up to the barrier.

And that's when we have to . . .

Fedora leaned forwards, his chin on Laura's shoulder. Shouted into her ear.

"IT WAS LIKE THIS ONCE BEFORE, IN ARGENTINA. . . ."

Laura nodded, registering no real interest.

"WE HAD TO BREAK A BARRIER, ADRIANA AND ME."

His chin was lifted, maybe a centimetre, as her shoulders stiffened slightly. The slipstream forced a grin on to his face.

"Oh?" Laura yelled. "INDEED?"

"YES. IN A CAR, THAT WAS, SHE WAS A BLOODY GOOD DRIVER."

Throttling back a little for the bend. "So all *right*. So you broke a barrier."

"We did, yes. No trouble at all. Well, I'm here now, aren't I?"

Opening out again. "YOU WON'T BE FOR VERY MUCH LONGER IF YOU DON'T BELT UP."

Fedora thought for a moment, considering alternatives. Bad, malicious Fedora. ". . . OF COURSE, LIKE I SAID, THAT WAS IN A CAR. A MOTOR-BIKE . . . THAT'S ANOTHER MATTER."

The pressure of the slipstream building up now. He turned his head away, tears trickling from his eyes. They took the last corner at a rakishly professional angle and levelled out on to the final stretch of grey-white tarmac; ahead of them, a low building, a dim light burning in one of its windows, and the high concrete shoulders of the dam. The orange overhead lights on tall thin columns, burning twenty feet above them. And between the lights, between the concrete shoulders, a lattice of red-and-white rectangles stretched across the road. The barrier.

Getting wider. Coming nearer. Streaking nearer. *Now*, Fedora thought, *throttle back. Throttle back. All they can see is the headlamp; it's that despatch rider, back again. He's* easing up now. Easing up to a halt. Now he could see them, in the orange light. Two shapeless khaki-clad figures, one on each side of the barrier. And a third in a kind of sandbagged crow's nest on top of the building. He'd have the machine-gun. He would be the one to watch. The others aren't even moving. Just standing there. Right. Now. "LIGHTS," he yelled in Laura's ear.

She cut the headlamp. For a second they were lost against the grey-black backing of the hills; then they came out into the pool of light, the vague outline of a splintered red-and-white shape careering towards them. Red and white, red and white. . . . Yes. It was odd. His shout was being echoed from the right—a yell of warning, rather than of alarm—almost drowned in the rising roar of the engine. She was timing it beautifully. Taking it dead centre, at the point of maximum weakness, lovely, just lovely, but going in fast, fast . . . *too* fast, surely? . . . His knees closing together frantically, desperately, as the great swinging beams blurred in towards his head. . . .

The collision. Harder, far harder than he'd imagined it could be. His brain shaken loose in his skull by a great jarring *whump*, his body flying away from him, his legs coming loose; he was off, he was spinning through the air. No, he wasn't. Or was he?... *Where* was he?... This was what he'd felt, that poor bastard. And really there was nothing to feel. It wasn't so bad. There was just ... bewilderment. Like a parachute jump, free fall, the air whipping at your sleeves and trouserlegs and your arms drifting open and your body left behind, far behind. *Stop thinking about it.* You can feel it now, your body's coming back, you can feel the metal between your thighs, bone-breakingly hard, and the pain there and the hard brown concrete whipping past you, faster, faster. ...

My God, he thought. *We're through. We did it.*

Reality suddenly returning as the headlamp flicked on again; the bulb wasn't even broken, though the glass had gone. Laura's body slim yet solid, pressed against his own. She was all right? ... She *had* to be all right. She was still riding, wasn't she? But that had been quite a wallop, yes, quite a wallop. With that fragile body between himself and the barrier, taking the brunt of the impact without even a gasp. ... *Fragile?* Fedora thought. *Fragile, hell. She has to be made of teak.*

And she was driving fast now. Really fast. Her body flattening over the petrol-tank, crouching into the demoniac howl of the engine. No gloves, no goggles. Blind with tears. Sixty, seventy? ... They were really moving. With the high concrete buttresses to either side flicking back the snarl of the motor, *boom ... boom ... boom*. ... Fedora, his head lowered, his mind a swirling emptiness, his body far withdrawn from all sensation; there was nothing now, nothing but noise and wind. Three minutes to cross. Three minutes to cross ...

They'd been going for twenty already.

No.

... More like twenty seconds.

There came by way of confirmation, though seemingly far

in the rear, the incoherent stutter of a light machine-gun. He wasn't trying to hit them, of course; he hadn't a hope. The tracer was passing high overhead, spinning in a shower of explosive fireworks off the high walls. He was warning the guards on the far side. *They* wouldn't be unprepared.

They'd be waiting.

Three minutes, that was far too long. Any fool could have seen that from the start. It gave them time to walk own to the Post Office and send a telegram. Tap Laura on the shoulder, tell her to stop? . . . A temptation, yes. But they had to go on. Or be trapped. There was no choice, no choice at all.

The BSA, juddering like a jet at mach one. The road—it *was* a three-lane highway—vibrating under the wheels, pulsating wildly beneath them like a damaged heart. A dead straight road, but even so. . . . This speed was suicidal. Fedora's eyes were narrowed into slits, his lips wrenched back by the slipstream into a gaping rictus like that of a mask of comedy; his cheeks were fluttering in the wind like flags. Eighty, ninety? . . . And other eyes, by the far barrier, watching the oncoming headlamp travel down the long straight road, its trembling velocity slowed by distance to something like a crawl. Other hands, steady brown hands, swinging the FAO machine-gun round on its tripod. Ready to fire on fixed lines, from four hundred to one hundred metres; those hands shouldn't miss. But still, they might. That was all you could hope for. They *might*.

A mile to go. . . .

The time, four minutes to six.

At the far end of the line, a voice speaking; its normal deep suavity touched with an edge of querulousness. "Yes? What is it?"

Feramontov's free hand felt for the scrambler button, pressed it down.

"Gutierrez speaking."

"I expected a report last night."

"There will be no further reports," Feramontov said.

"Circumstances have changed. I have to inform you that TIMELOCK goes into operation at six hundred hours. . . . You had better leave at once."

A moment's pause. "It's six hundred hours now. By my watch."

"You are three and a half minutes fast," Feramontov said.

". . . TIMELOCK is scheduled for tomorrow. You know that as well as I do."

"Circumstances have changed," Feramontov said expressionlessly. "TIMELOCK goes into operation at six hundred hours today. It's too late for orders to be changed or rescinded. I repeat, therefore . . . you'd better leave at once."

The voice now level, unperturbed as usual, its querulousness disappeared. "There will be a satisfactory explanation for this, no doubt."

"At the moment there's no time for explanations. There seldom is, when the cards are on the table. And now mine are. Get down here, General," Feramontov said. ". . . That's all."

He released the holder button, replaced the receiver. Under the tight white bandages, his cheek muscles moved. *Get down here. That's all.* He had waited a long time for that moment; it had been a good one.

And now the cards were down on the table all right. For what they were worth. Once again he was committed, completely committed; *les jeux sont faits.* With another good moment immediately ahead—perhaps the best moment of all. The moment of maximum danger. He saw it stretching ahead of him like a barrier; pass it, and the rest would be easy. Relatively easy. But it had to be passed. There was no stopping. From now on, there was no choice; no choice at all.

DANGER

CURVE AT 500 METRES

SLACKEN SPEED NOW

. . . The sign came up fast and blinked past them so rapidly that Fedora barely had time to read it. He leaned farther forwards as Laura's wrist rotated on the throttle; he screamed again,

". . . LIGHTS . . ."

. . . the speed dropping back, falling off fast; fifty, forty-five, forty. They'd be within range now. The lights snapping off, the motor-bike veering from side to side as Laura began a long series of sweeping curves. Then suddenly the first hot sparks of tracer, coming swinging slowly out of the darkness then zipping wickedly past them, close, blindingly close. The bike seemed to veer straight into them, then away from them to the right, far over to the right, till the towering vertical wall of the cutting seemed to be brushing Fedora's elbow. *The right thing to do,* he thought, *if they're firing on fixed lines. But if not, not. Doubles the risk, through the ricochets.* She had cut the engine right down, reducing the roar of its engine to a smooth purr; the walls would distort the direction of the sound, anyway, but if they based their estimate of angle on the previous speed of the bike, they'd be thrown off. So, the right thing again. Clever girl. Certainly the bullets seemed to be striking ahead of them, zooming and cannon-ading off the walls and road like angry red fireflies. And the bike drifting away to the left now, a little to the left, caught perhaps by some cross-current of wind from the high wall. . . .

Bad luck, if that was what it was. That was when the bullets hit them. There were three separate hammer blows, each with its accompaniment of buckling, splintering metal, and the bike swung back towards the wall; Laura corrected the front wheel in time, but the back wheel skidded badly and hit. The wall stripped the skin from Johnny's right leg in a split second, opening the leg of his trousers from the cuff almost to the hip; his thighs loosened their grip and he was thrown clear as the bike reared up like a wild horse and somer-saulted. There was a loud, an echoing crash; the tracer lashed the wall behind him into blue-white flame, then stopped. There was silence, except for the fast trickle of leaking petrol. Lying flat on his face, Fedora raised his head.

"... Laura?"

From behind him. ... How could that have happened? ... a voice said,

"Over here."

A bundle of discarded clothes in the road, she looked like. Only some ten feet away. Johnny hauled himself towards her; Fedora, the human caterpillar. "... Are you all right?"

"Yes, are you?"

"Oh, I'm wounded sore."

"Leg?"

"Yes. Against the wall."

"I thought so. Sorry. Is it broken?"

"No. I can walk. Maybe even run."

"Then for God's sake let's."

The tracer seemed to pass some six inches over their heads with a whipping hiss and a thump. Fedora cowered in terror.

"... You were saying?"

"Well, it seemed a good idea at the time."

"It was," Johnny said. "It still is. If you *have* to get hit, get hit early. It gives you time for a dignified retreat."

"Where to?"

"Yes, that's the problem."

They lay on the road for a few moments longer, in silence. Or not quite silence, because from the end of the road somebody seemed to be shouting. But there was no more machine-gun fire.

"They're coming out after us," Laura said suddenly.

"That makes it an even better idea than it was before. When they've gone about fifty metres, we'll skedaddle. They won't fire that bloody machine-gun, with their own boys in the way."

"But they'll catch us up."

"If they do," Johnny said, "we'll discourage them politely. Here. You'd better have the rifle."

He freed it from his shoulder, from which by some miracle it hadn't become detached. Then passed it across to her. His leg was burning now down all its length, was hurting more and more as feeling returned to it; he *hoped* he could still use it, but he wasn't sure. From somewhere ahead, another shout.

"Now," he said.

Laura raised the rifle slowly to her shoulder, fired one round. It might have gone anywhere, but appeared none the less to cause alarm and despondency. Fedora got to his feet. Yes, he could use the leg. Just. "Come on," he said.

They set off down the road at a fast hobble, zigzagging from side to side. He zigged. She zagged. She didn't seem, in fact, to be in very much better case than he was. Clip-clop, clip-clop. His feet made so much *noise*. Their shadows enormous on the wall, distorted in the overhead lights. They passed the notice again; SLACKEN SPEED NOW; no fear, Fedora thought, no bloody fear. "I thought it was . . . somewhere round here. . . ."

"What was?"

"Before we . . . passed that sign. . . . An opening."

"What kind of opening?"

But Fedora was short of breath. He saved it. On they ran, their shadows juttering about in front of them; clip-clop, clip-clop. Laura, too, was panting like a dog. He could hear her quite clearly, even above the bumping of the blood in his own head. Wherever it was, they had better find it soon.

He felt her catch at his shirt sleeve. ". . . Is *that* it?"

Yes. That was it. As near as a toucher, they had run straight past it.

An opening, he had said. Well, that was what it was. An opening in the sheer sides of the concrete wall; steps ran upwards from it, steps ran downwards. Some kind of inspection-way for the dam, no doubt. "Up or down?"

"Up," Fedora said.

It was the LMG that worried him, still. An LMG can be brought to bear downwards all right, but not upwards. Or not so easily.

They began to mount the steps. Wide concrete steps with eight-inch risers. Just the thing for people who've toppled off a motor-bike at thirty-odd miles an hour; brings a spring to the step and makes the hair curl. The first five hundred steps would be the hardest. Not that Fedora was counting them; he was too busy trying to stop his lungs from exploding through his ribcage. Sad, what a month in bed could do to a man. A month ago . . . Nothing to it. He'd have flown up those steps like a leaping gazelle. But as it was . . . Oh, *bed*. Don't think about bed. Just don't think about anything, if you can possibly help it. Just the steps—one after another, one after another—maintaining the same rhythmic pace, one-two-three-four, one-two-*three*-four, up and up and up. . . .

Laura's blistered hand skidded off the handrail. "Oh, wait. . . . Wait a moment. . . ."

"No, keep going. Keep going."

"But it goes on . . . f'rever."

"Never mind that. Keep going."

He took a quick glance round, through his wind-swollen eyelids. There was light, he was amazed to see how much light. The dawn was almost on them. They'd climbed up into it. Trees, hills, water. They were high up on the dam's great northward flank; the road was stretched out two hundred feet beneath them and still in the shadows. The overhead lights, of course, were overhead no longer, but far below. They couldn't be seen from the road, with all that dazzle. They were safe for the moment.

"All right," he said, and his shoulders slackened. "We can rest."

He sat down beside her and looked, for the first time at his leg. Most of the trousering had been ripped away, and the little that remained was sodden with blood and was stuck like plaster to his thigh. The leg itself was a dark and glistening mess; countless tiny trickles had reached his knee and turned there into rivers, and where the blood had thickened and dried, fresh rivulets had cut red channels. Only in one or two places did paler patches of sunburnt skin show through. It looked much worse, of course, than it probably was. That's the thing about blood. At least, Johnny thought grimly, that's the thing you always tell yourself. And it had to be true. Judging by how it looked, it was ripe for amputation.

He'd lost a lot of blood. That was for sure. An awful lot. Maybe too much.

He turned his head, looked down at Laura.

"Hey."

Her face, lifted towards him. "What?"

"I can see you at last."

"The way I have to look, I wish you couldn't."

"Don't be silly," Johnny said. "You look pretty good to me."

And not, apparently, too badly damaged. Which was probably more important. Under the laces of one of the canvas boots, though, her ankle was swelling outwards into what could be a *very* nasty sprain. "We'd better move on," Johnny said, "because in about another minute you probably won't be able to move at all. Ready?"

"I suppose I'm as ready as I'll ever be."

They rose creakingly to their feet and started to climb again. And, as so often happens, found that they'd stopped a matter of a few yards short of what had to be their ultimate destination. Another thirty steps, and they were there.

. . . There was a rectangular concrete apron, thrusting out of the very lip of the dam, an iron safety-rail running round all four sides. Thirty yards in length, maybe, by twenty wide; the size of a smallish university quadrangle. It was their ultimate destination all right; there was no place else to go. No other way in or out. There was damn-all in the way of cover, other than the narrowish four-foot-high wall that supported the safety-rail where the steps joined the parapet; in all respects it was like a hilltop, a natural fortification, and the only way up to it was via the curving flights of steps they had just ascended. Fedora looked back, and scratched his beginning-to-be-bristly chin.

Dubious, was what he seemed to be.

Laura, on the other hand, was full of girlish enthusiasm. "God, Johnny. We're in luck. Aren't we?"

"Yes," Johnny said. "We ought to be dead."

"We couldn't have found a better place. Why, we can hold an army from up here. All we have to do is cover the stairs—just one rifle'll do it. If they've got any sense at all, they won't even try and attack us. It'd be suicide."

"They don't have to," Johnny said.

"How do you mean?"

"All they have to do is sit at the bottom. And wait."

"Wait for what?"

"Don't say you'd forgotten," Johnny said. ". . . For the chopper."

"The *what?*"

"The helicopter."

There was rather a lengthy silence. Then Laura said, "Oh."

"That's about it, yes. Oh."

"Maybe we can go back again."

"No."

"But they may not have realised yet just where we've gone. I mean, they may have gone haring on down the road. . . ."

Johnny, sadly, raised his right foot. Put it down again. It went *squelch*. Laura looked down at the little puddle of blood in which he stood. She said, "Oh," . . . again.

"Sorry," Johnny said. "They can't miss it."

"I didn't know it was . . . Isn't there anything we can do?"

"Well, if we had a bandage, you could put on a bandage. But it might be tricky knowing where to begin."

"It's a mess all right," Laura said, staring at it.

That, of course, was Fedora's own opinion. "I expect it'll stop flowing," he said, with highly artificial cheerfulness, "as soon as I stop rushing round and round." He lowered himself with caution to the ground; or, more precisely, to the hard concrete floor of the rectangle. "We're in much the same position as they are, really. All *we* can do is wait."

"And enjoy the view."

"Yes, when the sun gets up it should be quite spectacular."

Laura sat down beside him, leaning her back against the wall. The sun, she thought, would be up at any moment; there was pink in the east now as well as grey. She closed her eyes. Why not? . . . It was the end of the road.

"Then just where have they got to?"

The sergeant's stubby finger pressed down on the large-scale map; withdrew. "There, sir."

". . . A shot was fired? You're sure about that?"

"Of course I'm sure, sir."

"I can't imagine what they're playing at."

The sergeant's face betrayed no emotion at all. It wasn't *his* business to imagine things, either.

"Well, they can't get down from *there*. *Más claro que el agua*."

"I don't see how we can get *up*, sir, that's the point. Not unless you're prepared to risk a few casualties."

"Of course I'm not, sergeant. We're not in a state of war, as far as I know." Lieutenant Soto was twenty-two years old. He didn't like the present situation at all. "I'm damned if I understand it, I'm damned if I do."

"Standard orders, sir, to report to Holding Detachment HQ, in event of firearms being used, sir."

"Well, I know *that*. But for God's sake. The unit's on operations, sergeant." Soto's fingers spread out the typewritten papers on the desk, the slitted envelope. "I haven't had time to *read* these orders properly yet, but the Detachment's on the move, they're coming *here*. It's some kind of an exercise. Every man jack from the CO downwards."

"I see, sir," said the sergeant, who self-evidently didn't.

Soto got up and took a little stroll, his hands clasped tightly behind his back. The obvious thing to do was to wait until the CO arrived. Yes, that was the obvious thing all right. But was it the right thing? . . . He didn't know. He'd never even *seen* the CO, as yet. Well, what about the Adj., then? Captain Bujas? . . . Always on about using one's initiative and all that codswallop. Still, *there* was a thought. Things have to *look* good, in the Army. *I had a little trouble here, sir, with the escaped prisoners. Cleared it up all right, though . . . The sergeant and myself between us. . . .* Like that. With the right touch of modesty about it. While the other . . . *Thought I'd wait until you got here, sir. . . .*

Decision-making, dammit, was what officers were *for*. Right. He'd make one. And besides, last night's orders had been definite. . . . *Detain at all costs. . . .* That meant dead, if necessary. Obviously, it did.

"All right, sergeant. We'll go in and get them."

His enthusiasm didn't seem to be contagious. "Very good, sir. If that's what you say, sir."

"You, and six of the stand-off guard. I'll take command myself. The Duty Corporal will remain in charge at the barrier."

"Sir," the sergeant said woodenly.

"I wonder what the hell they think they're doing?"

"They're shooting at us," Laura said.

"Yes, I'd worked that much out for myself. But they're getting quite spiteful, aren't they? I honestly believe they're going to try and rush us, the stupid nits."

"And do we shoot back?"

"Well, what else *can* we do?"

"Oh God," Laura said. "But it's murder."

"No more than the other was. It's like you said before—them or us."

"But they're bound to take us in the end. Why go *on* killing?"

"They're not going to take us," Johnny said. He patted the Luger where it lay on the ground just clear of his knee. "I'm saving the last two."

". . . You mean it?"

"It's that or Feramontov."

"Yes," Laura said. "It's that, then."

A bullet whined off the wall just above her head. She wriggled back a yard. "They're more than halfway up," Fedora said.

"Too close for my liking."

The breeze was blowing quite strongly now, strongly enough to lift the loose strands of her tousled hair. The surface of the lake far beneath them was ruffled, and occasionally a wave toppled over with a gleam of white foam. To their left, the sun was almost clear of the hilltops. It was going to be another hot day.

"We could jump," Laura said.

"Jump?"

"Into the water."

. . . Far beneath them. At least four hundred feet. Johnny shook his head.

"Why not? People have jumped that far and lived."

"I know," Johnny said. "That's the trouble." The pistol was in his hand now, nestling there comfortably. *"This is safer."*

"I see what you mean."

Somewhere below, a rifle cracked again. A wisp of smoke from behind the parapet; it hadn't been properly cleaned. *Bang,* Fedora said to himself. You're dead.

It was annoying to see the hills beyond the lake. The sage-scented hills and the oak trees. Because seeing them, you wished you were back there. Steep slopes, nagging brambles and all. It had been good there last night. Almost worth the rest of it.

". . . Not," he said, "that I'm gone on this for-whom-the-bell-tolls stuff, either. I've had about enough of it. You see that officer?"

"Yes."

"Can't very well *miss* seeing him, can you? . . . Take him. In the shoulder, if you're good enough. But take him."

"Wouldn't it be . . . ?"

"Take him," Fedora said patiently.

She raised the rifle, cuddling it into her cheek. She took up a nice position, anyway; well balanced. The shot was a long time in coming, to Fedora's mind; but when it came, it was a good one. Lieutenant Soto jumped up like a jackrabbit, his right hand leaping across to grasp his left arm above the elbow; then, predictably losing his balance, he rolled down a dozen steps and out of sight. "You're shooting low right," Fedora said unemotionally. "Make a correction."

"I *meant* to hit him in the arm."

"I told you the shoulder," Fedora said. "Nobody's *that* good. And we haven't any bullets to waste."

"Some people are damned hard to satisfy."

A shout came up from below, a cry of mingled rage and military ecstasy. The lieutenant had just realised that he'd been *hit*. And on active service, b'God. He was a *real* soldier now. A second or so later, a half-dozen rifles opened up in a ragged fusillade; and an arm, a striped sleeve emerged from behind a balustrade and beckoned furiously.

"I made a mistake," Johnny said. "We should have taken the sergeant. And killed the sod."

"Why?"

"He's calling up the machine-gun, that's bloody why."

. . . And it wasn't really a matter, he thought, of having bullets to waste. They could be sitting on an ammunition dump, and the problem for Laura would be the same. When all was said and done, this was *her* army. That was why her face looked dry and scraped now, why the bones were standing out in her cheeks; fighting Feramontov is one thing, killing your own side quite another. You need a special kind of callousness for that, and Johnny wasn't sure that she had it. In fact, he was almost sure she hadn't.

Here it came. The LMG. Poking its nasty snub nose round the corner, the flash-eliminator and part of the long blued-steel barrel. "Get back," Johnny said. "Back and down."

Laura wriggled away. The LMG opened up as she did so; a row of jagged white scars leaped into line in the wall beside her head; splinters flew; dust drifted down on to her back.

It made the most devilish racket, the steps amplifying the sound through some sinister trick of acoustics and banging it straight into their ears; Fedora breathed deeply, through his nose. It was no fun, no fun at all.

The machine-gun fired again, and then again. Slow, deliberate bursts, tiggety-tiggety-boo; eight rounds at a time. Fedora counted the seconds between the bursts. He could guess what the sergeant had in mind, and it was what he was most afraid of.

"They'll be coming up after us," he said. "Any moment."

Laura didn't answer. Her elbows were folded and her face hidden from view inside them. Probably, she was crying. It looked that way. Another, briefer rattle of shots, the bullets this time whining overhead: *Why* . . . Fedora thought, in genuine anger. *Why can't they sit there and sweat it out? Why do they have to be heroes?*

"They're changing the magazine," he said. "The machine-gun's going to give them covering fire. Make us keep our heads down. But when they're maybe halfway up, the machine-gun'll have to stop. For fear of hitting *them*. Now get that rifle of yours on automatic."

Laura's head lifted. Her hands moved. *Click*, said the rifle quietly.

"When I say *go* . . . wriggle forwards again and start shooting. And shoot fast. Right?"

"Oh God," Laura said, under her breath.

Fedora's hands jerked suddenly at the handcuffs, in a near-involuntary gesture of despair and frustration. If only, if only, if only. No. *If onlys* were no good to anyone. Here it came again, the screaming, banging rattle of the bullets. Shorter bursts this time; five rounds at a time; that was what he'd expected. They were on the way up now. He strained his ears to catch the scraping thump of boots on the steps, but his head was singing all the time from the after-impact of the machine-gun's blast; he couldn't hear a thing. He looked once more, quickly, at Laura.

"They'll be coming up together," he said. "They'll look like a row of ninepins. You'll think it's . . . too easy. Don't let that stop you." He paused to swallow saliva. "If we kill a few of them, that'll stop them. They'll call off the attack. It's the only—"

"All right," Laura said. "All right, all right, all *right*."

Silence.

And in the silence, Fedora's lips moving. He was counting.

Four, five, six. This had to be it. Seven, eight, nine. Yes. This was it.

"*Go*," he said.

. . . Thrusting with his good knee to push himself forwards. With the automatic rifle hammering in his ear, the spent cartridge-cases rattling beside him. Laura, firing down the steps like an automaton. And on the steps, nobody. Nobody at all. He knocked the barrel up, so hard that it almost twisted out of her hand. ". . . Who the hell d'you think you're shooting at . . .?

"I didn't . . . I'm sorry, I'm sorry." The breath coming out of her throat in great tearing sobs, the tears streaming wildly down her face. ". . . I had my eyes shut."

Johnny pulled the rifle away from her. His fingers pressed open the release catch, pried into the magazine. It was empty. He tossed it away. It fell with a clatter among the used cases. "I know," he said. Gently. "It's *your* army. And what's more, they're cunning bastards at that."

Or the sergeant is, anyway. Yes, that bloody sergeant has to be laughing.

And Laura might have been laughing, too, but wasn't. She lay flat, as though trying to press herself into the ground and disappear there, her head buried in her folded arms, her back and shoulders shaking uncontrollably in a soundless delirium of despair. There was saliva at the back of Johnny's throat again, a sticky wet ball of it. He tried to swallow it, but couldn't. His neck muscles seemed to be paralysed.

It had had to happen in the end, he thought. He'd asked too much of her. They'd been asking too much of each other, if it came to that, for the past twelve hours or so; each taking it in turn to push the other past desperation-point and on again down the hill. Some time, somewhere, inevitably, the wheels had had to stick. Against Feramontov, against the real enemy, she might have gone on and on, for as long or even longer than he himself; but the men below weren't the enemy —not to her. They were her own soldiers, obeying orders. Doing a job. In the end, he had asked too much of her. Inevitably.

He peered again down towards the corner of the steps; a movement had caught the corner of his eye. An optical illusion maybe. The men were better placed, now, and were sitting tight; the sergeant had taken over. And the sergeant knew his stuff. But then he saw it again. Parallel to the flight of steps and some twenty yards to the right there was a ladder . . . hardly even a ladder; iron rungs set at intervals in the concrete wall. It was screened, for the most part, from his view by the angle of the parapet; that was why he hadn't seen it before. But now, as the climber mounted, he could see an occasional movement of khaki cloth. . . .

Someone fired a shot. That was just to keep things going; they couldn't see him. Fedora didn't move. His eyes remained fixed, lazily contemplative, on the danger point. Not that he could see where the danger lay, as yet. The ladder ended well below the apron; even from the summit, the climber couldn't enfilade them; couldn't hit them or even see them. He'd be close to them, yes. But that was all.

Unless . . .

Yes. That had to be it. He was carrying grenades. From twenty yards, he could lob a grenade over the parapet with no trouble at all. The chances were it wouldn't do much damage, if he did; the grenade would be likely as not to skitter away over the smooth concrete and drop over the edge into the lake. But then he might, he just *might* get the timing right, or land it by some fluke up against the wall. Then that'd be bad. Very bad. There was nothing on that open space to absorb the blast . . . other, of course, than Laura and himself. The role of blast-absorber he didn't fancy. No, no. It couldn't be allowed.

The seconds were passing. The climber would probably be in position now. Screened, still, by the angle of the parapet. But he'd have to show himself to throw, have to lean back from the rungs to get his arm over. Fedora held the Luger in both hands. His thumb pushed down the safety catch. His narrowed eyes, watering in the sunlight, were watchful.

Lieutenant Soto, peering anxiously upwards. His pierced arm throbbing painfully under the emergency dressing.

"We'll never take them alive *that* way."

"I don't think they mean to be taken alive, sir."

"It sounded to me as though they ran out of ammo."

"They could be bluffing, sir," the sergeant said. "That fellow knows a trick or two of the trade. I wouldn't take a chance on it, I wouldn't really."

The khaki-clad figure, perched high overhead. His downwards-turned face a pink-brown blur. Waiting. Waiting for the signal.

". . . It's the woman I'm not happy about," the lieutenant said suddenly.

The sergeant shrugged. "She's the one with the gun, sir. We've fought women before, you know. In Africa."

"This isn't Africa," the lieutenant said.

He turned his head, looked at the crouching machine-gunners. Full magazine, long tilted barrel. They, too, were waiting.

". . . All right," he said. And sighed. "Carry on."

The sergeant raised his hand. Brought it down again in a chopping motion. Instantly, the machine-gunners opened fire.

. . . Covering fire, again. The bullets screaming overhead. Fedora didn't move. To the right, a man's head and shoulders in sudden view; the arm going back; Fedora squeezed the trigger. The Luger kicked once against his right wrist.

The soldier's arm, going back. And his body, with agonised slowness, detaching itself from the iron rung on which it stood.

Falling . . . thirty, forty feet? . . . to the steps beneath. He hit them with a sickening thump, started rolling. Rolling down the stairs like a sack of corn, faster and faster. His arms, his legs, thrown out at all angles. A dead man, rolling. A small, black, metal object rolled just behind him, bouncing, jumping about from side to side. It and the body travelled together a surprising distance, almost all the way down the steps to the sharp curve at the base. Then the grenade went off. He had had others . . . five others, probably . . . in pouches at his belt. They went off, too. All of them. The sound of the explosion whined plaintively away across the sun-splashed stillness of the lake; there was a thick cloud of dust on the steps, a wispy column of smoke slowly clearing. Then, clinging to the wall by the curve of the stairs, a thick dark glistening patch, an almost circular smear some six feet in diameter. It trickled.

"Christ," Lieutenant Soto said.

Fedora lowered the pistol.
Then lowered his head.
At the back of his throat now, the taste of vomit. An illusion, of course; another illusion. Psychological, or something. He hadn't eaten for thirty-six hours and, for a moment, was glad of it. Otherwise . . .
He wriggled back a couple of yards or so, squeezed the bridge of his nose between his fingers. The sharp morning sunlight was paining his eyes. Laura was sitting up now, her back once more to the bullet-scarred wall, staring out towards the far-off hills. She hadn't seen what had happened. It was just as well. Johnny touched her bare arm, but she didn't look round.
"Laura."
". . . What?" she said.
"You could have been right."
"I fired off the whole bloody magazine." She didn't even sound miserable about it; she had gone beyond that. Her voice was cool, dispassionate. "Every goddam round. I lost

my nerve. Completely."

"You could have been right," Fedora said. "I think you were."

"What about?"

"Going on killing people. What's the point of it? . . . It's all over now."

"You don't really mean that."

"It's all over now," Fedora said again.

He knew he was repeating himself. But there seemed to be no point, either, in hunting for other words to say the same thing. He was tired. He was tired of everything. He could see, though, that he wasn't getting through. A final effort, then. To put the whole thing very, very simply. . . .

"I've got six rounds left now," he said. "Two for us, like I said. And . . . four for them, maybe. That means four more dead, the way *I* shoot. Well, *why* four more? . . . They're just doing a job, the way I look at it. The same as we are. The man I just killed. . . . *He* had guts. So it's all such a *waste*."

Her lips seemed thin. Entirely bloodless. "We have a job, too. We have to go on with it."

"No," Johnny said. "It's finished. It's all over."

Her eyes turned towards him for a moment, then went back to their thoughtful study of the horizon; of the horizon, and of what lay beyond. "All right," she said. "Anything you say."

"We didn't do too badly."

What he meant by that, he didn't know. It was an epitaph, maybe. Epitaphs are by definition meaningless. Words are about things that *are*, not about things that aren't. Or things that were once, but aren't any more. Fedora pulled himself into a sitting position beside her and almost facing her; he rubbed the tip of his nose with the foresight of the Luger. Then turned his head, to follow the direction of her gaze across the water and past the trees to the distant hills.

The sun was well risen now. The sky the palest of imaginable blues, very nearly white. The hills blotched with brown and green and grey. The wind had dropped a little and the lake was unbelievably clear; the water a clean, steely grey; every ripple casting a dark shadow on the mirrorlike surface, damascening the depths in sweeping curves. Stretching away from them, mile after mile. And this time Johnny saw it before he heard it; far up the valley, just above the water, above the silent lake; a black speck in the sky. Moving towards them. He watched it until, in the air, a whisper of sound grew.

Here comes the chopper. To chop off your head. "Now it *is* all over," he said.

With the automatic rifle, it might have been worth a try. With the pistol, no. They could be picked off like targets at a fun-fair shooting booth, with the helicopter hovering out of range. Probably they'd come straight in, though; there was plenty of space on the apron for the 'copter to land, and Feramontov wanted them alive. Yes. The wash of the swinging blades was coming towards them, the angle of flight was flattening. They'd be coming in.

Laura was looking at him now. Big blue eyes, straight Grecian nose. A smudge of rifle oil down one cheek. He held the pistol in both hands again and his hands were steady. The barrel already aligned, motionless. The butt would kick in his hands again, there'd be the rattle of another cartridge-case as the ejector spat. And between the big blue eyes, a red hole. . . . The wash coming down now from almost overhead, lifting her hair, bringing up the dust in clouds, driving it into his own smarting eyes; the dust, sticking to his leg, mingling there with the coagulated blood. Through that dust they'd be peering downwards, rifles at the ready. . . . No point, he thought, in putting it off any longer.

Tired of everything. And yet, not quite. There was just one thing he wasn't tired of. She closed her eyelids, and that thing was gone. He still didn't fire.

The lever was there, in front of him. He had his hand on it. This was the lever, all over again. But this time he'd be backing a certainty. The one certainty there is, according to Feramontov. And maybe Feramontov was right. . . . The eyes, opening again. Now he had to do it. He couldn't keep her waiting. It wasn't fair. His lips curled back as he pressed the trigger.

Pressed it with all his strength. It wouldn't go back. It wasn't the trigger; it was his finger. It wouldn't obey him. He made a little sound deep in his throat. Laura put up one hand, pushed the barrel of the Luger sideways.

"No," she said. "No. Wait a moment."

He turned his head, once again following the direction of her gaze. Through the swirling dust he saw the helicopter, grounded now, its blades swinging idly in the empty air. From the open door, a man was leaping to the ground, the tail of his jacket flying loose as he dropped. There was something about him that was oddly familiar. . . .

"I *thought* so," Laura said. "It's Rivas, it's *Rivas*."

". . . I'll bet," Rivas said, "he never thought he'd be glad to see *me* again."

"S'shhh," Laura said.

The helicopter, swinging away from the dam and heading northwards. Fedora lay in the cabin, his head on Laura's lap. He had gone to sleep.